Blue Moon

THE LUNATICS ~ BOOK TWO

A.M. LEONARD

Raven Song Press

Freeville, New York

Cover design: Cristiana Leone
Editors: Nichole Nettleton and Brendan Dabkowski

Raven Song Press
46 Hammond Hill Road
Freeville, New York, 13068
(607) 844-8706
www.RavenSongPress.com

Publisher's Cataloging-In-Publishing Data
Names: Leonard, A.M., 1956- author
Title: Blue Moon / A.M. Leonard
Description: Freeville, NY: Raven Song Press, (2025)
Series: The Lunatics
The Library of Congress Cataloging-in-Publication Data is available upon request
ISBN 979-8-9907544-2-3 (paperback) ISBN 979-8-9907544-3-0 (e-book)

First Edition April 2025
10 9 8 7 6 5 4 3 2 1

For our son Benjamin, BSN, RN, who as Unit Manager provided care and leadership to staff and patients alike on Cayuga Medical Center's 4 South Telemetry floor throughout the COVID pandemic.

~ and ~

For the incredible health care personnel around the world who, despite overwhelming odds, stepped up to an impossible task and did their very best to save lives during the COVID pandemic. I am in awe of each and every one of you.

Thank you all.

Prologue

Let's get you up to speed before you dive into the insanity that is my life. My name is Raven Callahan. I'm a bi-racial kid—half Hidatsa Native American, half Irish. I'm also one of only two people in our world afflicted with the dubious distinction of having a body that changes age with the waxing and waning of the moon. It's an unpleasant side effect of being blessed with the ability to work magic. Yeah. You read that right. **Magic**. It's not as slay as it sounds. I'm actually 16, but depending on the moon's phase, I can look anywhere between one and my real age. It's a crazy way to live. That's why my Nan, who is the other "lucky" one, jokingly calls us Lunatics. The word "lunatic" comes from the Latin *lunaticus*, meaning "moonstruck." The belief was that changes of the moon caused intermittent insanity.

And true that! I just returned to my own dimension after having been kidnapped by Cerridwen, the Celtic goddess of the moon. She brought me to Tír na nÓg, a parallel dimension that resembles Ireland in its most perfect form. While trapped in the Celtic idea of Heaven, my Cait Sidhe bodyguard Kellas and I fought werewolves, dinosaurs, and other nasties conjured up from my childhood nightmares. I also learned to play a magic lute, which transformed into an unbeatable sword. We also rescued one of Cerridwen's sister moon goddesses, Rhiannon, from an ill-advised marriage to a Death god— who turned out to be a zombie. As a reward for my service, Rhiannon gave me a ring I could use to call on her for help—should I ever need it.

But this craziness is all in a day's work for me, sad to say. Yay me! The most insane part? It isn't what Kellas and I have had to face, or the unknowns we'll still face now that we have returned. It's the fact that when magic runs full tilt into family dynamics—things get tricky. *Really* tricky...

One

We crash-landed in the dark. Literally "crash landed"…like we had been dropped out of a tree or a low-flying airplane. I lay on the ground, stunned, my cheek pressed against the rough pavement. Nearby, I could hear my bodyguard, Kellas, cussing and spitting—not unlike his Cait Sidhe self. But this time it was in words, not growls.

"Brannaugh?"

Only Kellas calls me that. I saw his figure next to me now. When I groaned, he gave my shoulder a reassuring squeeze before helping me into a sitting position.

"Anything broken?"

"Don't think so." I struggled to my feet, wincing as pain sliced through my ribs. "Ouch!" I hurt so badly I couldn't even draw a deep breath.

"The landing was none too gentle," Kellas grumbled.

"Ya think?" I rolled my eyes at him, then tried to get my bearings. We were in the middle of a deserted city street. Streetlamps punched pools of light in the dark. Buildings towered over us ominously; they were sleek and almost weirdly uniform compared to Taliesin's hut or the wild forests of Tír na nÓg. In between the buildings' conformity lay shadows that could have hidden… anything.

"C'mon." Kellas took my arm. "Before a car comes along and flattens us." He guided me over to the sidewalk.

I leaned against a lamppost, still trying to take a proper breath. "Where are we?"

He glanced around and I swear, even though he was in human form, it was like he could flick his ears forward and back as he examined our surroundings. "Ithaca, close by the Commons. At least we know where we are. But it'll still be a hoof and a half to get us home to Amaris's place."

Amaris is my paternal grandmother. I call her Nan, which is what the Irish call their grandmothers. "What's that sound?" I was gradually becoming more aware, and what I was hearing made me uneasy. "It sounds...angry."

Kellas turned his head in the direction the sound was coming from. "It *is* angry. Chanting. Maybe a protest." It must have concerned him, because he grabbed my arm again and started leading me away from the source of the noise.

I wobbled along beside him, feeling worse than I'd ever had (and I'm saying this as someone who has experienced being offloaded by a bucking mustang). There would be bruises, for sure.

"I wish you were a bit older, 15 or 16 is not exactly an age to be gallivanting around at midnight in the city with someone like me. I'd rather not get arrested." Despite the flippant way he said that, Kellas tugged me a little nearer to him before pulling my hoody up over my head. "Stick close."

At least I was nearly my correct age again. That was something. Not that I had much time to dwell on that fact; movement in the dark street ahead caught my attention. There was something not quite right about it. "Kellas..."

He saw them too. A group of people had just come into view out of the shadows. They were dressed all in black. They blended into the darkness, nearly invisible except for their motion. As they came under a streetlamp, I could see they were men wearing riot gear, carrying shields and long batons. There was an eerie quality to the blackness that surrounded them. It swallowed up their faces, concealing them like phantoms.

They saw us almost as soon as we saw them. As of one mind, the men spread across the street, blocking our escape. They marched intently toward us, everything else silent but for the soft sounds of their booted feet.

I turned and bolted like a frightened animal. Stand my ground? No way!

The laughter that followed us was mocking, malicious, and grated like thousands of little shards of glass.

Kellas caught up and surprised me by grabbing my upper arm. "This way," he said, dragging me *toward* the chanting. "Safety in numbers."

Soon, we rounded a corner and came out on a well-lighted plaza—which, if it were daylight and we weren't being pursued, would definitely have been inviting. Instead, the scene that met our eyes was totally chaotic. The air was heavy with anger, and something else I couldn't quite place. The entire space was seething with people. They were carrying signs and shouting in response to a person with a megaphone, who was addressing the crowd from atop a large planter box full of pansies.

I caught a few words. "Push back.... Our choices.... Claim what's rightfully ours!" Or something like that. By then, Kellas was shoving his way through the crowd. He pulled me along with him, leaving me tripping over my own feet as I struggled to keep up.

"S'cuse us," he muttered. "Coming through.... Oops.... Sorry, gotta get through. Oof!"

He'd bumped hard into a large young Black woman, who swung around and glared at us over a white medical mask. Her dark eyes glittered in annoyance. I sensed she'd had a very long day, and that our crashing into her was testing the last threads of her patience.

She squared away, fists planted on ample hips, and sized us up with one clear glance. "Where are your masks?" she demanded sharply.

I stared at her, confused. "M-masks?" I stammered. Apparently, that was the wrong thing to say because she somehow looked even more annoyed by it.

"What are you, a Covidiot?" Scowling, she pulled a huge purse around to her front and dug into it. Then, she produced two cellophane-wrapped packages containing white somethings and shoved them at Kellas and me. "Put them on. It's required. We're following all the CDC guidelines for peaceful assembly, even if *some people* completely refuse to take any safety precautions."

Covidiots? The CDC? I was completely at a loss. What in the world was she talking about? What was happening? Apparently, this new masking thing was not optional. She watched like a hawk as we hastily opened the wrappings and struggled to put on the medical face masks she'd given us. She even reached over and helped me fix one of the loops behind my ear.

"Thanks," Kellas said, his voice muffled from behind the mask. He tipped his head politely, and I instinctively did a little half-bow of thanks. Although, I still didn't understand what all the fuss was about.

The woman's face softened a little under her own mask. She regarded me in silence for a second like she was about to say something, then shook her head slightly. "You should get your little sister home. This is no place for a kid," she admonished Kellas.

"Working on that!" he agreed swiftly.

Grabbing my upper arm again, Kellas began hurrying me back through the crowd. Angry shouts behind us heralded the arrival of riot-gear-clad men—and spurred us to greater haste.

Kellas panted, "The crowd will slow them down."

I fervently prayed that it would, though I didn't dare look back to check. The shouting and jostling in the crowd sounded more and more heated. I hoped that lady would be alright.

We cleared the outskirts of the crowd and broke into a run, pulling the masks from our faces as we went. The surrounding darkness was broken up by streetlights, but every flicker of movement still made my heart jump.

"What was that all about?" I wheezed.

"How the heck should I know?" Kellas shot back. "I've been out of town!"

I gave him a daggered glare. The pain in my side killed any chance of a snarky comeback.

Still, I ran. And we ran until I could run no longer. Then, I mixed running with walking—moving as fast as my legs would go. It wasn't nearly the speed I would have liked. But at least the noise of the conflict behind us was receding.

Kellas kept leading the way through the dimly lit streets until we reached a bridge arching over a wide waterway. "The Inlet," he supplied, answering my unspoken question. "Cayuga Lake is up there on our right. C'mon, we'll follow the Black Diamond Trail home."

The dark grew denser as we left the road and entered a park-like area—and even more so as we continued on, following one of the old railroad beds that the town had restored as a "rail trail." We could barely see the way ahead and I wished I had cat eyes, or at least a flashlight. Still, out here, away from the protest, black-clad men, and hard, sharp surfaces of buildings and city streets—I felt safer.

We settled into a strong walk. Kellas explained that we had a good eight miles to go before we would reach Nan's house. We'd be lucky to get home by dawn. I groaned pitifully at that. My muscles ached. I wished we could have just called an Uber. But we hadn't a nickel between the two of us, much less a smartphone.

I was getting used to the dark. When you can't see well, other senses take over. I became aware of the gravel surface of the trail crunching beneath our feet, and the night sounds that surrounded us: crickets singing softly, the trill of a toad. A warm breeze blew up from the lake below us. It carried the faint odor of rotting fish.

"Feels like August," I remarked.

"Smells like it too," he agreed. "Dead fish. Phew!"

I stopped in my tracks. "Wait! August? It was November when we left." But...it had felt like just a few days! I briefly glanced skyward, remembering how warm it had been in Tír na nÓg. I hadn't noticed it at first because of that.

"My, how time flies when you're having fun," Kellas muttered grimly.

"Huh?" I had no idea what he was talking about. What did that comment have to do with anything? Also, which of us was having *fun*, exactly?

He gave me a rough push. "Keep moving!"

The darkness hid the indignant look I gave him. But I did my best to pick up the pace. A couple of minutes later, he sighed heavily and spoke again. "Time works differently in other realms, Brannaugh. Something to keep in mind if you're going to insist on hopping back and forth between."

That was a bit unfair, I thought, but kept it to myself. There was quite a lot about my brand-new moon magic that I still didn't understand. Unintentional dimension-hopping, usually when I was dreaming, was one of those challenges.

We walked on in silence, setting a steady pace and making good progress up the trail.

"Do you hear music?" Kellas asked.

His sudden remark after such a long period of quiet made me jump.

"Boo!" he snickered.

"Jerk," I fumed.

"Seriously, though. Can you hear music in this realm?"

Oh! Point taken. I stopped walking and listened intently. Breezes rustled the aging leaves in the trees arching over us, a dry rattling sound like castanets. Crickets chirped like quick strokes of bows on violin strings, and somewhere nearby, a small waterfall splashed harp-like onto rocks. An owl called, *who's cooking for you? Who's cooking for you-all?* his voice reminiscent of a French horn. The sounds blended. Sang.

"Yes," I finally answered and began walking again. There had been nothing threatening, just quiet background music—like something you'd hear in a movie when the characters are slowing down and catching their breath. "It's not like the symphony orchestra in Tír na nÓg, but it's there."

"Good." Kellas sounded relieved. "So, we've got that going for us here too."

We walked on. Gradually, the darkness around us lifted to a dim twilight, heralding dawn. Our pace quickened as we "smelled the barn," as a horseman would say. Nearly home. I could feel my heart hammering in my chest, but I pushed on. I desperately wanted to get back to where I belonged—back with my family.

That's when I felt it, heard it: a nearly subsonic thrumming that felt like a sick ache in my belly. It came out of nowhere, interrupting the soft melody of the early morning.

Two

I grabbed Kellas's arm and dragged him off the trail and into the bushes. Twigs slapped me across the face and fallen branches tripped me, but this wasn't enough to stop my headlong rush to get away from the trail.

We finally came up against an ancient multi-floral rosebush. That effectively stopped my flight. I bent low, pulling Kellas down next to me. We crouched there, hidden by the bushes and the dark. Thankfully, Kellas didn't open his yap.

The thrumming came closer, swelling out of the darkness. I could barely make out the shabby figure up on the trail, pushing a heavily loaded bike downhill toward the city. I could hear its low muttering as it spoke to itself. The words themselves were unintelligible, half-formed, a babble of confused syllables.

The figure lurched to a sudden halt just as it drew abreast of our hiding spot. The muttering stopped. We hunkered down like rabbits hiding from a fox. Silent. Motionless.

Then it spoke, sending a shudder through my body. The voice was an odd singsong. "Kitty, kitty, kitty! Come out, come out, wherever you are! I know you're there. Come out, pretty kitty. I won't hurt you. Pssh, pssh, pssh." It made kissy noises, followed by a wild, high-pitched giggle that went on for too long…. Until it turned into a sob. It sounded like a man. An older man? The way his voice was shaking, I wasn't sure. The fear buzzing in my ears sure didn't help. "Aliens! I keep telling them: aliens! But they won't listen. No, they know too much. It's all my imagination…." His voice strengthened. "But we know better. Don't we, little kitty? We know aliens are afoot. And they are everywhere…." His voice trailed off. There was a heavy sigh, and he started pushing the overloaded bike forward down the hill again—slowly, ponderously—hopeless.

We waited for what seemed like forever until the crunch of tires on gravel and the low thrumming faded into the distance. Normal night sounds resumed, as if even the toads had been holding their breath. I got up slowly, my legs and back cramped from crouching down for so long. The rosebush had snagged my jacket and clawed at me like it wanted me to stay. I peeled the branch off me, wincing as it scratched and poked. Together, we made our way back up onto the trail. We moved warily, keeping an eye out for any sign of that guy's return.

Once we were sure he was gone, I made a faint retching sound. "Yuck." I felt a little bit guilty—but I couldn't help it. His music felt so discordant it made me feel ill.

Kellas made a sound that indicated agreement, then started uphill again.

"Talk to me," he said.

I told him about the sick feeling.

"Useful," he commented.

Oh, please. I thought we were past this monosyllabic nonsense. I felt like vomiting. "Somehow, he knew you were there!" Wasn't Kellas's superpower evading detection? Oh, right, only when he was in cat form. "And all you can say is useful?!" *Really?*

"Yup." He sounded grim. "Not the first time, either."

I huffed in annoyance. "Explain yourself, please. I cannot read minds."

He sighed, as if dealing with a human was a heavy burden. "That was one of the homeless people," he explained. "Years ago, he would have been in an institution. Nowadays, the powers that be let people like him look after themselves. Pretty much criminal negligence, I'd say. He's one of your dad's regulars. Every time he has one of his episodes, the paramedics pick him up and take him to the hospital. They keep him a while until he's stable again and then turn him loose. Back out onto the streets with nothing but the clothes on his back and no way for his situation to improve."

"And that's it?" I gawked at him, dumbfounded.

He shook his head and a brief look of sadness crossed his face. "Every time, it's the same thing. The poor sod goes nuts screaming about aliens. He gets sedated, they get him through it... And, well, nothing changes."

"Do you think he actually sees aliens?"

Kellas shrugged. "He knows when I'm around, apparently."

"But, how?" That's what I didn't get. Can some people just tell? Are they more in tune with the world or something?

Kellas looked at me patiently. "How did you know he was coming, hmm? You knew even before I did, and I'm no slouch."

I thought for a moment about how to explain the sensation. "There was this deep vibration. I almost felt it before I heard it."

Kellas nodded. I could see him easily now that dawn was coming. Soft pink and yellow rays painted long streaks across the sky and the darkness began to recede, softening into varying shades of gray. "Amaris has mentioned that. She's observed that for people with psychological trouble, it's as though their energetic boundaries get confused. Some spread out in wide pools; others shrink until they're almost smaller than their physical selves. That guy is one of the sprawling types. Ever notice how people give folks like him a wide berth? Even though they can't feel it like you can, their own energy senses another's is *off* and avoidance steps in."

"But why?" I asked. "It's cruel to just ignore them, isn't it?"

He sent me one of his one-eyebrow-raised glances. "You want some of that sticking to you?"

I shuddered. Guilty though it made me feel, that cringe sense attached to the man's ragged presence was too deep set. "No."

Kellas's knowing look was surprisingly nonjudgmental. "It takes a strong sense of self to keep it off—like your dad's. He deals with weird energies every single day."

"How?"

Kellas shrugged. "He'd be the one to ask."

The western hillside above us had gained a pinkish-lavender hue as we walked. Our way forward was easy to see now, the shadows still strong but somehow less solid. It was like watching a color pallet having more and more white added to it, slowly lightening up the shades—imperceptibly at first, then more noticeably.

We crossed an old railroad trestle. Kellas suddenly veered off the trail and stepped around some thorn bushes. "This way." He plunged downhill on a steep rock-strewn path that ran alongside a gradually deepening gully, where water splashed over shelves of shale rock. Off to either side, I could see scattered small pools of light shining from house windows.

We continued descending for what seemed an eternity, finally sliding on our rears down a very steep bank and into a deep ditch next to a hard-topped road. My thighs ached terribly, there was a painful stitch in my side from all the running, and I was trembling from exhaustion.

Kellas must have noticed I was struggling. "Hang in there, champ. Nearly there." He scrambled out of the ditch on all fours, then reached down and pulled me out. He trotted across the road and into the woods on the far side. I hastened after him.

"We're on our land now." The relief in his voice was palpable. "Amaris will know we're coming," he said, breaking into a steady trot.

"How could she?" I demanded, working hard to keep up.

"Her wards would have alerted her."

Right, the wards. "But how does she know it's us?" I still didn't really understand how they worked. Hopefully, Nan would clue me in sometime!

"No one else could have breached them."

A sudden loud burst of barking cut off any response I had to that, and a dark shape hurtled out of the shadows, threw itself upon Kellas, and knocked him flat.

"Kellas!" I tried to help, but the two were thrashing about so violently that I couldn't get close.

"Ugh! Get off me, you big oaf!" Kellas made a mighty heave and threw off his attacker, struggling to get to his feet while still being jumped at, by what I finally realized was a large black dog. Mercifully, it was a familiar black dog. "Off, ya great lump!"

"Bran!" I shouted with glee, recognizing Nan's hellhound. He paused his joyful jumping long enough to send me a tongue-lolling happy look, then flung himself at the Cait Sidhe again. Ah darn, no puppy-love for me, I guess!

"Oh, all right then, you asked for it!" Kellas exclaimed, and the two engaged in a pitched battle. Thankfully, it ended with them sprawled on the ground—panting heavily in a tangle of limbs.

"That was nuts," I commented, stepping over and offering Kellas a hand up. He accepted, levering himself to his feet in a single lithe motion. Then, he vigorously dusted himself off. Beside Kellas, Bran also lurched to his feet, then shook himself, ears popping.

Once everyone was settled, we set off again—the hellhound leading the way.

"Do you two always do that?" I wondered aloud.

Kellas snorted. "Every chance he gets. He's obsessed."

"Better you than me."

"You needn't worry, he only ever does that to me."

I valiantly resisted the urge to snicker. I sure didn't envy Kellas the hell-hound's version of dog love.

"Raven? Kellas?" It was Nan's voice, ringing with a high-pitched combination of alarm and hope that hit me like a punch to the gut.

"Nan! It's us!" I yelled. "We're back!"

We broke into a run, covering the remaining distance out of the woods and into the yard by Nan's house, where we could see several figures hastening toward us. Dad grabbed me in a hug and lifted me right off my feet. I hugged him back, crying with happiness and stress—so many jumbled feelings all at once. For a few minutes, there was a confused racket of laughing, crying, hugging, and back-thumping.

"This is wonderful!" exclaimed Nan, as we finally settled down.

I had my arms wrapped in a death grip around Dad's waist. Having his strong arms around my shoulders again was unimaginably comforting.

Nan's boyfriend, Elias, was beaming, his eyes warm with relief.

A tall, slender redhead had her arms wrapped possessively around Kellas's neck. I had no clue who she was. Had she been around before? I couldn't remember. As I watched, she kissed Kellas vigorously on the mouth. He kissed her back, then gently disengaged from her grasp, whispering something in her ear. She nodded and backed up, then sent me a sidelong glance that spoke volumes.

I promptly found a very interesting tree to stare at—in a different direction. During our time in Tír na nÓg, I'd grown very fond of Kellas. OK, more than fond. I admit; I was head over heels for the frustrating, wise-ass, pain-in-my-derriere, hot, handsome fairy cat-man. He'd never kissed me or anything.

And probably never would. But a girl can still dream—and I didn't much like the idea of him kissing anyone who wasn't me.

"We were just starting breakfast," Elias announced. "Hungry?"

I was ravenous, and apparently, Kellas was too. We lost no time trooping into the house, where eggs, bacon, and pancakes awaited us—along with a lot of questions. I let Kellas do most of the talking as I was far too busy stuffing my face. How I'd missed *our* kind of food—not that Taliesin's was bad. I appreciated the talented musician's cooking, *and* the time we'd spent together in Tír na nÓg when he taught me to play my magic lute. But home food? There was no substitute.

Kellas shot me his mocking *really, girl?* look. "Do you always eat like that?" he demanded.

"Hey, I'm hungry," I retorted around a mouthful of pancake. I glimpsed the lovely redhead out of the corner of my eye. There was a sardonic expression on her face. Was she being condescending, or was I reading into this way too much? Suddenly not as hungry, I set down my fork and pushed my plate away. "I need to call Mom. She's got to be going out of her mind."

I bolted from the kitchen and went upstairs to my loft bedroom, where I closed the door and flung myself across my bed, face down. Once I stopped to think, I vaguely remembered who the redhead was. Erin had been around before, when I had visited over summer vacations. She had seemed friendly enough the few times we'd chatted, but had never been front and center. She was more like one of Nan's friends who checked in semi-regularly, but that didn't hang around long. I'd never really focused on her. Now she loomed large—squarely between me and Kellas.

Kellas! Why should he matter? The Cait Sidhe was insufferable, arrogant, self-absorbed, infuriatingly wise-ass. (Maybe I mentioned this before? Whatever. It bears repeating.) I didn't need friends like him anyway. Only...

he'd seemed quite a bit more than that to me lately. He'd been...well...kind! And thoughtful and caring and.... Yeah, I must admit, he had those dark good looks going for him. Heck, we'd fought werewolves and velociraptors together...and.... Oh, darn it all!

I groaned and pulled a pillow over my head. That dratted cat meant more to me than I cared to admit. Not that what I felt meant anything to the Cait Sidhe. He was an "avowed bachelor," according to the Morrigan—and you'd think the Celtic Goddess of Death would know something about such things. Although juxtaposed against the tremendously affectionate reunion I'd just witnessed, I had to wonder if perhaps the Morrigan might be just the tiniest bit wrong in her assessment.

I needed to fix this. It would not do at all to be all teenaged dewy-eyed over a guy who was a whole lot older than me, and not even a *guy* all the time. I was being silly. And I really did need to call my mom. Hopefully, my Hidatsa grandmother would be there too. I call her Iku—what we Hidatsa call our grandmothers.

There was a gentle knock on my door. "Raven? I have my laptop here. Would you prefer to video call your mom and Iku?" It was Nan, thoughtful as always.

I rolled over and pushed the pillow back where it belonged. "Sure." Glad I hadn't gotten all teary-eyed at least, I scooted off the bed, went over to the door, and opened it. I took the laptop from Nan, avoiding her gaze. She always knew when I was upset, and frankly, I felt way too embarrassed right now to admit my stupid little crush to her. "Thanks."

"Let me know if you need anything," was all she said—but somehow, I knew she could see right through me.

I was already walking away. I didn't want her sympathy, didn't need anyone right now. At least, that is what I tried to convince myself of. Duty called.

It wasn't the time to get "The Talk" about first crushes. And I didn't really want to hear how they don't last or *whatever*, either. "OK," was all I said before plopping down in the big chair by the French doors and opening the laptop.

I heard the door close quietly behind me. On the computer, there was a verdant picture of Ireland, the green so intense it practically glowed. Effortlessly beautiful. Like Erin. How unfair was that? The rest of us were so dreadfully...ordinary. Oh god, was I really going there? I sounded pathetic, even to myself. I smacked my forehead with my hand, as if the gesture could somehow knock out my confusing feelings about my fae bodyguard. As if it were that easy.

Angrily, I signed in, opened the video app, and rang my mother. Margaret. Margaret Callahan. Or Meg for short. Dad sometimes calls her that, when they aren't being all formal and awkward because of their divorce. She never changed her last name back. She said it would make things easier for me at school. But honestly, a lot of kids these days have last names different from their parents. It's not that big a deal anymore.

Mom answered on the second ring, as though she'd been expecting me. Nan had probably alerted her of my call. She looked exhausted. Older. A relieved smile softened her stern features, reminding me that my disappearing for months into another dimension had probably been particularly hard for her. She wanted so badly to pretend magic wasn't real.

"Raven! Thank goodness you're back."

I did my best to smile back at her. "Hi, Mom. Yeah, I'm home."

A look of pain crossed her face ever so briefly, then it was gone. As if having said, *I'm home*, had hurt her somehow. She recovered rapidly, though, and started in with her usual energy—straight to agitated questions. "Where have you been? It's been months and no word! I've been going crazy with worry. We thought you'd been kidnapped!"

Actually, I *had* been kidnapped—by the Celtic goddess Cerridwen. She used a thoughtless geis to deprive me of my voice and then left me to wander the Celtic Otherworld looking for it. Because she, as it turned out, was unable to restore it. But how much of my experience would Mom believe and how much would she write off as my *overactive imagination*? Since the latter was her MO, I decided less was more.

"Ireland," I answered hastily. Without time to plan a plausible explanation, all I could do was blurt out the first country name that popped into my head. I knew she wouldn't accept *a moon goddess dragged me off to fairyland without my consent*. Even if it was true—especially because it was true.

"Ireland!" Mom gave me a flabbergasted look. "What in the world were you doing there?"

A whole lot of crazy stuff, actually. But I couldn't say most of what I was thinking out loud. "Learning to play the lute," I responded. I figured she could at least handle the lute part. Never mind that I'd never before expressed any interest in lutes, let alone in playing one.

Mom sputtered, rather like she had when she first brought me to Iku's house on my 16th birthday last year...when I'd first been afflicted with the moon craziness. It seemed like half a lifetime ago.

"A lute? Dear God, Raven, you've been missing since November of last year. It's August 1st. You've been gone nine months with no word at all, and now you tell me you were merely taking music lessons?"

OK, don't twitch, don't look down.... "Among other things." *Not that she could handle the other things, even if I tried to explain them.*

"Why didn't you call?" She was getting worked up into a proper rant.

"No phone, no internet. My teacher didn't have either. And I didn't realize that until it was too late to do much about it." Heck, there hadn't even been indoor plumbing or electricity, come to think of it.

"Really...?" Mom stared at me in total silence for some of the longest few seconds of my life. Thankfully, just when I was sure she was going to erupt like Mount Vesuvius, she breathed in slowly and gave me a concerned look. "You're not hurt? They didn't...*do*...anything to you?"

I shook my head firmly. "No. I'm fine."

"How did you get back?" I noticed she didn't say *home*. Neither she nor my dad really talked about their divorce—as if I couldn't tell how strained things were between them. I chose not to prod right now though.

I hesitated a split second. "We flew." I decided that explanation made the most sense. It was even sort of close to being true. Although the experience was more like the one from *Toy Story*; we hadn't been flying, we'd been falling with style. Yeah, that thought would really put her at ease. "It was a rough landing. The pilot pancaked us."

"Flew!" Mom sounded a combination of frustrated and confused. "Raven, air travel is all but shut down! How did you manage a flight? And with no money of your own?"

Huh? I was completely baffled. Air travel totally shut down? What could possibly cause that? "What do you mean, shut down?"

Her expression was priceless. To see my always-in-control-of-the-situation mother this confused was something I'd never experienced. I almost expected her jaw to unhinge and drop comically onto the table with a pronounced *thud*.

"Really, Raven? Since right after you disappeared, the whole world has practically been at a full stop. COVID-19."

"Like I said, I was way out in the countryside; my tutor didn't even have a TV. What's COVID?" My mind skittered back to that weird demonstration and how the lady had insisted that Kellas and I put on medical masks. Could that have something to do with this COVID thing?

Iku's face entered the video call meeting. She raised a hand where I could see it and wiggled her fingers in a teeny wave. I wiggled mine back too, overjoyed to see my grandmother.

Mom glanced over her shoulder briefly, then turned back. "COVID-19 is a virus that has caused a pandemic. It's killed millions worldwide since January this year, and you haven't heard of it?!"

"I had no idea." Then a thought struck me. "Is that why the masks?"

Iku was nodding. "It's an airborne virus."

I sank back against the seat cushions. A pandemic. Millions of people dead. How can you process *millions*? It felt weird in my head. Like...I was trying to solve a math problem, rather than thinking about lives lost. The scope was just too big.

Mom and Iku remained silent while I struggled with the news. I finally shook my head to clear it. "OK. What else is going on that I should know about? I saw a protest in town." But protesting *what*? The virus? What was *that* supposed to achieve?

"There have been a lot of protests—people demonstrating for Black rights who are clashing with reactionary militants, and people rallying to oppose mask mandates. It's been a horrible year in so many ways, and we're not out of the woods yet, by any means." Mom looked weary. "It's hard to explain," she sighed. "You really had no idea this was going on? Who took you, anyways? And why?"

"It's because of this weird aging thing. I'm dealing with all this, and I don't know how to manage it. I'm so confused all the time."

Iku settled on the couch next to my mother. "Pick one thing, sweetie. It won't seem as overwhelming that way. We don't need to do everything at once." I saw her dig an elbow into Mom's ribs, a prompt I'd seen her use before. A wordless way of letting Mom-the-lawyer know she should hold off on the cross-examination. "Just let Raven talk."

What could I possibly tell them that they would not instantly have more questions about?

"You mentioned lute lessons," Iku prompted gently.

"Yeah." Suddenly concerned, I felt over my shoulder for my lute, horrified that I had completely forgotten it until now. I felt an overwhelming surge of relief when my fingertips touched it in its hiding spot, a special dimension only I could access. I pulled it around to my front and cradled it in my lap.

Iku looked impressed. "That looks really complicated!"

"It's not bad once you get the hang of it," I said, tucking the lute close and checking its tuning. I wondered if it would play for me here. I touched the strings and a silvery chord rose in the surrounding air.

"Play us something," Iku urged.

'*Can you tell them what happened?*' I thought at the lute. '*Can you explain?*'

The wood and strings under my hands pulsed in response. "OK, here goes nothing." I closed my eyes and let the music flow through me like a mountain stream, pure and clear. My lute sang of sadness and fear, the joy of discovery, weakness and strength, triumph, loss, and overwhelming uncertainty—but underlying it all was hope. It was a song I'd never played before; it sprung from the living heart of the instrument, spinning its story unbidden, perfect. My audience sat spellbound.

I finished and glanced at the computer screen, unsure how my family was going to handle this latest bit of crazy.

Mom looked stunned. "You didn't just take lessons," she said faintly.

"You became a master," Iku finished the thought.

"It's not really me," I admitted. "It's this lute."

"Don't sell yourself short, Raven," Mom said crossly. It was one of her go-to lines. I'd heard it plenty of times. I know she meant well, but...well, the lute *was* magic. I couldn't take credit for that!

"That lute cannot sing without you," Iku added gently.

Under my hands, Fraegarthach's lute form vibrated its agreement. It brought tears to my eyes, and I fought to blink them away. "I love to play."

"Perhaps that is your calling," Iku said. She put a lot of importance on finding one's *calling*. Whatever that meant.

I managed a tight smile. Oh, the things they *didn't* know.... But that had to wait. For now, it was enough that I was back in my own realm of reality. No matter how out of whack it had become in my absence.

An enormous yawn forced itself past my teeth. Suddenly, I was dead tired. Considering when I might have last slept, who knew how long it had been since I'd gotten some ZZZs.

"Perhaps we should let Raven get some rest," Iku suggested diplomatically. "We can hear about her adventures once she's feeling more awake."

My mother reluctantly agreed, and I signed off with relief. That had gone better than expected. But I was far too familiar with Mom's lawyerly tendencies (for lack of a better description) to think I could get off quite so easily the next time we talked. Like a terrier with a bone, she would chew on me until she extracted every bit of information-marrow that she could. I wasn't looking forward to it.

I slid the lute back into its hiding place over my shoulder. Then I closed the laptop and set it on the bedside table, crawled onto the bed, and collapsed face down on top of the covers. I was asleep instantly.

Three

I awoke to full daylight, rays of sun spilling through the western windows. Someone had laid a blanket over me while I'd slept. I hadn't even been aware of anyone coming in. For the first time in a while, I felt well-rested and stress-free. It felt like someone had lifted a blue whale off my shoulders.

Rolling over onto my back, I lay staring up at the ceiling, listening. It was breezy outside; the house shifted and creaked a bit when a stronger gust hit it. Water dripped somewhere. Turning my head, I saw the French doors propped open. Rainwater continued to drip off the eves onto a corner of the deck railing. Must have been a recent rain shower. I could hear birds singing, picking up where they'd left off before the storm. Music. Peaceful and calm, no threat nearby. Good!

A shower. Now *that* sounded like a fabulous idea! I lifted my shirt to my nose and gave it a good whiff. Ugh! Long overdue. I rolled off the bed, grabbed some clean clothes out of my dresser, and headed downstairs at a trot.

Nan was in the kitchen working on supper. The entire house smelled of bread baking. Yummy! The others were nowhere to be seen. For a moment, I wondered what they were doing, but then shrugged it off.

"Good morning!" Nan greeted me, without sarcasm—despite it being clearly past noon. "Feeling a bit more yourself?"

"After I get rid of a few layers of grime and stink!" I agreed. "Where is everyone?"

"Your dad got called in to work. Elias is gathering wood for our Lughnasadh bonfire. Kellas is still passed out on the sofa."

So, I'd beat him up, had I? I peeked around the corner into the living room and saw Kellas in cat form curled up in a large black lump in the corner of the sofa. I tried not to just stand there and gaze at him. Tried to get my thoughts to focus. "Right, then. Shower!" I said, making a beeline for the bathroom.

Peeling off my filthy clothes, I discovered Taliesin's gift still around my neck. I took a moment to examine it. The medallion was made of some precious metal, likely gold, judging from its heft. It was about two inches in diameter, a delicate filigree of three spiraling circles attached to each other in the center, with an extra design that looked like ravens, all surrounded by another circle that went around the outside. It felt heavy in my hand, and somehow weighty in other ways—which I could not describe. For whatever reason, I had no desire to take it off. Ever. I got in the shower with it still around my neck.

The hot water felt beyond wonderful. After I had washed my hair twice to rid it of built-up oil and grime, I lingered under the water's warmth—far longer than necessary. The gentle spray pounding down on my back and shoulders was indescribably soothing. Finally, I reluctantly shut off the water; my dry-climate upbringing chided me about waste. I toweled off and wrapped my hair up turban-style in another towel to keep it from dripping all over. Perhaps I was mistaken, but my hair felt a good bit longer now than it was the last time I'd washed it. Maybe it was because of the nine months I'd been away?

Dressed in jean shorts and an aqua-colored tank top, I went outside to let my hair dry in the sun. With nothing else to do before supper, I headed down to the lake shoreline to find Elias. He was right where Nan had said he'd be, scrounging up firewood.

Elias had gathered a moderate-sized pile already, but still welcomed my help. "Mostly, we need some bigger stuff now," he explained.

We worked quietly for a while, collecting dead wood from the ash grove that grew nearby. It didn't take long before I realized that the ash trees seemed to have lost more branches than usual. I commented on that to Elias.

"It's the ash borer," he said sadly. "They're dying."

I wondered how that would affect our ceremonial fires, which required a combination of oak, ash, and thornbush branches. I decided not to comment on this, just listened to the wind in the ash trees—their leaves rustling a mournful minor key.

Elias cut larger branches into shorter pieces. I broke up the smaller ones for the fire starter pile. I stacked them log-cabin-style around a clump of finely torn white birch bark, tiny twigs, dry leaves, and pine needles in the stone fire ring we used for bonfires. Our fires were always small, cooking-sized, not monster conflagrations.

Done, I plopped my rear on a large flat rock nearby and watched the last of the thunderheads float away to the east. The sun sparkled and flashed off the myriads of wavelets on the lake. An osprey hovered high overhead, then folded its wings and dove. A moment later, it reappeared on the surface, lifted itself clear of the water, and flew away, a fish in its talons.

Elias, finished with his task, folded his saw, then came to join me. "You're pretty quiet."

I shrugged. Honestly, I just wanted to soak in the peace and serenity of my home. "Got a lot to think about."

He grunted in agreement. "I can imagine." He didn't press me for details though. That's what I like about him. Whereas my mother would interrogate me endlessly, Elias simply waited. Strangely enough, this made it easier to share.

And share I did, in as much detail as I could remember. I told him how Cerridwen had banished me and Kellas to wander about Tír na nÓg after she couldn't lift her own curse on my voice. How the Morrigan had suggested we find Taliesin, and how he'd taught me to play different stringed instruments. How he'd gifted me with a magical lute that was somehow both lute *and* sword, and how I transformed into a wild avatar when it became a sword. I also told Elias about how I'd unintentionally turned all my nightmares loose on Tír na nÓg, then had to go on a search-and-destroy quest to get rid of them all. I told him about the druid Uiscias, the former owner of the sword, and how he'd wanted to kill me so he could get it back. About how Cerridwen also wanted me dead. And how I'd finally managed to banish all my nightmares—regaining my voice in the process. I shared about Rhiannon and helping to save her from marrying a zombie. I even shared how mixed up and confused I was about Kellas.

Elias didn't laugh; he didn't comment. He just listened. Finally, as I ground to a halt in my narrative, he put his arm around my shoulders and gave me a gentle hug. "Wow."

We sat in silence for a bit, listening to those ash trees. Then Elias leaned forward, his elbows on his knees, his fingertips tented together (a sign he was about to say something big). "So, maybe you had your suspicions about this already, but I am also a Cait Sidhe," Elias announced. "Erin, too."

I bet anyone with a camera could make good money on the faces I make when those in my life just drop these little facts on me. No, I hadn't known. Sheesh! Am I clueless or what?

He sighed. "We all owe our lives to Amaris. Without her, we would have simply ceased to exist. As a result, we are duty-bound to her. Not like slaves," he added hastily. "It's more of a loyalty thing."

Apparently, my expression must have reflected how much I disliked the concept of being bound to anyone, even Nan. I didn't doubt she was good to them, but still...!

"Your grandmother is my *anam cara*, my soul mate. And I am hers." His forehead furrowed, he continued, "Erin and Kellas have an on-again, off-again relationship, more fireworks and catfights than lovey-dovey. That said, you are 16. He is ageless. Tread carefully. Never forget he is a fairy cat, and fairy cats can be.... Hmm.... Unreliable."

The wind picked up, and my emotions with it. "Are you unreliable?" I demanded, stung. What exactly was he trying to say? That Kellas would disappear on me the moment I least expected it? That *he* would?

"I have been, at times." He shot me a sideways glance. "I'm not saying Kellas would be unreliable with you, but..."

"Be careful. I get it." I was sorry I'd even mentioned it. I felt awkward and unhappy and wished I'd never said anything, let alone to another guy. Even if that guy was Elias, whom I'd known, like, forever. I don't know why I had even brought it up. I needed to guard my blabbermouth better. Wanting to guide the conversation to safer ground, I asked, "Is it really true Nan is 1,600 years old?"

He chuckled, seeing right through my attempt at deflection—but he went with it. "More accurately, she's ageless."

"Does that mean I will be too?" Obvious question. Though strangely enough, it hadn't occurred to me before now. I guess everything else had distracted me from asking. And the moment I said it out loud, I almost wished I hadn't. Suddenly, it didn't sound so wonderful. What if I was but the people I loved weren't like me? I'd be left alone. My stomach went sour. "What about Dad? Mom?"

"We've talked about that," he said gently. He must have seen the horror in my eyes. "Your maternal side is mortal. They will have normal lifespans. Your dad.... Well, you need to talk to him about that. It's not my place. You.... We don't know. It's a wait-and-see kind of thing."

"That's just weird." I felt completely miserable. I had to bat down the urge to scream—and possibly punch a certain moon goddess, if I could somehow get away with it.

"More questions than answers certainly," Elias summed up. Then, he got to his feet. He helped me up, too. "C'mon, enough of the heavy stuff for now. Let's go see what your grandmother's cooked up for supper."

We lit the Lughnasadh fire just as darkness fell. Flames licked up through my little cabin of twigs and caught hold on the larger branches until we had a lovely fire going that spread light to the far reaches of our rock-rimmed ceremonial circle. The familiar ritual felt reassuring after so much upheaval.

To anyone watching, it was just Nan and me. Nan's hellhound, Bran, had curled up to one side and was snoozing. The Cait Si, all three in cat form, kept to the shadows just beyond the reach of the firelight, waiting and watching. I caught an occasional glimpse of Elias, a giant yellow lion of a cat, and also once saw a slim, ginger-colored tiger cat. By process of elimination, I guessed it was Erin. There was nothing to be seen of Kellas. Black cats are at home in the dark.

Nan was dressed in a simple white knee-length shift, bound around her waist with a twisted cord. I hadn't changed, except to add my gray hoody in case I got chilly. But right now, between the fire and the warm breezes sliding down the hill toward the lake, I was fine.

Nan paced slowly around the firepit, murmuring words I didn't recognize, occasionally tossing something into the fire. Offerings to the gods, I assumed.

I had never paid all that close attention during my summer visits. Before, to my child's understanding, it had always been just a campfire.

I was beginning to feel very odd, though. It was a blend of nausea and lightheadedness combined with a prickly heat, like being vaguely disconnected. At first, I tried to ignore it; I brushed it off as lack of sleep, leftover nerves from my conversation with Elias and the terrifying prospect of being immortal. Or just complicated feelings about the strange, new world I'd been introduced to. All reasonable explanations for feeling anxious-sick, I figured.

I tried to sit with it and hope it went away, but the longer I sat there, the worse I felt. Finally, I was forced to admit that something was horribly, horribly wrong. Hopefully, it was just a *normal* sickness. Please, just let it be that. It had to be.

I still needed to tell my grandmother, though. She'd know what to do. She always did. I struggled to my feet. "Nan...."

But I pitched over. And as my senses deserted me, the world went black.

Four

I stood in a vast blighted field of wheat. Black mold had claimed the grain, and great swaths of the golden straw lay trampled on the ground. It looked totally decimated. I'd never seen anything like it.

People wandered aimlessly through the field, searching for the slightest hint of healthy grain. Small children wandered with their parents, crying, their faces streaked with tears of hunger. Even the adults's clothes hung off bony frames. Hands trembling, parents weakly clutched at their children to keep them close. Their cheeks sunken, their eyes dark and bleak.... These people barely looked alive. An awful shudder went down my spine when one turned my way. I stared into her face; she was a walking skeleton.

My attention turned from her to a fight that had broken out between two women over a single stalk of undamaged wheat. It fell to the ground and was lost under their trampling feet. Some men stepped in and the fight escalated until a terrible scream rang out. One of the women fell, blood gushing from a wound in her chest. I stumbled backward, horrified.

Parents hurried their children away while others crowded closer, hiding the dying woman from my sight. Sounding over all the chaos, a hollow, mocking laugh echoed from all directions, as if in a vast empty chamber....

~

"She's coming around."

I managed to crack my eyelids open. Nan and the Cait Si, all in human form, were clustered around me. I lay on the gravel beach, stones poking me uncomfortably. I tried to sit up, but Kellas pushed me back. "Stay put," he ordered.

I attempted a glare. "There are *rocks* digging into my back! Ow!" I tried again to sit, and this time Nan helped me. "What...what happened?"

"You tell us," Kellas said bluntly. "You added yourself to the fire just now."

"We pulled you off quickly," Erin added. "You might have a few burns anyways. Sorry about your hoody. And your *hair*." From her tone, I wasn't so sure she was all that sorry about my hair.

I was aware of searing pain on my face and right arm, and the awful smell of burnt hair. I'd been on fire. How? Why? Raising a trembling hand to my face, I saw burns from my shoulder down past my elbows toward my wrist. I started shaking uncontrollably. The smell suddenly made me feel sick; my stomach heaved.

"You'll need a new hairdo," Erin supplied. I thought I detected a hint of meanness in her voice. "Something short and sassy."

Burnt hair crumbled away under my exploring hand, and I whimpered in distress. No! I was proud of my hair. I didn't want it cut off!

"Can you walk up to the house?" Nan asked gently. "We need to get something on those burns right away."

"Yeah, I think so." I started to struggle to my feet. Both Erin and Kellas grabbed my arms to help, heaving me up. Blinding pain lanced through me where they touched my burns. "Ow!" I jerked my right arm away from Kellas.

He grunted something that might have been an apology. I pulled away from Erin as well. I wasn't going to accept any help I didn't actually need.

Brushing off dirt and rocks, I started a bit unsteadily toward the house, Kellas hovering nearby. Nan and Elias went on ahead to gather supplies, and Erin and Bran formed a rear guard.

My father came out the back door onto the deck just as we started up the steps, took in the situation in a single glance, held the door wide so we could all get in, then followed us into the kitchen.

"What happened?" Dad asked quietly, as he and Kellas helped me up onto a stool by the kitchen island.

"She took a header into the fire," Kellas told him.

Dad nodded; his expression tightly controlled. "I'll take it from here," he said.

The others left the room.

Nan reentered soon thereafter, carrying a large medical kit. She opened it on the counter and spun it around so my dad could reach things easily. I wiggled painfully out of my badly damaged hoody, so it was easier to reach the burns on my right arm.

I've had plenty of experience with Dad as a medical professional. I was always getting banged up while on vacation here. Not that I did it on purpose. There are a lot of ways to get bashed up when you're a kid enjoying the outdoors. Mom had threatened more than once to stop my annual visits because I always seemed to return home "damaged" in some way. Every. Year. I'd never given it much thought before, but what if it wasn't just being clumsy, as I'd always thought? What if it was because of *attacks from another dimension?* Crap! I didn't need yet another crisis right now. I pushed that thought aside. Not something I cared to entertain.

Dad carefully placed a large bandage by my right eye. "This one might leave a scar," he commented, "but at least it missed your eye."

"Kellas had her off in an instant," Nan said quietly. "You'll want to look at his hands. He used them to beat out the fire on her." I can't deny that my heart jumped at that. Kellas usually acted like my presence was a bother. But he did that? For *me*?

"See if he'll let me take a look after I finish here." Nan left to find Kellas and Dad continued to apply burn patches to my right shoulder and arm.

It made me feel like a car with too many bumper stickers. I moved restlessly on my stool.

"Nearly done, kiddo," he chided. "Good thing you're not going back to North Dakota anytime soon. Your mother would have my guts for garters."

Nan returned. "He claimed he's fine."

Dad grunted. "Kellas would be 'fine' even if he were half dead. Insist, if you would, please."

"I did. He still refused."

Dad shrugged. "His choice." He finished applying the last burn patch and straightened up, giving me an appraising look. "Feel better?"

Having the burns covered up made them hurt less, and I said so. My hand strayed to the one high on my right cheekbone. I went to brush my hair behind my ear and froze when I felt it fall apart under my fingers. My hair!

I moaned and hopped down from the stool, making a beeline for the bathroom. I took one look in the mirror and wailed like a child. The hair on the right side of my head was ragged; in one place it was nearly burnt to my scalp, in others it hung in damaged clumps, some of which crumbled and fell off the moment I touched it.

Nan came in as I stood and bawled, sympathy bright in her silver-blue eyes.

Turning away from the mirror, I threw myself at her, knocking her back a step. "I'm so ugly!"

Taking care not to touch the painful spots, she wrapped her arms around me and laid her cheek against the top of my head. "No, you're not," she soothed. "Your hair will grow back."

"It'll take forever!" I moaned.

"Sweetheart. It's hair!"

How did I tell her my hair was the only thing I really liked about my looks? "I liked my hair the way it was!"

"I liked it too. But still, it's *hair*. It will grow back. Meanwhile, we can play with it a bit. Maybe punk it up some?" She set me back at arm's length so she could look me in the eyes. Her own were twinkling with a bit of mischief. "Come on, sweetie. It might be fun!"

I groaned. Nan was such an optimist. "OK for you to say. If yours were any shorter, you'd be bald." Now that was rather rude, and I regretted it the moment I'd said it. But Nan only laughed.

"Short hair has some significant advantages, Raven." She set me back at arm's length and locked her eyes with mine. "You'll be *fine*, dear. Your hair *will* grow back. Meanwhile..." she released me and opened the medicine cabinet, taking out a lethal-looking pair of shears. She slipped her fingers into the holes and snipped them open and shut a couple of times. "Shall we?"

I gave my reflection a last sad look in the mirror, then nodded grimly.

"OK then, wet your mop down and let's get going."

I dutifully followed orders and went to the kitchen, where I sat in a chair with a bedsheet wrapped around my shoulders. Nan walked around me, studying my wrecked mane for a few minutes, then went to work. After the first long chunk of hair fell to the floor, I squeezed my eyes shut. I couldn't bear to watch.

Nan worked steadily for the better part of an hour, leaving once to fetch a set of clippers and another time to get a hairdryer and brush to style my new 'do. She clicked off the dryer and studied me from every angle. Then nodded, satisfied.

"Go take a look and tell me what you think."

I flung off the bedsheet and headed for the bathroom, filled with trepidation. A stranger stared back at me from the mirror: high cheekbones; dark, haunted eyes; a hard jawline that said, "stubborn." Where the fire had burned to my scalp, Nan had buzzed three lines and three dots...the Awen symbol. Everywhere else, my hair was somewhere between three to six inches long. The gel she'd used kept it swept back from my face. This new hairstyle made me look older, stronger, and maybe...even a bit fierce. I had to admit, I looked *good*.

Nan had just finished sweeping up when I returned to the kitchen. "Well?" she asked, smiling. As if she didn't already know.

I tried to look downcast, but I was a poor actress. I broke into a huge grin. "Pretty amazeballs!"

Nan laughed. "I take it that's good, then?"

Dad and Elias came in then, and I basked in their compliments.

Kellas came in a bit later. I'd gone back into the bathroom to admire my reflection again but heard him out in the kitchen. "How's the little burnt sacrifice doing?"

Annoyed, I went back out to the kitchen and Nan pointed to me. Kellas turned. His reaction was priceless, a wordless double take that was all the better for being completely natural. He gave me a hard look. "Always knew you were trouble, kid. Now you look like it."

Strangely enough, this was the best compliment of all. I grinned and bounced up and down on my toes. "I know, right?" I touched the Awen symbol on my scalp. "This is epic!"

The clock in the living room chimed 11 p.m. Our party broke up shortly thereafter. Just as I drifted off to sleep, I remembered the vision I'd had when I'd fallen into the fire. I needed to tell Nan about that in the morning....

I was back in the blighted wheat field, but this time there were no people, just a deep feeling of foreboding, of an imminent menace. Instinctively, I reached over my shoulder for Fraegarthach.

Again, I heard that deep, mocking laughter. It echoed and swelled about me, coming from every side. I pulled my sword free and felt my body transform.

"Stupid child. You think you can defeat me with a sword?" Fog condensed around me, swirled in cold droplets. A haggard, gray face formed in the mist, twisted, reformed, then hung midair, bodyless.

"Who are you?" I gasped, holding Fraegarthach in front of me with both hands. Cold, I was so cold...

The mocking laughter again, chilling me further until I was shuddering like a leaf. My stomach ached cruelly, as if I hadn't eaten anything for days.

"All creatures fear me. I am nothing, yet everything. I birth death and cruelty, destruction and despair. Where I am, darkness follows. I give nothing. Fear nothing. Love nothing!"

"You're a monster then," I gritted out, gripping my sword with failing strength.

The demon in the fog laughed at that, continued laughing as I grew rapidly weaker until I fell to my knees on the hard ground.

"Die, stupid earth girl. You alone cannot save the world from me. Die and let me get on with my work..."

With the last of my strength, I raised Fraegarthach. "Not. Gonna. Happen. You. Freak." I plunged my sword to the hilt into the blighted soil.

Five

I awoke with the monster's screams echoing in my ears. I was soaked with sweat, bedsheets tangled and tossed about me. Wide awake too, despite it being 3:11 a.m. Disgusted, I changed into dry clothing and headed downstairs, my stomach complaining loudly.

A light was already on in the kitchen. As I came in, Kellas emerged from behind the refrigerator door, a stack of leftover food containers balanced precariously in one hand.

"Might have known you'd show up," he grunted, pushing the fridge door shut with one foot. He set the containers down on the counter. "What'll it be? We have roast beef, ham, three kinds of cheeses. Looks like we have some ciabatta rolls. A sandwich perhaps?"

"I'd eat about anything right now," I said, rummaging through the fridge for lettuce and condiments.

"Famine will do that to you." He started assembling our sandwiches, but scowled at the proffered lettuce. "Don't want any rabbit food, thanks."

"But I do," I retorted, setting the lettuce down on the counter next to where he was working, along with the condiments. "Make mine with the spicy mustard, please."

"Like you need spicing up," he grumbled. But I saw he applied the stuff liberally to one of the rolls.

"Famine, you said." I straddled one of the bar stools, put my chin on my hands, elbows on the counter, and watched him work.

He sent me a dark look. "Yeah. Famine. I thought you would realize by now when you were dimension-hopping."

My stomach growled audibly and, despite myself, I giggled. Kellas sent me a reproachful look. He set the finished sandwich on a plate and slid it across the counter to me, then leaned one hip on the counter and bit into his own. We ate in silence for a while until the raging emptiness in my belly eased— helping clear my head for more critical thinking skills. "So, famine...."

Silence.

When Kellas did not respond, I added, "That was an invitation to explain, Cat Man."

He quirked one eyebrow in response, then slowly and deliberately finished his sandwich before responding. Dratted feline anyways! He licked off his fingers one at a time. "Yeah. Famine." Returning to the fridge, he disappeared behind the door again, this time emerging with a gallon of milk. He poured two glasses full and set one in front of me, then slid onto the stool next to mine. "You know the legend of the God Lugh and the battle with Carman, right?"

"The fight between feast and famine."

He gave me a mocking salute. "You got it. It's why we Celts celebrate Lughnasadh, with bread-making and fire ceremonies giving tribute to the god Lugh and so on and so forth. Too bad you had to go insert yourself into the whole battle scene and steal Lugh's thunder. Thank the gods that insane sword of yours knew what to do."

I finished my sandwich, trying to digest what he just said. "I take it you were there, too."

"Dragged there kicking and screaming the whole way." He drank his milk in one long go.

I shot him a quizzical glance.

He set his glass down deliberately. "It would appear I'm still bound to you somehow, despite your more intemperate impulses. Kindly try not to get me killed in the process, OK? I rather like my life."

It was selfish of me, I realized, but my spirits soared at the news. I felt less alone in this crazy rabbit hole of an adventure.

"I'll try."

He sighed. "'Do. Or do not. There is no try.'"

I recognized the line from the movie *The Empire Strikes Back*. "Oh, man, now you're Yoda? I am definitely *not* Luke Skywalker, so get that analogy out of your little cat brain."

Dad shuffled into the kitchen at that point, looking distinctly bleary eyed, and made a beeline for the coffee maker. "You two realize it's not even four in the morning, right?"

"Me, too!" I prompted as he reached for the coffee beans.

"And me," Kellas added.

Dad nodded acknowledgement and started the brewing ritual. With that underway, he took advantage of all the sandwich making materials still strewn on the counter and started assembling his own sandwich. "I feel like I've been eating subtraction stew," he said. It was a reference to one of my favorite books, *The Phantom Tollbooth*, when Milo and his friends were eating a stew served by the Mathematician, getting hungrier and hungrier until the Bug realized they had been eating Famine.

"You would. That's because junior, here, has been flirting with Famine herself," Kellas informed him.

Dad sent me an alarmed look. "Raven!"

"In my defense, I had no idea!" I protested.

Then, Nan walked in, closely followed by Elias. How she could look reasonably alert after such a crappy night's sleep was anyone's guess. Elias, I noted with some satisfaction, looked nearly as sleep deprived as the rest of us.

"Raven, you've been lucid dreaming again." Nan sounded cranky. So maybe she wasn't as perky as she looked. Great. Just my luck. Here comes the lecture!

Dad set out five mugs and filled each part way before running out. "I'll make more," he assured us, and set about doing so.

"Can we all please talk about what just happened?" I asked. "Apparently, everyone here knows what's going on but me."

"Actually, we don't, really." Nan opened the fridge door and stood studying its contents for a minute before emerging with two containers of yogurt. She handed one to Elias, and he handed her a spoon as though he'd known exactly what she was going to get out of the fridge even before she brought it out. Awesome invisible communication skills.

They were hungry too. Apparently, we were all experiencing the fallout of dimension-hopping.

Nan leaned back against the kitchen sink and spooned yogurt into her mouth, tasting it thoughtfully. She swallowed before responding. "What we *do* know is that our Lughnasadh ceremony yesterday evening triggered something. Your reaction," she pointed at me with her spoon, "was to pass out. Thank the gods Kellas was close-by and pulled you off the fire before you were seriously injured. Then, apparently, when you fell asleep, you started a lucid dream, dimension-hopping to where Lugh and Carman were dueling..."

"How do you know that?" I demanded.

"I was there too, this time."

"But...!" I protested.

She'd taken another bite of yogurt but hastily pulled her spoon from her mouth and waved it at me, swallowing quickly. "We don't blame you, Raven!

We know it wasn't deliberate. What I don't understand is how we all got pulled into it with you."

"All of you?" I managed weakly. I looked around our little circle. Dad nodded, and Elias merely tightened his lips a little. Yes, him too. Gods.

"I was there too." Erin stalked in, distinctly unhappy, her red hair mussed like she'd been tossing and turning. Like the rest of us, she beelined to the fridge. "I, for one, would have appreciated a little advance notice." She leaned back around the open fridge door to send me a daggers-drawn stare.

"I had no idea!" I protested.

Nan waved down the impending argument with her spoon. "None of us did," she said soothingly. "So...you really didn't know we were there with you?"

"No!"

"Hmm." Nan pondered that. Finally, she shook her head. "I've no idea. But the problem remains. How should we handle this going forward?"

"Send her back to North Dakota?" Erin muttered ungraciously, earning an icy stare from my dad. Go Dad! She harrumphed and stalked off to the opposite corner of the kitchen from the rest of us with her food.

"Alright," Nan continued. "Let's work on that and see if we can figure something out quickly. Meanwhile, we've got a game plan to bring Raven up to speed on everything else we could think of. We're all up anyways. Shall we get started?"

~

I did not regret having missed out on winter, I decided, but August in upstate New York was proving unusually hot and humid. Mornings were wonderful, filled with sunshine, birdsong, and fragrant breezes, but huge thunderstorms built up in the heat of the afternoons, turning the sky and lake gray as gun-metal, filling the air with blinding flashes of light, ear-splitting thunder, and the lingering smell of ozone. Not that it rained all that much. Nan informed me we had been in a drought all summer, and more rain would have been welcome.

It had been a week since Lughnasadh, but we had already fallen into a schedule built around the weather, spending almost all of our time outside, retreating indoors only when the storms blew in and watching them play out their fury over the lake below. Today, Nan and I watched one as it worked its way slowly eastward. I had sprawled on a giant beanbag chair near the front bank of windows in the living room. Nan sat on the sofa nearby, making notes in a spiral-bound notebook. Often, I fell asleep listening to the storms, but today I just felt restless. I'd been spending nearly every waking minute with Nan, trying to memorize everything she was teaching me, practicing the simplest things repeatedly, trying to get them right. It was proving a challenge.

At least I'd pretty quickly picked up on the simplest of ward crafting...it had nothing to do with the video game versions, and everything about your intent while following a set series of steps.

Wards are a magical way of setting up a boundary that, *in theory*, humans or non-humans cannot cross. *In theory* because there have been instances where non-humans have crashed through and made a nuisance of themselves. It works better on humans, who come up against a ward, suddenly remember they had an important appointment elsewhere, and leave in a hurry.

Casting a ward is a lot like following a recipe. For wards, you need sunlight—which is available even on a cloudy day, it's just not as strong. It also requires chlorophyll (the green stuff in plants) and water. Ward casting uses the energy that the chlorophyll pulls from sunlight and water, and instead of creating a plant with it, creates a ward. It also requires moon magic, which few people have, but the magic comes with some not-so-great side effects.

And, like with any recipe, different cooks get different results. My wards aren't nearly as professional as my Nan's, but she keeps telling me I'll get better at it with practice. I think she's being overly optimistic.

I still haven't mastered the spell of seeming, which is currently my biggest frustration. I hate looking like a little kid. Right now, I'm about 10 or 11.

"It was easier in the Summer Lands," I said, as the thunder rumbled away across the hills beyond the lake.

Nan looked up from her scribbling, pen suspended in midair. "Pardon?"

I had shared the saga of our adventures in Tír na nÓg with Nan shortly after our return, not that I had any other choice. She was as deft a cross-examiner as my mom. I'd showed her Taliesin's gift, and she'd echoed my instinctive reaction about never taking it off. "A talisman of great power," she had told me. "Who knows what all it does. Time will tell, I guess."

I had yet to tell my own mother (whom I owed another video call...ugh!) about my adventures. I dreaded it, suddenly wondering how Mom would handle me turning into my wild avatar warrior self. Doing so in front of her was something I wanted to avoid, if possible.

I rolled over on the beanbag and rested my chin on folded forearms. "Learning," I told her. "It was easier, almost instantaneous. Like magic, or osmosis."

Nan chuckled. "Osmosis. I like that analogy! But remember Raven, time there works differently. What you felt as only a few days was nine long months here. Think how much you can learn in that amount of time."

I waggled my head back and forth, seeing her point. "Whatcha writing?"

Nan had gone back to scribbling. "Notes," she supplied. "I'm trying to make order out of chaos, cover all the bases in a reasonable progression. Lesson plans, if you will."

I groaned and rolled off the beanbag onto the hardwood floor before pushing myself to my feet. "Lessons and more lessons!" I grumbled. Both Nan and Elias had kept me busy with instruction as varied as setting wards on doorways to Aikido. Elias was teaching me how to be a better swordsman also, not that he ever allowed me to draw Fraegarthach. We practiced with wooden sticks. Kellas popped in and out, but often he was gone off somewhere, doing something no one felt necessary for me to know anything about. That was annoying, because, well, I still had feelings for him. I rather liked having him around, annoying as he could be! Dad was gone 24 hours at a time for his job as a paramedic, often with Erin shadowing him. A lot of his off days were spent catching up on sleep. "The crazies are out in force" was all he ever said when asked. Pressed for details, he'd just smile. "You have enough on your plate with everything your Nan is throwing at you." I'd given up asking.

I picked up my lute. It was always available just over my shoulder, invisible and without substance until I consciously thought about it. I was reaching for it in another dimension, one made available to me by right of ownership of that very special instrument. It was remarkably handy having it always close at hand without lugging it around all the while. I plopped down on the chair near Nan. I'd grown accustomed to how alive it felt; there was always a latent energy about it, even when it was silent. When I played, however, it felt like a living thing under my hands. I touched the strings now, sounding a soft arpeggio.

"Apparently, when I played by the cliff in Tír na nÓg, I called in the werewolves and all the other creepies." Another arpeggio. "That just didn't make sense to me. How could I have done that?"

Nan put down her pen with a sigh. "To understand that, you must consider how magic works to begin with. It's not evenly distributed," she explained. "There are areas of concentration. You sat at the edge of a tall cliff between the highlands and the valley, which is a very clear boundary—a particularly powerful place for magic. Consider how people are drawn to those kinds of locations: cliff edges, mountaintops, ocean and lake shores, just to name a few.

All beautiful views are compelling, but views such as these, even ordinary people describe them as *magical*."

"It was a really great view," I agreed.

"So, when you combine a magical place with the sword that divides light from dark, even in its disguise as a musical instrument, you call really powerful forces into play."

"This lute." I lifted its neck slightly.

Nan nodded. "Fraegarthach, like many talismans of great power, has a lot of nicknames. Nuada's sword. The sword that divides day from night, or light from dark. The Unbeatable Sword, the Protector, the Whisperer, the Answerer, the Retaliator. And my personal favorite, Claimh Solais. It means sword of light. It is one of four magical talismans of the Tuatha Dé Danann, and had been missing for many centuries. Its last known *chosen one* was a bard, and accomplished magician, who magicked it into the disguise it now carries."

Yeah, I'd met the dude. Uiscias. He was a prize jerk, in my opinion.

Nan continued. "That disguise was a stroke of genius. Otherwise, the bearer was forever a target. The Claimh Solais is a creature of magic far more powerful than even the other three."

"What are those?"

"A stone, a spear, and a cauldron." Nan picked up her notebook again and made a note in it. Outside, the storm continued unabated.

"Like Cerridwen's cauldron?" Cerridwen was the Celtic full moon goddess, and a right royal pain in my backside. I guess she thought the same about me, though.

"One and the same."

"Who has the other ones?" I plucked the lute's strings, sounding a minor chord.

"Arianrod possesses the stone, and the Morrigan carries the spear."

Arianrod was yet another moon goddess; they were practically a dime a dozen in the old religion. The Morrigan was the Celtic Goddess of Death, and one utterly terrifying lady. I'd come up against her a time or two as well. "What are their powers?" They couldn't possibly be as awesome as mine.

Nan merely smiled. "Their gifts tend to rely on the strengths of the ones entrusted with them. You will, in time, discover your own version of Fraegarthach. It might be *very* different from before."

I sent her a puzzled frown. "Why should that be?"

Nan looked like she knew a secret. "Well, you are the first female to wield it, for one."

Oh. Huh. I went back to practicing arpeggios. Nan returned to working on her notes. Bran groaned a little in his sleep and a hind leg twitched as though he were chasing something. The storm outside continued.

Really, it was lasting an awfully long time for a thunderstorm. I looked up from my lute, scowling out into the twilight cast by the storm just as a thick column of orange fire slammed into a solo white pine tree in the yard, accompanied by a blinding flash of light and a crash of thunder that happened all at the same time.

Six

It was so violent, so sudden, that for a couple heartbeats I couldn't process what had just happened. It took several seconds before my body finally came out of its shock. I jumped up and ran to the window wall.

"Nan, the tree!" It was fully engulfed in flames.

She was already beside me, her breathing shallow and fast. "Oh, gods, no..." She was yanking open the door and dashing out into the pouring rain as she spoke. Bran squeezed past her and ran at the tree, barking madly. Like an idiot, I dashed out after them as thunder continued to rumble and groan like the drone of death itself. We were instantly soaked to the skin, not that we noticed. The fate of the pine held our entire attention. It had been there for as long as I could remember: huge, ageless. But it was now clearly dying, scream-ing in agony like a woman, high and shrill, fully engulfed in flames from the base of its trunk into the highest branches.

How could that be? I wondered, the shock of it making me lightheaded and dizzy. A living thing, burning like tinder, sounding like a woman burning alive. The horror of it was carving deep into my mind.

Nan was screaming an incantation at the flames, her hands outstretched, standing so close to the conflagration that her clothes were steaming, sur-rounding her in fog. I struggled to stay close to her, wanting to help. But my shocked brain was not processing. What could I do? The flames nearest her hands were dampened, but the remainder of the tree continued its disastrous immolation unchecked.

Abruptly, the screaming stopped. Nan fell to her knees, sobbing uncontrollably. The fire continued unabated. The rain couldn't get close enough to drown out the fire, changing to steam before getting anywhere near the flames. It finally registered in my brain that Nan was steaming too, which meant that she could catch on fire...Gods!

Snapping out of my shock, I grabbed Nan under her arms and dragged her away from the fire. Her clothing was almost too hot to touch, and I gritted my teeth against the pain of it.

When we were far enough away that we were safe from the flames, I lowered Nan to the ground, dropped to my knees and wrapped my arms around her. I could feel her trembling in my arms, shivering as she wept. My heart ached for her. Bran whined and licked her face. Nan looked ancient, her spell of seeming dispelled by the effort she'd poured into trying to save the tree.

It hit me like a ton of bricks then: while I grew stronger with the full moon, she did not.

Elias appeared out of the downpour and scooped Nan up in his arms. "Come," was all he said, and I followed him into the house.

The storm abated soon afterward, leaving everything dripping wet, clouds floating away over the lake, flickering bits of lightning like snake tongues in its wake.

The pine tree burned steadily. We sat in the living room, bundled up in oversized fluffy towels, and watched it burn. I couldn't stop looking at it. Couldn't stop hearing the screaming as it echoed in my brain. I started shivering uncontrollably. Someone...Kellas, I think...settled another banket around my shoulders and I pulled it close, managing only a nod of thanks.

Nan looked utterly devastated. "I couldn't stop it," she choked out. Gods, she looked beyond ancient. So fragile...

"Not your fault, you did your best," Elias tried to comfort her.

Nan's jaw tightened and she sent him a wild look. "It wasn't good enough. She died anyways! The moon is still too close to being full and I am too weak. Besides, my wards should have stopped a direct strike like that!"

Elias said nothing. I guessed that there must be some truth in what Nan had said about the wards. I knew they were designed to keep intruders out. Not that they worked all that well against the gods themselves. Take Cerridwen. Her flashy entrance last year, right through the closed windows, is one such example. The wards were designed to allow natural phenomena like wind and rain and sunshine, but not truly violent weather. Until now, that is.

"She saved me," Nan said sadly. "When it was my turn to save her, I couldn't."

I blinked in confusion. Maybe it wasn't terribly sensitive of me, but I had to know. "How could a tree save you?"

Elias glared at me, but Nan lay a hand on his arm. "She should know." She gazed at me, her pale blue eyes still swimming in tears. "That tree was the home of a very old friend...a tree nymph. You remember the stories about how different spirits protect the trees and rivers?" She waited until I nodded before going on. "Back when I was first made into...what we are..." she gestured to herself and then me. "Cerridwen's idea of saving me, it was just past the new moon, like you were when you changed. Orinthia, the nymph who's been protecting the pine here, snatched me up and hid me just as the warriors arrived, so they never found me."

Gads. "So, you were an infant!" I exclaimed. Pretty shortsighted of Cerridwen, but I didn't have much faith in her discretionary powers, given my experiences with her.

She nodded. For some odd reason, this was helping Nan get a grip on herself. She mopped her eyes on her towel, then sniffed several times. Elias handed her a box of tissues. She sent him a look of thanks and took a moment to blow her nose.

"As Taliesin told you, my family was targeted for death by another powerful druid. First, they killed my father, then when my mother and I fled into the forest, they hunted us like wild animals until we could run no longer. Mother appealed to the goddess Cerridwen to save me, and the goddess demanded a sacrifice. Her own life was the only thing my mother had left to give, so she killed herself. Orinthia witnessed the whole thing and snatched me up just in time, or else all of this would never have been. The hunters would have killed me as surely as they killed my father and caused my mother's death."

"A baby? They would have killed a baby?" My mouth hung open for a moment until shock gave way to righteous fury. "Monsters!"

Nan nodded, her eyes dark with sadness. "Without even a second thought. They were possessed of Dother."

Oh boy. More new names. This was *not* a good sign! "Who's Bother?" I was clueless, never a fun situation.

Nan managed a watery smile. "Dother, with a 'D,' sometimes called Olc. The spirit of evil, or wickedness. What we now call trolls. He is one of Carman's three sons."

"You're losing me!" I exclaimed. "No one I recognize." *Carmen? What, like Carmen Sandiego? No, why would I be that lucky?*

Nan managed another weak smile. "Carman was a Grecian witch goddess who invaded Ireland with her three sons, Dub, Dian, and Dother. These four are collectively known by the Celts as 'the Old Gods.'"

"Oh bother, it's Dother," I muttered. "Yes?"

My stupid rhyme brought a wan smile to Nan's face. "Carman laid waste to the crops. Her son Dub is a god of darkness, Dother a god of evil, and Dian a god of violence. All of them perpetrate cruelty that could be tied in some way to their mother's domain: famine."

"What a happy family," I said faintly. "Thanksgiving and Christmas must be a riot at their place. Imagine the party games!"

Nan sent me an amused look, which I took as a win because I hated seeing her so distraught.

"We Druids celebrate the winter solstice, Alban Arthan...the light of Arthur, not Christmas, but never mind. It took all the Tuatha Dé Danann to defeat the Old Gods and cast them out," she continued. "Lugh, the god of plenty, overpowered Carman herself with the sword of Nuada...*your* sword. Carman was imprisoned, but required a feast to be carried out in her honor. We do so at the feast of Lughnasadh, our harvest ceremony, where we celebrate our triumph over famine. Her sons, as you can see from the news, have been hard at work all over the world, doing what they do best, spreading chaos and cruelty."

I let that information bounce around my mind for a beat before the realization of what this meant all but punched me in the chest. "So maybe that's what I saw last week, at the fire when I passed out? Could Carman be back somehow?" This was so not cool... This was what we were up against? Just no way I could manage all that. I felt panic starting to overtake me.

Elias and Nan exchanged looks. Elias was the one to reply. "That's what we're afraid of, Raven."

～

I wandered out the back door and down the lawn toward the lake, feeling utterly overwhelmed and scared. Nan had quickly explained about Carman and her sons—and what they were capable of: wholesale murder, mayhem, and despair. The Old Gods left chaos and ruin in their wake, and they weren't just flippantly uncaring moon goddesses like Cerridwen; they were...monsters. The monsters you believed hid underneath your bed as a baby, the kind you were supposed to realize didn't exist when you grew up.

Except that they did. There were real, actual monsters. And now, they were targeting us. The enormity of their existence and their power crashed down on me like heavy waves on the surf. I felt helpless. There was no way we could possibly win against them. No way. Not when they could always draw willing minions, like flies to dead meat. Not when they could just make monsters out of anyone. Because—who wouldn't be driven to rage if they were pushed hard enough? It made me want to run and hide someplace where the world couldn't find me, to crawl into a hole in the deepest wilderness and vanish.

There was a time when I thought my parents and Nan were invincible, that they would take care of everything, that I would be safe and loved always. Now, I wasn't so sure. Nan was *old*. Iku was too—although not nearly as old as Nan. Mom was a nervous wreck; although I didn't fully understand why. And Dad was...Dad. He just carried on as always, like a good soldier—doing whatever came his way and saying nothing about it. I didn't know how he felt about any of this. As for Elias and Kellas...and Erin too (not that I cared much for her), all relied on Nan to a degree that was just disturbing. How much longer could she hold on, anyways? Sixteen hundred years is a long time to live, even if you are magically rejuvenated every month.

I stood on the lake shore, looking at but not seeing the water in front of me. My mind was miles away. Sixteen hundred. I'd first learned that from Taliesin when I'd been in Tír na nÓg. But just how old that made my Nan hadn't really hit home. Now it did.

My stomach twisted with a familiar panic when my thoughts looped back around to the immortality question, but I banished it before it overwhelmed me again.

I plopped down on a nearby boulder and stuck my feet in the water. It had gotten ungodly hot and humid after the storm, and I was sweating bullets. The water didn't offer me any answers, but the soft ripples soothed my spirit a little.

"Want some company?" Kellas appeared out of nowhere, startling me. He snickered, of course.

"Jeepers, Cat Man! Don't you know how to approach someone without scaring them out of their wits?"

"I could leave," he offered with a lazy smirk.

Grabbing his wrist, I pulled him down on the rock next to me. "I could use some moral support right now. Think you could manage that?"

He snorted, leaned back on his hands, and sent me a wry grin. "I'm told that's not one of my strong suits, Brannaugh."

"I tend to agree, but you're all I have at the moment, so please at least try to show some empathy," was my retort.

He raised that quirky eyebrow at me. "OK, so try me."

I thought for a second about where to begin. "Nan's ancient."

A faintly amused look crossed his handsome features. "So am I."

"But you don't age like she does."

"Thank the gods for small favors," he grunted. "We're not tied to moon phases like you two are."

"What are we to do?" I spread my hands out, palms up. "I have no idea what to do, or even if there's anything I *can* do. It's all so new and so sudden and I—Ugh!"

Kellas was silent for a moment. "That pretty much sums it up, kid."

Really?!! I punched him in the arm. "You're no help!"

He rubbed his arm where I'd hit him. "Easy, tiger! You pack a wallop."

"Sorry." I wasn't, much. Well, maybe a little. "It's just...I'm so confused. And scared. What can I do against ancient evils that can't be killed, if even Nan can't prevail against them?" Right there was the crux of the problem. "Did she ever tell you why she came here from Ireland?"

He thought about that for a moment, then shrugged. "She never said, directly. We came because she did."

"Nan's hiding. That's what she just told me." I stared at the water, feeling helpless and lost. "For the last 400 years, she's been hiding here in the United States, out in the country, hoping none of those old immortals would find her and bother her anymore. She doesn't think she can manage what they like to throw at her because she gets so old and weak at the full moon." I kicked the water in a sudden flash of frustration. "But then Dad married Mom and they had me, and that messed absolutely everything up. Because of me, Nan's no longer safe. And neither are the rest of you. It's all because of me! How am I supposed to handle that guilt trip, huh?!"

Kellas pondered that for a while before responding. "Amaris doesn't stay weak for long, right? Just while the moon is full, and again when the moon is dark. That means she's strong the rest of the time. While you, you're at the peak of your powers when the moon is full but weak at the dark of the moon." He shot me a sidelong glance. "And that's when we're the most vulnerable. That's why you need Erin and me, Elias, Bran, and the help of Nan's warding magic—"

"Which was just breached by that monster lightning bolt," I reminded him. Tipping my head back, I closed my eyes and groaned. I was led to believe that what had happened today wasn't supposed to be possible, even if it had been a naturally occurring lightning bolt—which Nan and Elias found doubtful. I planted my elbows on my knees and bent over, grabbing my hair with both hands. Harder to do now, since it was so short in places. "What am I supposed to *DO*?!" I cried.

Kellas pondered that quietly, while I wallowed in self-pity. I was as good at that as anyone else. So why not? Considering everything!

Finally, he drew a deep breath and let it out slowly. "Well, try not to let this go to your head, OK? Let's go over what you are good at, and frankly, it's a fair bit. With that sword, without a lick of training, you've taken on and defeated...single-handedly, mind you...the ghouls of the Dark Lands *and* the werewolves of human imagination. Right?" He jostled me with one elbow, as if to make sure I acknowledged that point. "And even with minimum training, when you play your music, you can do considerable healing magic. Even the rocks pay attention."

I sent him a skeptical sideways look. "Rocks, you say?"

A faint grin twitched his lips. "Hmm. Yes. Rocks. It's hard to get their attention, by the way. It's like they have rocks for brains."

I groaned and straightened up so I could roll my eyes at him. "Har de har, har." However, his dumb joke helped me feel a bit less desperate, like it was OK to breathe again.

He grinned and waggled his eyebrows a bit. "That's your superpower, I think. That and singing. You need to sing more. You're really pretty good... or you could be if you practiced more. Have you played to heal your burns? You should try at least." He paused and gave me an intense up-and-down look, scrutinizing me. "How are they coming by the way?"

I'd almost forgotten about them. I'd healed incredibly fast. Even the bad one near my eye was almost gone. I had a bandage there, but mostly to be careful. I didn't want a scar if I could help it. Hey, I'm as vain about my looks as the next girl, OK? "They're mostly healed." Could that have been because I'd been practicing my music? Wild. "How about your hands?" I asked Kellas.

"They're coming along," he said—while attempting to hide his hands.

But I grabbed Kellas's right wrist and turned his hand over. I winced: the skin was puckered and raw looking, some areas still oozing lymph fluid. Natch, he hadn't even bandaged his wounds. Crazy cat.

"They look awful," I said bluntly. Reaching over my back, I pulled out my lute. "Let's see if this works for you, too. What shall I play?"

"Doesn't that depend on the lute?" he asked quietly.

"Hmm! Probably." Bending over the lute and touching its strings lightly, I asked it what to play. The arpeggios I'd been practicing earlier sang forth, pulled together, and formed a hauntingly familiar pattern. I was singing Shubert's *Ave Maria*, the version I'd heard so many times on Dad's Celine Dion recording. I poured everything I had into it, striving to achieve the same golden tones as my musical hero.

Finishing that song, I immediately segued into another: *Heal the World*. I belted out Michael Jackson's lyrics like they were written on my soul. It wasn't until after the few final chords had faded away that I noticed it. Total silence. No wind, no birdsong. Nothing. I opened my eyes and looked around in confusion. "What happened?"

Kellas was staring at his hands. He met my gaze with his own and slowly tipped his palms toward me. They were completely healed. Strong new skin covered them entirely. You couldn't even see where the burns had been.

Maybe I was getting used to crazy miracles; I managed not to freak out quite so much. "Wow, that's amazing." I'd done that? Me and my magical lute?

"Somehow Brannaugh, I don't think we have as much to worry about as we thought we did."

Slowly, normal sounds were picking up around me again, as if the world had held its collective breath and was finally letting it out again. I slid my lute back into its hiding place over my shoulder, wandered over to the ash grove nearby, and listened intently. Where before they'd sung in a mournful minor key, it had now changed and sounded happy. Peaceful. The worried knot in my chest loosened a little.

"The trees feel better too," I called over to Kellas, who was still staring at his hands like he'd never really looked at them before. I laughed in sheer relief. "This is incredible!"

A heavy flurry of wings startled me as an enormous raven landed on Elias's wood pile nearby. I gasped, and Kellas shot to his feet as though the rock had become too hot to sit on.

"What are you doing here, Huginn?" Kellas stalked toward the bird, who merely ruffled its feathers and trained one beady eye on him.

"You know this bird?" I asked. "He's beautiful." He really was, too. As large as ravens get, this one was much larger, his black feathers iridescent with a rainbow of color laid over the dark. Anyone who thought black was a boring color was not very observant.

Kellas moved close to me, a low snarl in his throat, like a cat warning away a threat. "That's Odin's bird, and he has no business being here. Scat!"

"Odin?" I rather hoped he was joking. Gods help me, the Norse pantheon was a thing as well?

'Why so quick to get rid of me, Cait Sidhe?'

The thought came into my head like it was my own, but it wasn't. It rumbled low and powerful, like a string bass. From Kellas's reaction, he'd heard it too. And it did not make him happy. The snarl grew louder.

'Relax, Cait Sidhe, we are not enemies in this fight. The child has healed me, and I am appreciative.'

"I'm...confused," I admitted. Should I be playing peacemaker here? No need to offend *another* deity. I already had the Celtic gods to deal with! "Maybe, explain?" I prompted cautiously.

The bird trained its bright eyes on me. *'I had an encounter with one of your birds of prey. I was injured and could not return to Odin. You sang. I was healed. Thank you.'*

"You're welcome," I said reflexively. "Really, my singing healed you? Like Kellas? Like the trees?"

Huginn ruffled his feathers. *'Likewise.'*

"Don't trust him, Brannaugh." Kellas was visibly bristling, despite being in human form. What was I missing here? "He's a raven. Ravens are…"

'Tricksters?' the raven thought at us. *'Unreliable? Like Cait Si, perhaps?'* The bird stretched its wings out to their full length…they must have been six feet long, wingtip to wingtip…and flapped them several times, sending a flurry of dead leaves and wood chips flying. *'I tire of your delusional attitude toward me and my kind. You, however,'* somehow, I knew he meant me, *'As a symbol of my gratitude to you, you may call on my aid once. But be careful. Be sure that it is truly needed, for once requested, you cannot undo it.'*

"Thank you," I said. Aid? From a raven?

'Again, I am underestimated.' Huginn sounded disappointed, as though he'd read my thoughts. *'Don't prejudge, child. The smallest amongst us have the greatest power to enact change. Think of the microorganisms in the soil. Without them, nothing would grow. The creatures of the world would starve. That is untold power. Remember this.'* With that, the raven spread his wings and leapt into the air, wheeling in a large circle over our heads. *'Until we meet again, Raven Light Bringer.'* And abruptly, he disappeared into thin air.

Seven

Wow, a positive interaction with another pantheon...maybe things were finally looking up! I grinned. "That was so cool!"

"That was just nuts," Kellas said at the same time. We looked at each other—me laughing, him scowling.

I reached for his hand and clasped it in mine. "C'mon, grumpy!" I demanded, tugging him back toward the house. "That was a raven. I'm its namesake. I love ravens!"

"You can't rely on them; Ravens are tricksters," Kellas grumbled, continuing to let me lead him along. "And 'Light Bringer,'" he fumed. "Where did he come up with that wonky name?"

Was I missing something? Why would something as harmless as a bird get under Kellas's skin so badly? "He's not the first to call me that," I said, "although I have no idea why. Maybe because in Hidatsa folklore, Raven stole sunlight from the gods and brought it into the world. Iku used to tell me the tale as a bedtime story when I was little." I knew it by heart. "Raven was once pure white. He was punished for his audacity by having all his feathers turned black. How unfair is that?"

Kellas mumbled something under his breath I couldn't make out. Then he spoke louder. "Raven did it for his own good. It was only an accident that it benefited the world."

"Killjoy," I scoffed. "So what? I love to sing, and by chance, it benefits others too. How wrong can that be? C'mon. Lighten up!"

"And that wasn't a pun or anything, given what we were just talking about?"

I thought about that a fraction of a second and shrugged. "Yep! Guess so! Heh!" I grinned at him. After a moment, his face relaxed, and he smiled too.

"You're a piece of work, Brannaugh."

It was one of those warm, fuzzy moments you see in chick flicks, but it couldn't last, of course. As we approached Orinthia's destroyed tree, Kellas quick-squeezed my hand and let go. All my family were standing near the tree and looking at it. It felt like a wake, although we lacked the clothes and music to send off the tree nymph in the manner she deserved. Dad was there in his scrubs, looking weary. Elias was inscrutable. Nan had recovered enough that she had reinstated her spell of seeming. But now, when I looked at her just right, I could see through the glamour to the old lady inside it. When had I managed that bit of skill?

"Hey, what's up?" I asked lightly, feeling the tension and wishing it would go away.

Dad sent me a tired smile. "Hi, fledgling." His pet name for me. "The fire is out."

Considering there was enough tree there to have continued to burn for a good day and a half, that was notable. "Really?" I hustled the last few feet up the hill and stood next to him, catching his right hand in both of mine. I looked at Orinthia's tree. The fire was indeed out. The remaining wood wasn't even hot! "What the heck?" I caught Nan's gaze. "How could this happen?"

"Good question," she said quietly. "We'd hoped you could shed some light on the matter."

That caught me flat-footed. Why me? What could I have possibly done? From down by the lake. To put out a fire that had been raging out of control. Not even an hour earlier.

"Brannaugh has been playing the Claimh Solais and singing," Kellas said in a matter-of-fact tone of voice. He spread his hands out palms up, so everyone could see. "She gets results."

Oh. That. Had I really reached out that far? I'd only been focused on healing Kellas! But I felt the shock wave that went through my dad's body. "Really!" was all he said. Dad is not one to effuse.

I let go of his hand and peeled the bandage off my temple. "How does it look?" I asked. Dad had just re-bandaged it this morning, fussing over it and warning me that it could still scar.

Everyone looked. Dad blinked twice, rapidly. "Good as new."

"That's not all," Kellas assured them. He relayed the news about the ash grove and Odin's raven. "It's not the first time, either," Kellas went on. "In the Summer Lands, after we fought the werewolves, she sang Taliesin and me back to life."

"Not!" I protested. Back to life? No, not possible. It hadn't been that severe! They'd been in danger, sure...they'd been badly hurt, bleeding everywhere... "No way!"

"You think we'd have survived those injuries otherwise, Brannaugh? I think not." He sounded absolutely convinced.

I looked around at my family. The way they were staring at me made me exceedingly uncomfortable. I didn't like that shock and awe, like it made me into something I wasn't. "It was just playing and singing," I whispered. "No big deal."

A slow smile spread across Nan's face. "Big enough," she said softly. "Look." She pointed to where a small sapling had started growing near the dead tree.

I watched in amazement as the sapling grew rapidly, gaining a decade of growth in just under a minute before slowing down to a more decorous pace. A figure shimmered into being from the heart of the young tree and stepped out. An ethereally beautiful young child, maybe five, dressed in greens and browns. Her pale green hair flowed in the breeze.

"Hi!" the child said. "My name is Orianthi. I am Orinthia's daughter." She looked directly at me then. "I heard you calling, and I came. I love your music. Will you teach me to play too?"

~

Of course, there were lots of questions. Many, many questions. Too many. I was quickly overwhelmed. We'd retreated to the deck. Elias brought everyone fruit drinks. Although, I suspected the adults had more in theirs than just juice. Who could blame them after everything we'd seen today? But getting tired of repeating "I don't know," I finally clammed up, scowling at everyone from beneath my new bangs.

At least Dad knew what was going on. "Too much, Mother," he said quietly when Nan continued pushing me to describe what exactly happened with the Claimh Solais. "Maybe later," he suggested.

I sent him a grateful look over the top of my juice glass. Clamming up had been my only protection against my mother's frequent cross-examinations. She probably meant well, but Mom did not know how to turn down the intensity. Dad had seen me clam up before and perhaps experienced the need for it himself. I had some questions I wanted to ask *him*, too. But not here. Not in front of everyone else.... *Especially not* in front of the annoying Erin, who was hanging out at the edge of the group, scowling.

After I'd promised to come play with her as often as I could, Orianthi skipped off to explore the premises. She'd given me a smile that could light up the dark corners of a room, then had taken off like a shot to explore. I liked her intensely already. If Nan had felt this same way about Orinthia... Ugh. Not something to think too hard about right now.

"Maybe we've been taking the wrong tack with Raven's training," Nan mused, almost to herself.

Elias nodded. "I was wondering the same thing."

Kellas finished his juice and set the glass down on the side table between us. "Nope," he declared. "But maybe add music lessons? And she still needs to know how to do Druidic magic and defend herself—even if she doesn't take on her big, scary Celtic warrior avatar form like she did in Tír na nÓg. And..." He looked at me intently. "We need to get you stronger. Faster. Right now, you are the human equivalent of a cream puff. You're not ready to take on the Old Gods."

Cream puff?! Ah geez...thanks, Cat Man! I didn't appreciate his candid assessment of my physical fitness. I stayed silent and conveyed my total lack of enthusiasm via a glare.

Erin, who was now smirking, probably found my humiliation hilarious.

Kellas grinned at me, and there was a "cat ate the canary" look to it. "Shall we get started?" He grabbed my hand and hauled me out of my comfy deck chair. "No time like the present!"

I reluctantly followed him off the deck and around the side of the house, where he faced me, gripping me by the shoulders. The teasing look was gone, replaced by complete seriousness. "In all honesty, Brannaugh, no offense intended, but you aren't terribly fit. If you are to survive, you'll have to bring your A-game. Can't do that in a couch potato's body."

As unpleasant as it was to admit, he was kind of right. When your favorite physical activity amounts to being bucked off by barely trained mustangs, you develop little in the way of endurance. Unless the ability to heal from multiple bruises counts. Amazingly enough, I had never broken anything, not so much as a pinkie.

I groaned, knowing I was beaten. "OK, tough guy. What do you suggest?"

He released his grip on my shoulders and grinned. "We'll start with running, shall we?"

Eight

Running is not my strong suit, I decided, pressing a hand against the stitch in my side and groaning. A little voice in my head was screaming "dear god why me?" in an endless loop. My lungs were burning from the effort, and I was wringing wet with sweat. Kellas waited nearby, stretching his hamstrings, while I struggled to regain some semblance of normal.

"Can we be done with this already?" I wheezed painfully. It stung my pride that he didn't even look winded. Was I really that wimpy? "How many miles did we just do anyways?"

He glanced at his wrist, where he'd strapped a fancy GPS heart monitor thingamajig. "Just six miles. You did more after we got dropped off by the Commons last week."

I moaned a bit. Seriously? "We did a bunch of walking too, and the hills weren't steep like these!" And stairs. Hundreds and hundreds of stone steps that went on forever.

He grinned. "Hill workouts really make you realize where the weak spots are for sure. Take heart, Brannaugh. We're only half a mile from the car."

Right now, a half mile seemed an insurmountable distance. We were just four days into my new regimen of torture, and it felt like I would never get any stronger. At the rate I was going, I might manage to "up my game" in a hundred years or so, give or take a decade. Dad kept assuring me this was normal, and I had to be patient, but it was really disheartening.

At least it got me out exploring the state parks and forests in the area. So far, we'd run twice in Taughannock State Park (a kajillion stone stairs) and once in Hammond Hill State Forest (endless trail loops, all uphill). Today it was Treman State Park, where Kellas told me a local business hosted a 10K called Lucifer's Crossing. He'd delighted in telling me a 9-year-old girl had done the challenging six-mile course in 1 hour and 27 minutes earlier that year. I'd been too tired to ask if that little girl was some kind of superhuman. At the pace I was going, I'd be well over that time. Frustrating! I was about five years old now and still unsuccessfully attempting to adjust to the rapid changes in my bodily status. My body got younger as the moon waned from being full until it disappeared over about a two-week period, which isn't particularly fast, but it can be disorienting when you wake up each morning looking a year younger every single day. It doesn't sound like much, but it adds up. Fortunately, after the new moon, the reverse would be the case. I was looking forward to my body matching my actual maturity again. People really do act differently toward little kids. Some are nice, and others...well, don't get me started. Ugh!

We were following the same course as the race. Within minutes, I decided it had been designed by an expert in torture, or at least Lucifer's advocate. We had just come up a very long, very steep set of stone steps that zigzagged up a cliff overlooking the falls some wag had named after Lucifer. It was incredibly gorgeous; why anyone would name it after the devil himself was a mystery. Maybe it was someone who'd been running up past them and practically dying of oxygen deprivation, like me. That I could sort of understand.

"Come on, kid, I'm getting hungry. Let's finish this, eh?" Kellas was jogging in place, still looking fresh as a daisy. (Who'd come up with that silly metaphor anyways?)

"I'm coming," I groaned, straightening up again, the stitch in my side less awful than it had been. I broke into what only a truly generous person would call a run—more like hobbling along at a snail's pace.

Kellas made a deprecating snort. "I'll meet you back at the car," he said. "Stay on the main trail. It'll take you right back to the Old Mill parking lot. See you in about an hour or so!"

"Jerk." Sadly, it was my go-to insult for him, not that it packed any power. More of a pet name now than anything.

He grinned and took off like the devil was on his tail (yeah, har de har har), and I struggled to keep up, failing miserably as the stitch in my side immediately started back up. He was out of sight in less than a minute. I muttered something uncomplimentary and slowed to a walk, seeing as how my running wasn't exactly going to help me catch that stupid cat anyways.

The trail here was easier going, rolling a bit, following along the top of the gorge. Ithaca was famous for its gorges; there were many such water-cut clefts all around the lake, and I was told there were others in the surrounding region, too, all around the Finger Lakes. Kellas had promised to take me to Watkins Glen next week, where, he gleefully told me, the trail made Treman's gorge trails look like child's play. Ugh! I wasn't looking forward to it, no matter how beautiful it might be.

Up ahead a woman screamed, causing the small hairs on my neck to stand at attention.

I broke into a run, faster than I'd managed all day. Adrenaline can do that. I spied a good stout stick as I ran, stopping just long enough to grab it before continuing towards what sounded like a dogfight in progress.

I dashed over a small creek via a stone bridge and found myself in the Old Mill parking lot where we had left Nan's Prius. Just in front of me, a furry black dog the size of a small bear was attacking Kellas. Not in the playful way dogs will jump up on you when they don't know their own size, either. It was snarling and lunging at him, its lips pulled back in a snarl full of large, white teeth. Kellas was fending it off, but it was an uneven battle given their respective sizes and the fact the dog meant business. Kellas was just trying not to get hurt. The woman, whose screams I had just heard, stood nearby, wringing her hands uselessly. I raised my stick and swung it at the dog, ready to murder it.

"No!" The woman jumped at me and grabbed my arm, stopping me. She looked horrified that I would attack her dog. "Don't hurt Junior! He's never done anything like this! He's just a big lovebug!"

I sent the lady a look of complete disbelief and struggled to break away from her. We're all attached to our pets, but hers was trying to maul Kellas!

She clung on desperately. "Please! Really, he's a big baby."

"He's trying to kill my friend!"

She shook her head vehemently. "Not really. Junior wouldn't hurt a fly!"

"News flash!" I exclaimed. "He's hurting Kellas right now!" And in fact, the dog had finally managed to connect, drawing blood on Kellas's arm. "If he's such a big baby, call him off!"

"A little help here?" Kellas yelled; his voice strained—in what sounded like the beginning of panic.

The lady was in tears, and had gone back to wringing her hands. She seemed confused and terrified at her dog's *abnormal* behavior. "He won't listen. I tried."

At that point, the dog himself glanced over at us. Its eyes glowed an unusual, sickly green color that seemed wholly unnatural, reminding me of the movie *Ghostbusters*. I realized immediately what had happened: something had possessed the dog and was using it against Kellas. Outrage bubbled up in my chest, not only for Kellas but also on behalf of the poor pup who was being used as a disposable attacker. What was doing this or why I did not know, but to kill or injure the dog would be wrong. He was not the problem; he wasn't consciously choosing to be a bad boy. Whatever the thing was that possessed him was the problem.

Kellas took advantage of the dog's temporary distraction to land a telling kick to its chest, knocking it backward several feet. The dog howled and staggered back on its feet. With his owner still not doing a thing to intervene, it was time for me to make my move *now*. I jumped forward and grabbed the dog by its collar. "Junior! Good doggie, sweet doggie! Do you want a bickie? Some num-nums?"

The dog twisted around so its slavering teeth were inches from my face. We were practically eye to eye. I glared into the green glow emanating from those eyes and snarled at the thing that had possessed the poor dog. "You are not welcome here, troll. Get out, now!"

"Or what, small and insignificant one? What could you possibly do to harm me?" The words emerged from the dog's mouth in a growl. Its voice reminded me of the troll who used the police dog against me on my 16th birthday—the one Nan's hellhound, Bran, had fought off.

"I could sing!" I declared viciously. "Want some music, you disgusting creep?"

The dog struggled violently, trying to break away.

But I wasn't going to let him. Wrapping my arms and legs around Junior's neck and body in a bear hug, I dragged him to the ground. Then I began singing the refrain from *Yellow Submarine* at the top of my lungs in as obnoxious a voice as I could muster (which was truly awful, to be honest). And though it was terrible and completely inappropriate for the occasion, gods help me, it was *working*. I yelled the refrain over and over until the spirit finally screamed in agony and lifted out of the dog, dissipating in a cloud of green smoke.

For a long, frozen second, nothing happened. Then, Junior the dog started licking my face like he felt I needed a bath. As his overly enthusiastic energy felt like *normal dog* again, I let go of him in relief, pushing him away. "Yuck, dog! Stop slurping me!" I sent a look over at the woman. "Some help here, please!" I found the end of the leash, still attached to Junior, picked it up, and held it toward her.

She was standing stock still, as if she'd been turned to stone. Her hands were clamped over her ears and she was staring at me in dismay, making no move to give help of any sort. Dang. Some people!

"Ah...Kellas?" I struggled to my feet, still fending off the dog—losing my hold on his leash in the process. I looked around for the Cait Sidhe. He was standing not too far away. He also had his hands clamped over his ears. But at least he didn't act like he'd been turned to stone.

He looked at me with something akin to horror on his face. "Safe to take my hands down now?" he asked cautiously.

"Yeah, why wouldn't it be?" I bent and scooped up the dog's leash, still fending off its overzealous slurpiness.

"Gods, you just unleashed an earworm bad enough to exorcise a demon, and you wonder why I worry about my sanity?" He did, however, bring his hands down, and started examining the raw wound left by Junior's teeth. "Urgh..." He sent me a glance. "Gonna need some of your magic healing powers again. This one's deep."

"And a tetanus shot too, no doubt." I turned to the woman who'd finally unfrozen herself and come over to take Junior's leash. She was petting him and scolding him at the same time for frightening her. Way to send the dog mixed messages, lady! "Is your dog up on his shots?"

She nodded vigorously. "Oh, yes, he certainly is! Why, we just came from the vet. I thought a nice walk would help him feel better after he had his teeth cleaned."

I grinned at Kellas. "Hey, he bit you with teeth fresh from the dentist!"

"I'm honored," he grumbled. "We're going to need your name and number, ma'am. Junior is going to have to be watched for a while, in case he's rabid."

"But he's had all his shots! Oh, no, you're not going to report him, are you?" She was clearly distressed at the thought, probably terrified that her precious pup would be put down. I felt a little sympathy for her. After all, it wasn't really Junior's fault he bit Kellas.

Kellas looked dumbfounded. He wasn't nearly so inclined to be sympathetic—which was totally understandable, considering he was the one who'd been on the receiving end of Junior's fangs. "Lady, he bit me! I really don't want to take any chances." He showed her his arm, where blood was running liberally down his forearm and dripping onto the macadam.

It was like she'd just realized he was bleeding. Her attitude did an abrupt about-face. "Oh no, that's awful! I will pay for the doctor, absolutely. Oh, I am so very sorry! I have no idea what got into Junior. He's never done anything like this, ever! And he's nine! It's not like he's a puppy or anything." She was babbling nonstop.

Eventually, though, we got everything sorted out. We finally got away from the lady—whose name was Melanie Crispin—after a *here was her cell and her work number and text her anytime, and she was so very, very, sorry, and she would take Junior back to doggie training, maybe he needed a refresher course in his clicker training.*

Gads! I was beginning to feel sorry for Junior, having to live with Melanie's blathering all the time. She was way too frantically energetic, which perhaps made them the perfect pair in that regard. We escaped to Nan's Prius after assuring her we would let her know how everything went. Kellas had wrapped a buff around his arm to slow the bleeding a bit, but he still managed to get blood on the seat and the steering wheel.

"You're cleaning that, not me," I said, lamely attempting to make a joke about the mess.

He sent me a look that could curdle milk. "Wanna walk, kid?"

I immediately shut my face. Tired enough from my run and the dog encounter, I had zero desire to hoof it the ten miles back to Nan's place.

"So," Kellas started after we'd left the park, wended our way through Ithaca traffic and headed up our road toward home. "What made you decide to call in an earworm to shake off that troll?"

"I didn't," I admitted. "It was just the first thing that popped into my head."

He smiled. "I have to admit that was genius, using an earworm to dislodge a nasty."

"Next time you're being nasty, maybe I should try one on you?" I grinned, starting in again sotto voce. "We all live..."

"Gah!" he groaned. "La la la, I can't hear you! La la la."

I laughed long and loud. It helped make up for all my aching muscles. Note to self: Earworms can come in handy when battling trolls and dealing with annoying cats.

Nine

Much was made of Kellas's bitten arm when we returned. Dad was home, fortunately, and was awakened to take care of the wound. Tetanus antitoxin was pulled from the medical stash and administered. (Nan and my father had an impressively complete home pharmacy, way more than Mom's bandages and triple antibiotic ointment.) No surprise; Cait Si are no fonder of shots than cats are. Mom would have been all over Kellas with her toilet-cleaning threats. I wouldn't have been surprised if she could hear him cursing halfway across the country. My own contribution eased his pain, but it seemed a bit of time was also going to be necessary before it was fully healed.

We finished up, and Nan pulled me aside. "While you were gone, Margaret texted me. She'd like you to video call her at two this afternoon." She glanced at the kitchen clock. "It's nearly that now. Best get going. My laptop is in the office."

The last phone call with Mom had been a struggle, one I was in no hurry to repeat. Video calls would be infinitely more difficult. My face must have revealed my dismay because she gave me a brief side-to-side hug around the shoulders. "No worries, dear, you've got this! Anyone who can exorcise a demon with *Yellow Submarine* has mad skills."

"You don't know Mom very well, do you?" I muttered. But I still dutifully took myself off to Nan's office and shut the door behind me. I didn't want anyone else to hear our conversation; I suspected it would not be an easy one.

It wasn't.

Mom signed on in a foul mood. I knew the warning signs: a furrowed brow, tight lips, flared nostrils. Oh boy, here we were, off to a great start already! At home, I'd always made myself scarce under those circumstances. At least I was 1,615.5 miles away and could always just shut down the computer if she got to be too much for me.

"Heya, Mom!" I said breezily, trying to keep things light.

She took one look at my new haircut and blanched. "What do you call *that*?" she demanded. At least she hadn't fainted at seeing me as a six-year-old!

"What?" I tried to look innocent, raising my hand to touch my new 'do. Good thing I came prepared with an explanation! "Oh, you mean my hair? Yeah, there was a bit of an accident, and we had to cut a bunch off." I struggled to stay light and breezy. Not easy when a hurricane was brewing on the other end of the connection.

"Another accident?" she demanded, in a tone that could instantly freeze Lake Superior. "Why? You are always getting hurt at your dad's place. That's it. You need to come home."

Wait, what?! It's a ruddy haircut! It's not like I was hurt anywhere, and I wasn't upset about it at all. That should be obvious! (Good thing she hadn't seen me with all those burns.) I squared my shoulders and did my best to be firm while keeping things light. "It's 24 hours one way, Mom, not stopping for meals or pee breaks. I'm not going anywhere!"

"Your Nan has a private jet. She can bring you."

"Actually, that's not hers. It belongs to a friend." I'd been disappointed to learn it wasn't Nan's after all. Private jets are cool. "She borrowed it last year when all that...well, on my birthday."

"She can borrow it again." Mom was obdurate. She was used to getting what she wanted, used to me obeying her. As far as she was concerned, she was the only one who knew what was best for me and what I needed, including myself. I did my best to bear with it. Boy, did I try! After all, her anger used to scare me—but that was before I met spiteful goddesses and trolls in another dimension and went face-to-face with death. Now, all I felt was a violent, searing stab of frustration that she refused to respect Dad or Nan...or even me.

Light and breezy wasn't going to do it; I could sense that now. I was going to have to match her storm and raise her one. There was a hard edge to my voice now, and I could see from her expression she recognized it. "No, no, and no! Mom, you don't know what's going on here. Nan needs me right now, and I can't leave her. I know you don't believe any of this moon stuff, but it's real and..."

"I really don't care, Raven! The longer you stay there, the more you are at risk." Mom steamrolled right over me.

I hissed through my teeth, my fingernails digging into my palms in anger.

"If Amaris is really in that much danger, she doesn't need you in the middle of it. You're just a kid!" Mom continued. "What are you now, like five? Six? What can *you* do to help anyway?"

She meant it as a rhetorical question, but I answered it as though it wasn't. "A lot more than you might think," I retorted. Bad enough I got condescended to by Cerridwen; I sure didn't need it from her as well.

"Like what?" she snapped. "It doesn't matter. You are *my* child, and I simply won't let you stay in harm's way. If I must, I will drive all the way there and bring you home. Don't think I won't."

"Suffering how many speeding tickets?" I snapped back waspishly. "Even if you do drive over here, I'm not going back with you!" She started to say something, but I spoke right over her. "Mom, no. I won't go. I'm tired of the way you treat Dad and Nan…. And me! Would it kill you to show us a shred of respect?! I'm staying right here until…well, whenever I'm not needed anymore."

"Young lady, you—"

Too angry to continue the conversation, I shut the lid on the laptop.

~

Dad was outside on the back deck dozing in the sunshine when I stormed out of the house. I was ready to murder anything that got in my way. Send me all the trolls! I felt capable of performing an extermination campaign and usurping the Morrigan's role as the Goddess of Death.

"Hey, kiddo, hold up there a minute." His calm voice slowed my headlong exit somewhat. "Please," he added.

That stopped me. I whirled around, breathing hard through my nose. "What?!" I snapped nastily. I really didn't need a lecture right about now, please and thank you.

He rolled to his feet off the zero-gravity recliner he had been lying on and came over to where I stood at the top of the stairs leading off the deck. "C'mon. Let's walk."

Which was where I had been headed anyway, so why not? I wasn't in the mood to talk, but if he wanted to tag along, so be it. We struck off in silence, headed for the path that meandered around Nan's 100 acres. Thankfully, he didn't even attempt to ask me about my anger. We walked without talking for a while until I finally had gotten myself under more control. I don't know how he does it, but Dad just seems to know when I'm ready to talk again.

"I take it the call with your mother didn't go so well," he said quietly.

"She says she's going to come get me," I shared through clenched teeth. "I don't want to go." OK, so maybe I wasn't as calmed down as I'd thought. "Why does she always have to be like this?!"

"Hmm," was his only response.

"She doesn't want me in danger, she says." I kicked a pebble hard, sending it flying into the grass.

"None of us do," he conceded.

I groaned in exasperation. "So, how is going back to North Dakota going to make me any safer?" I demanded. "That was the first place the trolls attacked me! Iku's wards didn't hold up. If I went back, I'd go from having a houseful of people who could back me up, to being alone trying to protect Mom and Iku all by myself with who only knows what! Mom doesn't seem to understand that refusing to believe in trolls and the Celtic gods won't make them go away. She'll only make surviving harder for all of us!" I was building up to a real rant now.

"Agreed," he nodded. Just one word again. Argh!

"Dad!" I stopped in my tracks, whirling around to scowl indignantly at him. What the heck was I supposed to take away from that?

He stopped also and turned to face me. "Yes?" His expression was infuriatingly calm.

I stomped a foot, ignoring how childish that made me look. "Something more than monosyllabic responses would be good!"

A slow smile spread across his face. "What, you want me to become an orator, just like that?"

"Dad!" I protested. "I need some support here. I don't want to go back to North Dakota! I like it here, in upstate New York. I want to learn everything I can about this lunacy thing, and I can't do that at Mom's place in Kestrel. I can help! Running away and sticking my head in the sand won't make any of my problems go away. Or make the trolls, or the Old Gods—or anything else—stop looking for me. If I can heal people..."

He held up a hand to stop my onslaught of words, beckoned me to come with him, then started walking. I followed at his side. "We will call your mother," he said. "We'll do what we can to talk some sense into her, but you know how bullheaded she can be." He grinned. "Kind of like you." More soberly, he added, "She's hard-headed, proud, and fiercely loyal. A fighter. Again, *just like you.*"

The comparison was infuriating. I glared at him. No way was I as stubborn as her!

He continued. "Yes, the two of you send sparks off each other. But there are also advantages to that. Because you are so alike, you are one of the few people who know how to reason with your mom—in a way that makes sense to her."

My turn to be monosyllabic. "How?" I packed all my doubts into that one word.

"Tell me, Raven, what would convince you, if you were in her shoes?"

I thought for a moment, but my mind was a complete blank. Mom was so obstinate, so inflexible; maybe it was a lawyer thing. I couldn't remember a time when I'd convinced her of *anything.* "I haven't the foggiest."

"Sure, you do. You use arguments that could work for you."

Like I didn't do that all the time! Mostly my internal arguments went around and around in circles, never getting anywhere. And I said as much.

"Maybe take a different approach," he suggested. "I would start with her most pressing concern: your safety. Pointing out why you're safer here with us would be a good start. But also don't forget to consider how she feels about you. She misses you, Raven. She misses you terribly. When you were in Tír na nÓg, she was inconsolable. Even the dream trip your Iku made to meet you failed to ease her pain." He put a hand on my shoulder. "To you, it was only a few days, but your mom spent months unable to believe where you were and that you were safe. It was really hard on her."

"Now you're giving me a guilt trip," I muttered, thinking about how I'd slammed the laptop shut on her earlier. My anger was promptly undermined.

How my actions must have made her feel...ugh. "I hadn't thought of it that way," I admitted.

"Now, what do you think might help her feel better about letting you stay here a while longer?"

I kicked a stone out of the path. "Less fighting?" I muttered. As if I had complete control over that!

"Could help," he agreed. "What else?"

"Dunno."

He looked a bit exasperated. "Come on, kiddo, what are some ways to connect with someone you want to be friends with?"

I knew what he was getting at, and it didn't make me feel any better. "More sharing," I muttered. "Spend time together. More communication. Texting, emails, phone calls, video calls," I added after a brief hesitation. I dreaded all these options. My stomach twisted into an emotional knot. When had I gotten so defensive around my mother?

"So, what do you need to do when we get back to the house?" he prompted gently.

～

I texted my mother to ask her to get back on a video call, and I apologized. The odd thing was, she did too—at the same time I did. It startled both of us so much, we started laughing—also at the same time. Then things went vastly better. Apparently, Mom had a particularly nasty case she was working on, and it had put her in that lousy mood she'd signed on with before. *Note to self: it isn't always about me. Note to Mom: please leave your work crap elsewhere when calling me. Thank you very much!*

Then I brought up staying with Dad for a while longer.

Her face fell. "Raven, honestly, I don't know. You're always getting hurt. Look at your poor hair!"

I reminded myself to stay calm. "It's hair, Mom. It'll grow back." (Now, where had I heard that before?) I took a deep breath. Knowing my mother, this next bit was not going to be an easy sell. "I need to keep working on my music," I explained. "There are...things...I can do with my music that make people better." There. I'd said it. Sort of.

Mom looked confused.

"I can heal people," I explained. "Kellas had some bad burns on his hands. I sang and played my lute, and it healed him." Probably best not to mention the raven, the ash trees, nor the baby pine tree that had managed 10 years' worth of growth in under a minute. "And I'm really worried about Nan. She gets very old at times, and it weakens her."

"What do you mean, 'at times?'" Mom asked quietly.

"When the moon is full," I said. Let's see what she made of that. "You know, when I turned two on my birthday? Well, Nan changes too, and when the moon is full, she's like, ancient." How do you explain 1,600 years to someone who thinks it's all smoke and mirrors?

Mom sat there staring off into the distance for a very long time, so long I was getting increasingly nervous that I'd pushed harder than I should have. Finally, she focused back on me. "You remember when you asked me why your father and I split up?"

"You said he hadn't been straight with you," I said sadly.

"That's right. He wasn't. But I'm realizing that maybe I hadn't let him be as straight with me as he would have liked." She stopped, got that faraway-elsewhere look again for a while, then slowly refocused. "Raven, I don't pretend to understand all this *lunacy,* as your Nan likes to call it. It's crazy for sure.

But what I've seen of it with you, my own child, has helped me understand that whether or not we want to recognize facts when they smack us upside the head—not admitting something is happening, when it *is* happening—is lunacy in the other sense of the word. Craziness. Idiocy. I may not want to admit you and your grandmother have this...*unique* condition...but it affects you both, and like it or not..." her voice trailed off.

"It's real," I finished for her. "Mom, it's OK. Really. I'm getting used to it. I'm not thrilled about turning into a little kid over and over again either, but there are upsides to it as well. Maybe, eventually, I'll figure out how to put up a decent spell of seeming..."

"What's that?" Mom interrupted.

"It's glamour, like the fairy-tales tell us about how fairies appear as something other than what they are. Usually, more beautiful. For me and Nan, it just helps us look more normal."

"So..." Mom hesitated a bit. "When the moon is full, you are your normal age."

I nodded. The anxious knot in my chest was easing. She was finally trying to understand.

"What happens when it's new? Fully dark?"

The truth: I became immaterial. But telling her that now would likely freak her out. Best to break her in slowly. So, I lied. "I'm not sure. I haven't hit that moon phase yet."

Mom looked puzzled. "But it's been over nine months since your birthday."

"Yup, but most of those I was in Tír na nÓg. To me, it was only a week or so."

"Oh," she said. Although judging from her face, it wasn't clear that she'd really processed all that. I know I hadn't, not completely. "I guess we're about to find out, huh?"

I nodded, biting my lower lip.

"You will tell me what happens, right? Be straight with me?" She got that fierce look in her eyes again, more mom-like. "Because I'll know if you aren't."

I held up my right hand, pinkie raised. "Pinkie swear."

She mimicked my motion with her own hand. "Pinkie sworn," she agreed.

I guess that meant I could stay with Dad. Good.

Ten

I wandered back out to the living room—after I'd said goodbye to my mom and promised to do better in the staying-in-touch department. If future conversations went as well as this one, things might just get easier, I thought. I was humming *Heal the World* and thinking about what I'd like for a snack when the doorbell rang. Huh? That was a first. I didn't remember us ever getting company here, what with Nan's wards making us invisible to the rest of the world. Was there another person in our little loop I hadn't met yet? Honestly, it made me very curious.

Since no one else seemed to be answering the bell, I went over and peeked out through the sidelights to see who it was. A tall young man was waiting patiently, arms full of grocery bags. They looked heavy. I opened the door. "Hey!"

He looked down at me (yeah, I was little kid-sized, remember?) "Sgę:no!" he grinned at me. "You're new! Are you why I have so much ice cream in these bags?"

I stood there wordlessly, staring at him like I'd seen a vision. Well, OK, I might look six, but I was 16, with 16-year-old hormones—and this guy was gorgeous. Like, Hollywood handsome: tall, broad-shouldered, chiseled features, dark skin taut over muscled arms...OK, I had to stop staring at him before I started drooling. (Bad form, Raven! Focus your brain!) "Yeah, probably," I managed and stepped back out of the way. He walked past me and deposited the bags on the kitchen counter.

"You might want to put the ice cream away," he suggested. "I have more stuff out in the car." He left to fetch the other stuff.

I dug into the bags and pulled out my all-time favorite ice cream, three containers of it, and put them in the freezer. I knew what I was going to have as a snack now. But not until tall, dark, and handsome left. I wouldn't get caught dead stuffing my face in front of him! No, I needed to look as mature as possible, for obvious reasons.

Dad came in from the back deck where he'd returned to resting after our walk and talk. The grocery guy also came back in the front door, loaded down with more groceries. "Hey there, Archer! It's been a while," Dad greeted him.

Archer set the bags down on the counter. "Quite a while, Michael. You're usually at work or sleeping when I get here." He jerked his head toward the door. "More in the car..."

"I'll help," Dad said and followed. I went too.

Archer leaned into the back of an ancient red Subaru hatchback, pulled out more bags, and handed two to my father, then saw me standing there as well. "Well, peanut, think you could manage one of these?"

Grrr. Why can't I be my proper age when a gorgeous guy shows up? So not fair! I nodded silently, and he handed me a lightweight bag. I sent him a glare as I shouldered it easily, and reaching into the car, grabbed a bag that was obviously loaded to the brim with canned goods, hefted the carrying straps onto my other shoulder, and stalked off back to the house. An appreciative whistle followed me. "Go, tiger!" he called after me.

I turned and glared at him. "Raven," I declared. "My name is Raven. Get your species right, mister!" And I escaped to the house.

Archer followed with the remaining grocery bags. Dad had started putting things away. I dumped my load onto the counter and slouched away into the furthest corner of the kitchen, glowering at the new guy, who was pretending not to notice my bad mood. He set his load on the counter and dusted his hands together. "That's all of it," he said unnecessarily.

Dad nodded. "Much appreciated, as always. The funds to pay you are over there." He motioned toward a fat business-sized envelope on the side table near the front door. "Raven, this is Archer. He's our link to the rest of the world."

"Meaning, I grab your groceries," Archer explained, his teeth very white in a wide smile. "What with COVID and all, and Michael here working 24/7. Least I can do!"

"Archer is Haudenosaunee. Cayuga, to be more precise," Dad added.

"We call ourselves Gayogo̱hó:nǫ.' Means *people of the swamp*," Archer added cheerfully.

"Our families go way back," Dad relayed.

I was getting a weird sort of vibe, not that this was a novel sensation given everything that had been happening in my life for the past year! "How far back?" I asked suspiciously.

Archer rocked his head back and forth the tiniest bit. "Maybe something like 400 years?"

Oh. OH! Now I get it. He was definitely someone who was somewhat in the loop. "OK, Dad. Tell me, just how much does this guy know about us?"

"About you Celts?" Archer's dark eyes lit up with mirth. "A fair bit, peanut."

I glared at him.

"I mean Raven," he amended.

Dad chuckled. "Full disclosure, Archer. Raven shares a certain unusual aging condition with her grandmother."

It was Archer's turn to look awkward. "How old are you, Raven? Actually?"

Oh, to have mastered that lousy spell of seeming! Well, here goes nothing, I thought, squinted up my eyes and tried that dratted spell one more time. Really, *really*, tried. The air around me shimmered in rainbow hues, just like it did around Nan when she assumed her glamour. I felt a rush of *something* happening within me, and.... I felt different! I felt like, well, *me*! Full-grown me, not mini-me.

I wished I had a camera because the look on Archer's face was one for the record books.

"Hey, fledgling, you did it!" Dad exclaimed.

I smiled.

"First time ever!" he added, for Archer's benefit.

"...OK...." Archer managed in a tentative voice. He looked me up and down before carefully looking over my shoulder. "Can we maybe...wind a bit here? Like...all the way back to the beginning, as in "Hi there! My name is Archer. What's yours?"

Dad guffawed. "I'll leave you two to it," he said. "I need a bit more shut-eye before I head out tonight again." He wandered back outside and shut the door gently behind him, leaving me and Archer alone in the kitchen.

We stood looking at each other like two dummies. My brain was a complete blank. So much for words being my power!

"I..." he started.

"Hey..." I said at the same time.

An awkward pause.

"Go ahead," I offered.

"No, by all means, you first!" he countered.

We stood looking at each other, momentarily silent again.

"OK!" I managed at last. "Yeah. I'm Raven. Michael's my dad, which makes Amaris my Nan. And, short version, I'm a Lunatic too. I'm also half Hidatsa, on my mom's side. So, I'm a bit stuck between two worlds. It's not easy." Umm. At least that's a start? Was that too much information at once?

"Hidatsa." There was a brief pause before his face lit up. "North Dakota!" he said, suddenly putting some pieces together. "Your mom and dad...ugh, sorry." He looked abashed at almost having said the *divorced* word. "That's why I haven't seen you here before."

I nodded. For me, the divorce was old news. I wasn't really fazed by it anymore; it had only really bothered me when I was a kid. "Mostly, I'm just here for a couple of weeks in the summer. But I'm going to be staying longer this year."

"COVID?" he asked, as if this was an obvious factor. I nodded, not knowing how much he knew of our situation and not wanting to be the one to share information that maybe shouldn't be shared.

"Want something to drink?" I asked, suddenly wondering if I should be more hostessy. "Water, iced tea?"

"Make mine lemonade, since you're volunteering," Kellas stalked in with, as usual, the worst possible timing. I sent him an indignant look. Which he ignored. As usual.

"Hey, Cat Man!" Archer greeted him with unfeigned enthusiasm. "How's life?" He noticed the bloodied bandage on Kellas's left forearm. "Still finding ways to get torn up, I see."

"Ran into a possessed dog," Kellas grunted, as if that was all in a day's work. "Makes a guy thirsty," he added, sending a pointed look my way.

Oh, right. I was doing *the hostess with the most-est* thing. "Coming right up," I said, sending a glare Kellas's way, and made myself useful. I glanced at Archer, because he hadn't actually said what he'd like to drink.

He seemed puzzled, but then realized the reason for the look. "Lemonade," he said hastily. "That would be great. Thanks!"

Kellas looked from me to Archer and then back again at me. "Makes sense that you'd finally figure out how to look your age when a good-looking guy comes around, huh, Brannaugh?" Sarcasm practically dripped from every syllable coming out of his mouth.

I flamed bright pink.

Archer ducked his head, embarrassed. "Hey dude, take it easy."

Pouring everyone their lemonade, I set the glasses in front of the two guys. They took up positions on the stools by the kitchen island, and I backed up against the sink. "Archer just brought groceries," I managed, trying to break the awkward silence that had descended.

"No COVID germs on you, apparently," Kellas grunted.

Archer merely nodded.

"Umm...?" Way to sound intelligent, Raven. (Not!)

"Amaris's wards wouldn't have let him in otherwise," Kellas explained, as if it should have been obvious.

"Oh!" I nodded. Silence descended again. This was getting old. Pick a topic, any topic! "So! How do you two know each other?" I finally blurted out.

The guys exchanged long glances. "Where to start?" Archer fiddled with his glass a little, whistling thoughtfully.

"Long-standing history," Kellas said. "Goes way back."

"All the way back to a certain pine tree, the story goes," Archer agreed.

Kellas blanched. "Yeah. Right. About that pine tree..."

"Orinthia!" Archer again. "She's amazing, that dryad. How's she doing these days?"

Remembering her death was a punch directly to my gut. Orinthia's voice, screaming with pain, echoed in my ears. The horror of being burned alive...

"Umm. Not so good," Kellas muttered, focused on his lemonade glass.

A frown furrowed Archer's forehead. "What do you mean?"

"She's dead." I didn't mean for it to come out that bluntly, and cringed at my lack of tact. How well had he known her? I hadn't even known she was there, until suddenly she wasn't.

Archer shot off his stool, nearly knocking over his lemonade. "Dead! How?" There was a look of total panic on his face.

"Struck by lightning late last week." Kellas took a deep breath, as if the memory was as difficult for him as it was for me. "Wasn't a thing we could do to save her."

"How about her tree?"

Kellas just shook his head.

Archer looked like he'd seen the end of the world coming; all the color drained from his face and his hands started shaking. "That's not good, dude. Not good at all."

His reaction both alarmed and confused me. "Why? What does that matter to you?"

Archer looked at me with eyes dark with worry. "Orinthia's pine is a special tree, Raven. Our people buried all our weapons under her roots when we formed our confederacy. She was the guardian of the pine and our nation's peace. With her gone, well, who knows what might happen." He glanced back at Kellas. "How about the eagle? Have you seen it lately?"

"It attacked Odin's raven Huginn recently. That's the last I know of it."

"I saw a bird circling way up a few times," I added. They looked at me. "I couldn't swear it was an eagle," I had to admit. That didn't seem to lighten their moods. "Umm, well, there's Orianthi? Her tree? Right next to Orinthia's old one. Would that help?"

"Show me," Archer said, and it was a request even if put a wee bit bluntly.

I shrugged and nodded, finished off my glass of lemonade, and set the glass in the sink. Maybe seeing Orianthi and her pine would help him somewhat. I led the way out the back, tiptoeing quietly past my dad, who was fast asleep and snoring just the tiniest bit on his recliner in the shadiest part of the deck.

We walked across the lawn toward Orinthia's pine. Archer groaned as he took in the extent of the damage to the grand old tree. "She was older than all of us," he said sadly. "Older than our confederacy, even. At least the pine was. Your grandmother summoned Orinthia to guard this tree, all the way from

Tír na nÓg, I think." He focused on Orianthi's tree then. It had continued to grow rapidly over the past few days and was now about six inches in diameter and 15 feet tall. "What's this?"

"That's Orianthi's tree," I told him, feeling just a speck of pride. "She says I called her here. She's Orinthia's daughter."

A girl's figure shimmered into being from the heart of the pine, and she threw herself at me, wrapping her arms around my waist in an enthusiastic hug. "Raven!" Orianthi exclaimed in glee, then looked up at me. "You got big!"

I hugged her back. "Finally figured out the whole glamour thing, girlfriend."

"Yay you!" Orianthi cheered, then spotted Archer. "Who's this guy?"

"Sgę:no, Orianthi," Archer said graciously. "I'm Archer. My family and I are friends of your mother. We are deeply saddened to hear of her passing. I offer our most sincere condolences for your loss."

"Sgę:no, Archer man," Orianthi said somberly, wrapping her arms around herself as if to ward off a sudden chill. "And nya:węh. I never knew my mother, but she gave me life—so I will fulfill her promise to you and your people."

"Wait, what?" I interrupted. "How do you know all this, Orianthi? Because I just got left at the starting line."

Orianthi sent me a big smile. "It's easy, actually. Everything Mother Tree had: knowledge, nourishment, even history and language—she passed on to me. It's in the soil; a big web of fungus stores everything I need to learn and grow. Even though my mother is dead, she provides for me. Pretty nifty, right?"

Wow. I looked at the dead pine with renewed respect. Trees knew how to be better parents than many humans, apparently. Imagine providing every-thing a child needs, even after your own death. Amazing—if also a bit morbid and sad. "More than nifty, I'd say."

Orianthi started skipping around me, not unlike a dog in need of a walk. "Yup, I know! Hey, can we go climb some trees now?" She grabbed me around my waist from behind and peered around me at Archer. "Or are you going to be too busy for me now that Archer is here?" she added teasingly.

Kellas snorted in laughter and Archer turned pink. "Actually, little lady, I have to get back to work today." He sent me a quick glance. "I'll be off tomorrow though, if..."

"Amaris and Elias keep Brannaugh busy with lessons most of the day, and we're running every day too," Kellas interjected. "She's booked."

I gave Archer a *gee I'm sorry* look, but the Cayuga was not to be dissuaded so easily. "I like running. When are you going? We could meet up."

For some inexplicable reason, Kellas looked disgruntled by his offer. "She's slower than molasses in January." He gave me a know-it-all look. "And the swamp monster here," he said nodding at Archer, "he's always winning his age group, placing in the top five overall at most local races. The man's a machine. You don't want to run with him."

I wasn't thrilled to have Kellas managing my social calendar. "Maybe I want to run with him!" I declared. "And if he just happens to be running at the same time and place we are, why not run together? After all, who knows if you'll be attacked by another demon-possessed dog and need rescuing...again?"

Kellas shot me a dirty look.

I smiled sweetly. "Turnabout is fair play, Cat Man."

He grunted, but to be honest, he didn't look as grumpy as he could have. Maybe he liked the idea of having Archer along for our runs? Maybe it would give him someone who could challenge him, speed-wise? "I guess that would work," he admitted grudgingly. "Tomorrow we're doing the Taughannock Falls loop from the bottom parking lot. 2 p.m. If you're still game, Swamp Monster. We hope to do a couple loops, if Brannaugh here can manage the stairs." He sent a wry look at Archer. "We did Lucifer's Crossing today. The stairs really kicked her butt. No way she'd have kept up with McKenzie."

"That girl is a freak of nature," Archer said. He looked at me. "She's nine, and she won her age class…against 15- and 16-year-old kids who are top-notch runners on their high school track teams. No dishonor in not being able to match her stride for stride!" His gaze narrowed thoughtfully. "How long have you been running, Raven?"

"Four days," I admitted sheepishly.

"Four days!" Archer wheeled on Kellas. "Cripes, Cat Man, you can't go comparing apples and oranges. Give Raven…or is it Brannaugh?" He looked puzzled as to the doubling up of names "…a chance to build some strength first. Then, we'll have a better idea of what she's capable of."

Kellas didn't look the least bit ashamed of himself. Dratted cat! He just grinned ear to ear. "You be the carrot, I'll be the stick," he said, sounding way too cheerful. "Maybe, between the two of us, we can whip her sorry butt into shape faster."

"Hey, I'm standing right here!" I interjected. "I'm not some side of beef you're discussing! And my name is Raven," I clarified for Archer. "Kellas persists in calling me Brannaugh—even though he knows better." I glared at Kellas, who just gave me a Cheshire-cat grin. Dang it! The darn cat had managed to get my goat…again.

Archer, however, looked a bit abashed. He apologized. Then he glanced at his watch and did a hard double-take. "Gotta go, I'm already past due at my next job. See you two tomorrow!" he said, taking off.

Orianthi was swaying back and forth from one foot to the other. "Archer and Raven, sittin' in a tree, K-I-S-S-I-N-G, first comes love…"

"Shut it, little sister!" I yelped at her.

Then, I changed my approach. "Last one to the climbing tree is a rotten apple!" I challenged her. (Hey, it was the only way I could think of to stop her from teasing me and get her away from Kellas. I didn't need him to decide to lay it on thick as well.) I dropped my glamour and the two of us took off stride for stride toward the big oak tree, which spread its ancient branches invitingly on the eastern side of the lawn. I'd like to say I got there first, but my legs were still like wet noodles from my run earlier. Orianthi was in heaven about winning. And her happiness...made me happy.

Eleven

August was passing quickly, the days packed with many lessons in Druidic lore, Aikido, and the sword. I spent my few spare minutes playing with Orianthi, either fooling around or practicing our instruments. She quickly fell in love with a set of pan pipes Nan had in her stash of instruments, and together the lute and pan pipes made lovely other-worldly-sounding music. She could sing like a lark too. I wished I could spend more time just listening to her. But there was so little time—and so much for me to learn.

Kellas's idea of training often felt like torture. My running lately seemed to be faltering. Archer tried to reassure me this was natural, that my body just needed to build up a tolerance. Still, it was a little discouraging—and worrisome for another reason. Nan also seemed to be faltering again. It was not because she was so very old, either. Just the opposite. The new moon was approaching, and I had no idea what was going to happen to me this time.

I wasn't prepared for what happened. Kellas, Archer, and I were jogging in Buttermilk Falls State Park in mid-August when I stumbled and fell hard. I went to push myself up off the ground, caught a glimpse of myself, and screamed. I could not see my hands. An instant later, I couldn't see *any* of me.

I was well behind the two guys when this happened, so they didn't realize right away that I wasn't with them.

Ever wonder what it's like to be invisible? Well, it's weird. Very weird. And completely disorienting. I stood in the middle of the path shaking in my invisible sneakers, mortally terrified to move, afraid I'd float away into nothingness. Sweating, my breath came in gusty short bursts. I was dizzy—and panicky. Was I going to pass out? No! Mustn't! Wobbling over to a nearby boulder, I sat down and dropped my head between my knees. I willed my breathing to slow.

Wait one stinking minute! I had moved and not floated off into nothingness. I had felt my rear sit on the rock. I could feel my breath going in and out, the sweat trickling down my ribs. The only difference was that I could not *see* myself. I was not incorporeal. I hadn't just teleported out of the mortal realm and left my body to rot somewhere.

I let out a sigh of relief. I wasn't a ghost at all. I was merely invisible. Which made sense. Just because we can't *see* the moon when it's dark doesn't mean it has become *nothing*. It's still there, like me...just...not visible.

But moons are one thing and people are another. I soon discovered this invisibility thing was going to get problematic.

When Archer and Kellas finally realized I wasn't with them, they started shouting for me. Kellas jogged back down the trail toward me, Archer on his heels.

"She can't have gone far," Kellas said. "It's not like there are any side trails she might have headed off on by mistake."

They drew abreast of me and I, thinking I could give them a bit of a surprise, yelled, "Boo!" But they kept on jogging as though I wasn't there, as if I hadn't spoken. I wasn't sure if I was disappointed, annoyed, or worried by this. Maybe all of the above.

"Wait till I catch up to her," Kellas growled. "I bet she ditched us and headed back to the car. The little punk."

"Why would she do that?" Archer asked. "It's not like her to give up on our runs."

Wait! They were leaving me! I jumped up onto my invisible feet and dashed after them. "Hey, I'm right here!" I yelled, or tried to. They still didn't hear me. It seemed I was voiceless again. Yeah, like that was so fun the last time I'd experienced it. At this rate, I was going to start breaking Mom's rule about using bad language in a really serious way.

They picked up the pace and started pulling away from me, despite my best efforts to keep up. At this point, I decided drastic measures were needed. I could always apologize later. Scooping up a good-sized chunk of rock, I hurled it after them. It hit Archer between the shoulder blades.

"What the…" Archer stopped in his tracks, turning to see what had hit him. "Kellas! Wait a minute!"

Kellas hauled up and turned, hands on hips, a worried expression on his face. "What is it?"

Archer stooped and picked up the rock I'd hit him with, then frowned and looked up at the cliff face above him. "I just got hit with a rock."

OK! I had their attention. I cast about and found another rock, which I tossed underhand at them, so it landed nearby. They both jumped like startled deer. I laughed aloud (or rather, voicelessly) and started chucking more rocks their way. I wasn't aiming to hit them, but oops, some did. My bad.

"Someone is throwing rocks at us," Archer said flatly.

Kellas grunted. "And I think I know who, too. Anyone coming?" He sent a quick look around.

"Nobody," Archer said.

"OK, let's see if this works," Kellas muttered, shifting into cat shape. Archer didn't even blink. I guessed this wasn't a new experience for him. Must be nice, not being surprised by just about everything—like me!

'Brannaugh! Are you here?' he thought-yelled.

'No need to yell!' I grump-thought at him.

I could feel his relief. Yup. However, it was not just thoughts now. I could feel what he was feeling, and his relief washed over me like a warm shower. Huh! Nice.... Maybe. He couldn't feel the feelings I had about him, right? At least, I hoped not! That could prove awkward. Very. Awkward.

'You're in dark moon phase,' he said, stating the obvious. *'But I can hear you while I am in cat form, just like in Tír na nÓg.'*

'I can hear you even when you're not, though.' I responded, starting to feel distinctly spacey. Almost like that episode by our Lughnasadh fire. Like I was separating into tiny pieces—that were drifting away from each other. Fear curled in my stomach like a venomous snake. *'Kellas, something's wrong,'* I managed weakly. *'It feels like I'm coming apart...'*

Faster than I thought possible, Kellas shifted back into human form. "Archer! Grab her! We must hold her here. She can talk to me while I'm in cat form, so I'll shift back. C'mon, we've got to find her."

"Where is she, though?" Poor Archer was making grabbing motions with his arms, stumbling about trying to connect with me, but he was simply too far away.

Kellas shifted back into cat form. *'Where are you?'* he thought-screamed, running back and forth trying to locate me.

'By...the big rock...' I managed. It was hard to speak, like I was halfway under from the sleeping gas they use on patients before big operations. Even though I was only whispering, it took titanic effort to say anything. My knees went wobbly and I sank back against the solid form of the boulder behind me. Kellas dashed over—and ran into my legs.

"Here! She's here!" he yelled at Archer as he shifted momentarily to human form, and then back again. *'Hang in there, Brannaugh. Don't disappear on us!'*

Archer lunged at the rock and felt desperately about until he connected with my right arm. "Gotcha," he exclaimed. But his relief was short-lived. "Kellas, she's squishy-feeling. What does that mean?"

Kellas made a loud and terrible *mroowing* noise, like a lost cat calling for help. But the sound was fading from my ears, and I could barely feel Archer's arms around me anymore. I was losing consciousness...

Then Orianthi was there, appearing out of thin air in front of me. She pushed Archer to one side and wrapped her arms around me. "I've got her."

It was the last thing I heard. Everything faded to nothing.

~

Slowly waking up, I found myself in my own bed, darkness soft around me. I could hear someone else breathing, low and even—so that someone was likely asleep. I pushed up onto one arm. By the dim light from outside, I could make out a lump under the covers next to me. It was someone small, someone who smelled like fresh breezes and warm earth. Orianthi. She had come for me when I was disappearing into nothingness. She'd saved me, just like her mother had saved Nan centuries ago. We owed the dryads our unfailing allegiance.

Sinking back against my pillow, I reviewed the whole episode in my mind. Nan had never mentioned becoming immaterial, only invisible. Was this something new, perhaps? Or was it like the time in Tír na nÓg, when I'd become only light? Was this a whole new wrinkle in the lunacy paradigm? Why was this happening? I wish I had a clue.

When I was fading, Orianthi had just appeared—out of thin air! How did she do that? And what would have happened if she hadn't? I was going to have to quiz her on all this when she woke up. Would my atoms have been scattered to the winds, never to reassemble themselves as "me?" Would I have been a mere consciousness floating around the world on the wind...forever? Would that even qualify as dying? The idea made me shake with horror. Becoming a ghost-like thing—not exactly a happily-ever-after ending.

I stared at the ceiling, wide awake. Outside, the wind pushed against the house, making it creak. The huge set of D minor wind chimes Nan had hung outside on the deck sang softly as the wind pushed its striker against the long metal tubes. Normally, the sound made me feel peaceful. Not right now. I had come too close to becoming nonexistent. Probably not dead—but without form or voice.... What would you even call being neither alive nor dead? I shuddered. It wasn't anything I wanted to experience again—ever. But how would I avoid it?

It was pretty obvious I wasn't going to be able to get back to sleep. I slid out from under the covers and padded over to the French doors, which were shut tight. Unusual. In good weather, they were normally left wide open. Maybe.... Nope, I would not dwell on that right now! I pulled the lever handle down enough to release the door latch, tugged the door open slightly, and slid out through the opening, leaving the door ajar. I wanted to make as little sound as possible.

The railing was taller than I was now. Plopping down on the deck by the railing, I sat with my feet dangling over the edge. I pressed my face against the spindles, staring out over the backyard. The dead hulk of Orinthia's pine was a dark mass in the middle of the lawn. The lake at the bottom of the hill shimmered with the tiniest bit of ambient light. Crickets sang their *summer is dying* song. A few toads still trilled. Somewhere a barred owl hooted. The wind brought the wonderful smell of drying hay from further up the lake, where a neighboring farmer had cut his alfalfa field just the day before. It was perhaps the best smell in the whole world. If someone could bottle it as a perfume, I would be first in line to buy it.

Below, on the lawn, a dark, four-legged form wandered out of the woods. A doe. She looked about carefully, then wandered farther out into the middle. Soon, two half-grown fawns followed her. They gamboled and frisked around their mother as if they were too full of energy to even bother with eating. The cautious mother would take a bite of grass, then raise her head to check for danger as she chewed her mouthful. The doe froze when a distant fox barked, its voice harsh and strangled-sounding. But then she relaxed, as though she knew the fox was no danger to her or her babies.

The door hinges creaked quietly behind me and Kellas's black cat form padded over. *'Are you here, Brannaugh?'* he thought at me.

'I'm here,' I thought back at him. *'Am I still invisible?'*

'Yes,' he responded, wandering back and forth searching for me. When he bumped into my shoulder, he stopped and sat down beside me. Together, we looked down upon the picturesque scene of the doe with her fawns.

'You scared me out of a few lives back there,' he thought at me. He sounded like someone who'd come very close to losing a friend. It heartened me to know just how much he cared.

'You were scared! How do you think I felt?' I retorted. But there wasn't any oomph to it. Neither of us were upset with the other. Mostly we sensed just how close to disaster we'd come.

'Is this typical?' I thought-asked.

'No.'

My heart sank. *'Gee, that's fantastic...'*

We sat in silence for a good five minutes. Behind us, the door creaked again and Orianthi emerged. She sat down next to me, dangling her legs between the spindles as I was.

"You can see me?" I asked. She hadn't blundered around looking for me like Kellas had.

"You're shining around the edges now," she said simply. "Pretty soon you'll show up again."

"Do you know what happened...back there?" I realized I wasn't being terribly specific, but I found it hard to talk about. Just thinking about it sent shudders down my spine.

Orianthi sat silently for a space. "Well..." she started, then stopped again. "I heard Kellas's call for help, and somehow, I knew I was the only one who could get there in time..." Her voice trailed off again. When she started again, she sounded tense. "I space-traveled to where I'd heard his call and realized you were...coming apart...and.... I did the only thing I could think of. I grabbed you and space-traveled you back home. I knew the house could keep you safe until you pulled yourself back together again."

"You space-traveled?"

"That's how I got here in the first place," she said, as if it were no big deal. "All we dryads can do it. I mean, I'd never tried bringing anyone with me before—but I had to try. It's not like you had anything to lose. If it hadn't worked, you'd have been a goner anyways."

That made me gulp hard. "And you could hear Kellas's cat call?" I realized that had another meaning from the one I'd meant, but I left it at that.

"That cry? All of us fairy folk can hear it. That's why it's a cry of last resort."

"What?!" I blurted in astonishment.

"It brings the baddies, as well as the good guys," Kellas supplied. He'd switched back into man form and was studying me. "I can see you now. Kinda like a shadow."

I looked at Kellas with a surge of relief. *Well, thank the gods for that!*

Then I turned back to Orianthi. "But how did *you* know where I was?" I continued.

"Archer. The power of his will was holding you there just enough that I could find you—a shadow you."

"Squishy," Kellas added.

"Yup. Definitely squishy," Orianthi agreed.

"Am I squishy now?" I shuddered. What a nasty-sounding word "squishy" was. Especially when applied to oneself.

Orianthi leaned over, wrapped her arms around me, and gave me a sisterly hug. "Definitely not squishy," she reassured me. I leaned into her, hugging her back.

I cast about for the right words to express the depth of gratitude I felt, but my word bank was at a deficit. All I could come up with was *thanks*—which hardly began to cover it.

My friends nodded with a look of understanding.

Somehow, I think they knew.

But...this squishy bit had me worried. When Cerridwen had messed with the moon in Tír na nÓg, forcing the moon into dark phase, I had ended up being immaterial but still "there." Pure energy. This time, I'd felt like I was *coming apart.* "Why?"

I didn't realize I'd asked my question aloud until Kellas answered. "Something must have attacked you."

What?! Who? How? I needed to know.

"We knew something was wrong, but we didn't know what. Or why. Or even how it was being done. And we still don't." His voice deepened with an emotion I couldn't place.

I didn't react—but it had an immediate effect on Orianthi, who abruptly hopped to her feet. "Gotta go! Things to do, people to see!" she declared in a chirpy tone. She dropped a kiss on the top of my head, then disappeared into thin air.

I was baffled. "What just happened?" I demanded. "Why did Orianthi take off like she was stung by a bee?"

Kellas's answer was a soft huff, a cross between frustration and disgust. He stood up in a single lithe movement, caught me under the arms, and lifted me onto my feet.

Being a baby next to this man was not something I was excited about. So, I swiftly assumed my glamour; I'd gotten good at it lately. Although, right now, I was surprised I could even think straight enough to do it. He was so close, so...darn good-looking! (Geez, Raven, get a grip! You're practically drooling!)

Kellas didn't seem to notice how much he affected me that way; he just stared down at my face like he was trying to memorize it.

Kinda hard to stay neutral under the circumstances! (Kinda hard to want to.) Gods, he smelled good.... My heart was pounding in my ears.

"Brannaugh," he started, then fell silent.

I could feel his breath on my face. I inched a little closer. "What?"

"I thought.... No." He grimaced. "*We* thought we'd lost you forever." He leaned his head down, our faces mere inches apart now.

Gods, was he going to kiss me? I was mesmerized by his beautiful mouth. I stared at it, hoping he would. Maybe my eyes even closed a bit...anticipating...

But he didn't kiss me. Instead, he groaned, his breath a hot gush on my cheeks. He drew me into his arms with a hug that felt more like *just friends* than the sweethearts I desperately wished we were.

"You're so young," he said.

Argh! So close! And then he chickened out. Darn the Cat Man! I glowered at him. "I'm nearly 17!"

"Still too young," he said, gently setting me back at arm's length, his hands on my shoulders.

I stared up at him, my heart dropping to my toes. *No, no, no!* This was not how I'd wanted the conversation to go.

He looked apologetic. "Don't think for a minute I don't know how you feel about me, Brannaugh. You don't hide your emotions well. They're right out there in the open, all the time. A blind man could see it. Believe me, I'm honored, really honored. And you…" A grimace flitted across his face, like he was in pain. "You're amazingly hard to resist…but…" Kellas shook his head. Then he dropped his hands from my arms and shrugged. His face was stamped with regret. "I'm too old for you."

Too old? *That* was his excuse? Hot tears stung the back of my eyes. "Isn't that my decision to make?"

One of those lousy tears must have escaped my eyes because he lifted a hand and gently brushed it away with his thumb. "No," he said.

"Kellas!" I protested. But it didn't sound at all like me. My throat was too tight.

He had started to turn away but looked back over his shoulder. "Archer is 19, nearly 20. He's a far more appropriate match for you than I am." Kellas's eyes saddened. "He about lost his mind when you disappeared on us yesterday. The man is seriously taken with you, Brannaugh. You should see where that goes." And with that, the coward turned and walked away.

The angry tears poured down my face, although I did not cry out loud. I just stood there; my arms wrapped around myself in silent misery. How dare he declare himself *too old* and then casually fob me off on another guy? Even if the other guy *was* undeniably good-looking and more age-appropriate (according to Kellas, anyway). I was also unbelievably embarrassed and ashamed. He was *honored* that I was *obviously infatuated* with him. Cringe. If he found me so *hard to resist,* he wouldn't have just patted me on the head and told me to go play with kids my own age. I balled my hands into fists at the thought. How *dare* he!

I did not go downstairs right away. I couldn't bear the thought of seeing Kellas down there, eating breakfast in the kitchen like nothing was different. How could I even look him in the eye after what he had just said, let alone do our daily workouts together?

In the end, I did go down to breakfast. I was driven there by an unrelentingly grumbly, undeniably empty, belly. No one was there, which was fine by me. No need for awkward conversations. I grabbed a bowl of whole wheat cereal, then went looking for Nan. I needed to get good at everything ASAP. And I needed to not waste a single moment more thinking about a certain condescending, irritating, pain-in-my-derriere, *old* Cait Sidhe.

Or...so I told myself. Repeatedly. Ad nauseam, even.

Yeah. I couldn't convince myself of that, either.

Twelve

August 26th was back to school—regular school. Although, because of the COVID-19 pandemic, it was to be held online instead of in an actual classroom. Dad signed me up with the local high school, just in case we returned to in-school classes before the year was out. I managed to test out of most of the sophomore classes. I had no idea how, but it seemed I no longer needed to make up classes for my "gap year"—Dad's diplomatic way of referring to my time in Tír na nÓg. Calling it "those months where I was kidnapped by a spiteful moon goddess" probably would not sit very well with school officials.

I was now officially a junior, which was kind of nice. However, the added hours in front of a computer really put a dent in my time studying "moon craft," as Nan called it. Fortunately, my music practice and daily runs counted toward music and PE requirements. That helped. By basically giving up my free time (of any sort), I could cram it all in. It was difficult, but doable.

August blended into September as we fell into a predictable routine, which for me, included learning all the basics—from "normal" education to Druidry practice and self-defense. My running definitely got stronger...I mean...at least now I could *almost* keep up with Kellas and Archer without becoming too oxygen-deprived—or dying of heart failure. What's more, I accomplished this *while* breezily pretending nothing had happened between the Cait Sidhe and me.

Kellas went along with it all, treating me like he'd always had: teasing, nagging, pushing me to my limits. But he...never...spent time alone with me anymore. And what was worse, he never once touched me. Never once sent me one of his sidelong sardonic looks—the kind that would always send my heart racing. I told myself it didn't matter.... But I lied.

~

The new moon came and went in mid-September without incident. I was careful to stay inside and not do anything stupid, like open a window. This time, as before my near miss with immateriality, all I experienced was being invisible. Nothing "squishy" about it. Thank the gods! We still didn't know why I'd nearly *come apart*, but we were going to have to figure that one out if I was to manage the dark moon phase without hiding in my room every single month. No way I was risking ghosthood.

Then there was the Archer problem. Now that was "interesting." It was bad enough to be kid-sized so much of the time, let alone enduring the added torture of being around the kindest, very considerate, incredibly handsome guy—and having him treat me like I was a porcelain doll. I finally lost my patience and pulled off a Kote Gaeshi technique I'd been learning, a nice little Aikido throw that put Archer flat on his back gasping for air.

I got in his face. "You need to stop treating me like that!"

He stared at me like I was nuts. "Like what?"

"Like I'm made of glass or something. I'm not breakable."

He went to get up. "But you *are* breakable!"

I put him in an arm bar and drove him back to the ground. "Promise me you will treat me like a normal kid—unless I pull another squishy. Then you can fuss over me."

"Fine! I promise," he groaned. He tapped out and I let him go.

It made me realize that it wasn't kind to focus on a person's disability to the exclusion of everything else, including things it didn't really affect. It might be meant well, but it was surprisingly grating.

~

September was beautiful in upstate New York, I decided. The humidity of August had relented. The morning air was crisp and refreshing. The leaves were starting to turn, mostly on trees that were stressed in one way or another. The soft maples had a gorgeous red hue to them.

"Fall's my new favorite season," I told Nan one day when we were practicing our ward-making on the back deck one afternoon.

"Every season has something to recommend it," she smiled. And I was glad to see that it was a real one, unlike the forced smiles she'd been giving everyone lately. Even so, something was bothering her. I could see it in her face as she stared out the window just a little too long, lost in thought. I needed whatever she was thinking to be out in the open. No more tiptoeing around it.

"OK, so this might seem a bit pushy, but I need to know. What's really going on?"

Nan's smile faded.

"Why are you so grim all the time? Where are Kellas, Erin, and Elias off to most days, and why is Dad such a washed-out wreck?" I demanded. "You all might think I'm still a kid, but honestly, I have a stake in this too, and being left out of the whole process is...well...just not useful."

It rushed out of me all in a breath. Until I had put it into words, I hadn't realized how tense and anxious I'd been. I guess part of me had simply been waiting for the next shoe to drop—unconvinced I was "out of the woods," so to speak.

Caution was on Nan's face now, and I knew I had to convince her I was mature enough to handle *whatever* it was. "Really, you can trust me not to be an idiot about things."

Nan dropped her arms, letting the spell she was weaving fall apart in shimmering strands that soaked into the wood of the deck. She stared mournfully at the wrecked hulk of Orinthia's Peace Tree, her spell of seeming wavering enough that I could see the elderly lady inside it.

Finally, Nan drew a shaky breath. "Come on, let's walk together." She reached for my hand and we headed for the perimeter walk, the same one I had wandered with my dad the day I'd lost my cool with my mother.

As we passed Orinthia's once-flourishing tree, Nan took a moment to put a hand solemnly on its fire-ravished trunk. I commented on how Orianthi's pine was doing well. Then, we continued on.

We walked in silence for probably five minutes. I tried simply enjoying our walk together, but Nan's prolonged silence was frustrating. I paused to watch a flock of redwings that had settled in an ash tree nearby, filling the air with their cries. Made an effort to admire the brilliant fall foliage. But, despite my best attempts not to be, I was impatient. When was Nan going to start talking?

Finally, she drew a deep breath and began.

"It's complicated; it will take a while to explain. So, forgive me if I leave out details or repeat myself. And *DO* feel free to ask questions."

Oh, you better believe I was going to ask questions! But I just nodded and matched her pace as we continued on.

"Ok. The short answer: We still don't know what's going on. It's bad enough the entire country is in an uproar and COVID keeps killing so many people—but to have this to worry about, too?" Nan couldn't keep the concern from her voice.

I moved closer to her for reassurance.

"The longer answer is still mostly guesswork." She continued. "And our best guess, as I already told you, is that after 400 years of us hiding here, the Grecian witch goddess Carman and her three sons...the Old Gods...have finally located us. We have no way of confirming that, however. So far, the only incursion here was that lightning strike."

"But why would they do that?" I interjected. I bent down, caught up a pebble, and flung it in frustration against a tree. None of this made sense.

"It could have been a test to see if they could breach our boundaries. Or they may have accomplished their mission by killing Orinthia. We don't know what they're planning next, or even if they are planning anything further against us here."

Nan shook her head sadly. "I also have my suspicions that it's Dub, Dian, and Dother behind all the pandemonium going on in our country right now. It would be typical of their way of working: creating havoc, then stirring up hate until people act out in hideous ways."

"But lightning," I stated, wanting her to expand on that thought. "Why lightning?"

"Not your typical bolt, that one," Nan admitted. "It was larger and more powerful than usual—and it had a target. It wasn't by happenstance that Orinthia's tree was struck."

I gnawed on my bottom lip. "You think the brothers...whatever they are... were targeting the Peace Tree?"

Nan nodded. "That tree represents the power of the collective choice for peace. With it gone, the collective weakens and falls apart. Arguments become more frequent, then deepen into bitterness and fighting of all sorts. We can't let that happen."

"And one of the sons, Dother or Dian—his domain is evil or something, right?" He was probably the one who killed Orinthia. She and her tree were a direct hindrance to his powers. Then another question popped into my mind. "Does it only affect the Haudenosaunee?"

"It affects everyone." Nan shook her head, looking a little rueful. "As for who is behind this, my bet is on Dother, Raven. He's pure evil. He thrives on hate—and hate grows like cancer. You can't let it get a toehold."

"Seems like there is plenty of it going around already," I said darkly. "All this crazy talk you hear in the news."

She sighed in agreement. "Misinformation is a tough one. People choose to believe something, then it's almost impossible to dislodge from their psyche. Like a cancer that's metastasized."

"So...what can we do?" I asked helplessly. If hate and conflict fed directly into Dother's powers, then he was probably feasting away at a banquet right now. "Is there some magic we can call into action to stop all this?"

Nan smiled sadly. "Magic can only do so much. The rest is up to people and their choices."

"Then we need to influence their choices," I insisted. But how on earth could that be done? "Is there a spell or something for that?" I added.

"It's called charisma," Nan said quietly. "With it, someone can stand up and shine a light for others to follow." She looked at me with her face more serious than I'd ever seen it. "Think you can manage that?"

I stopped in my tracks. "What?! Are you nuts? I'm 16. Can't you, the Cait Si, and Dad do something?"

"We are doing everything in our power; trust me on that point. A lot of what we are doing is behind-the-scenes stuff. However, you're nearly 17, Raven. People underestimate children, claiming that they're too young, when, in fact, they are often wiser, stronger, and more sensible than the adults who call the shots. At 17, Greta Thunberg was a powerful voice combating climate change. Malala Yousafzai was 17 when she was awarded the Noble Peace Prize for her fierce advocacy that every girl has the right to choose her own future. And there are many others around the world taking up the fight. Age is immaterial."

I was trembling. Apparently, Nan thought I could join these incredible young women and make a difference somehow. But I had no idea how. "Where do I start?" I managed at last. "What can I do?"

Nan squeezed my hand. "You do exceptionally well with poetry and music," she said. "So here's a suggestion." And she quoted the following (from what I learned later, was Charles Kingsley's "A Farewell"):

Do the work that's nearest,

Though it's dull at whiles,

Helping when you see them,

Lame dogs over stiles.

Like that made any sense. I must have looked confused because Nan squeezed my hand again.

"Baby steps, Raven. You start close to home, doing what may seem like little things. Greta started by encouraging her parents to adopt planet-friendly actions—and look where it's led. Malala gave a powerful speech when she was just 11. But she sure didn't know at the time that it would be so earth-shaking." She stopped walking and took me by the shoulders, a serious look on her face. "You can do this, whatever *this* happens to be. And given your own abilities with that amazing lute, and your lovely voice—I think you could pretty much achieve anything you decide to." She let me go and started walking again.

"Through music," I said, hurrying to catch up. "You must be kidding me."

"Through music," Nan repeated. "Music has inspired humanity through-out the ages. It takes the spoken word and empowers it manyfold. It quietly works its way into the collective consciousness and spreads its message in the most effective way possible. In short, when it's used by those who desire to spread hope and create change, it is a vehicle for mass inoculation against hate."

I stopped to take that in as Nan turned toward me, a look of knowing twinkling in her eyes. "Now," she declared with a smile, "can you think of any magic more powerful than that?"

Put that way, it sounded like I'd have superpowers after all. Huh! Why, then, did I still feel so powerless? "Can you tell me what you all are doing? Maybe it would help me with perspective."

Nan smiled again. "Your dad works overtime helping people who are dangerously sick or injured. He learns a lot about what is going on just by being present for them. He listens carefully to those who have mental problems and sometimes can get them the help they need. Homeless people, whom no one gives the time of day to, are often our best source of information about what's happening in the local landscape."

A memory pinged at the back of my mind. "Like that strange man who knew Kellas was nearby, even though we were hidden?"

"As creepy as his energy field feels to us, that unfortunate gentleman is acutely sensitive to the presence of other worlders. And lately, he's been reporting some unusual activity to your dad. Unfortunately, doing so landed the poor man back in the mental ward again. So, we've temporarily lost that source of information."

My stomach twisted into a knot, wishing there was a permanent solution for the man. Also, what had he told my dad that got him hospitalized?

"What kind of activity?" I wanted to know.

"Michael said he kept crying about ghosts and ghouls."

I shuddered. "And the Cait Si?"

"On the prowl, to put it succinctly. Few folks notice cats. Those who do can usually be evaded. Erin had a near miss with an overly enthusiastic cat-saver lady yesterday. So, everyone is being especially cautious."

Ohh! "What constitutes a near miss?"

"The gal had a net and almost trapped Erin in it. She scooted out from under it just in the nick of time."

I giggled, thinking of Erin's tiger cat nearly getting scooped up in a net. "What would you have done if she had gotten caught?"

"Claimed her as ours." Nan grinned. "We had to adopt Kellas from the pound once. But please don't tell him I told you that. He's been humiliated enough."

What did that mean? I wanted to know, but didn't dare ask.

Nan hesitated a moment, then quietly chuckled. "The lady at the SPCA offered to sign him up for a free spay/neuter clinic. We declined, though, saying he was one of the few remaining felines of his kind—which is true, considering there are less than 100 Cait Si worldwide now. We did some quick thinking and made up the excuse that we needed him to reestablish the breed. She bought it, hook, line, and sinker. Fortunately for Kellas. I don't think he would've been too happy had she not believed us."

I grinned ear to ear, and I swear Nan knew exactly what I was thinking.

"Please, Raven, not a word to anyone. I probably shouldn't have even mentioned it."

I zipped my lips with a quick one-handed motion. But I was still sorely tempted to lean into Kellas about this later—and would have, if we were still on speaking terms. Which we weren't. Not after his condescending behavior recently! The thought chilled me and my humorous mood died.

I shifted the subject to Nan. "And you?" I asked, carefully. "What have you been doing? Besides trying to get my sorry butt up to speed, that is."

"Teaching you, as you say. Although, I wouldn't have characterized your abilities quite like that!" She sent me a chiding look. "I've also been doing my best to improve our wards here," she said quietly, "looking for the weak points and shoring them up—and teaching you to do the same. That way, you can take over...when I'm not able to."

She didn't say it, but we both knew what she was referring to. Her age was a distinct disability, and it was steadily worsening. I skittered away from the thought. Nan was immortal, wasn't she? She wasn't going away anytime soon. Right?

"What's my role in all this, then?" I asked. Even though I thought I had a pretty good idea...considering everything.

But Nan's reply sent cold shivers down my spine.

"Remember how badly the trolls wanted to kidnap you when your moon magic kicked in?" she questioned grimly. "You are uniquely powerful, especially now that you possess the Claimh Solais. As long as they see you as a threat, you remain at risk."

I blanched.

"I don't say this to scare you, Raven, but it's the fact of the matter. As hard as you think you are working now? You need to double down and work even harder. Your life depends on it—perhaps ours too."

Gee. No pressure. I kicked at a rock. *What was I supposed to do now?*

"Do the work that's nearest," she continued more gently. "For you, that means learning your magic as fast as you possibly can. I know it doesn't seem like you're helping us solve anything, Raven—but it all adds up."

I nodded, unable to say anything. My throat was too tight. I wasn't ready to have lives depending on me. I understood what that meant; I'd seen Kellas and Taliesin almost die trying to protect me back in Tír na nÓg. Her words sat on my shoulders like a thousand stones.

At this point, we reached the side trail that led back to the stables. Nan's night mare, Moon Dancer, stayed there whenever she came to visit. It wasn't a fancy barn, but it fit the role we needed it for. Nan headed in that direction. "Moon's here. Want to say hi?"

Still unable to say much, I just tagged along. It had been quite some time since Moon Dancer had paid us a visit. I was looking forward to seeing her again. We came out of the woods to a gate in the paddock fence. Fencing wasn't necessary for the night mare, but if we ever wanted a regular sort of horse, it would come in handy. Plus, having a barn with no fencing...well...it would look rather odd.

Moon was out in the paddock. She was grazing on the thick green grass—which we mowed regularly. The mare wasn't around frequently enough right now to do the job herself, and if we didn't...it would be a jungle.

Moon wandered over to us as we approached and leaned her face against Nan's chest. The two stood there quietly, Nan stroking the mare's lovely neck. I stood by, not wanting to interrupt the moment, wondering if they were having the sort of silent communication I used to have with Kellas when he was in cat form. The thought made my heart hurt. I banished it almost immediately, then stood respectfully, waiting for the pair to part.

Finally, they both gave a sort of deep sigh. Nan stepped back and Moon wandered off to graze again. Somehow Nan looked younger, stronger. Happier. I looked from her to the mare, then back again. I must have looked confused.

"Horse magic," Nan said, answering my unasked question.

There was a peacefulness in her voice that I hadn't heard in a long time. The lines in her face were now relaxed, her shoulders had released their tension, and she was smiling—really smiling. What was that about?

"Moon heals me in so many ways; it's impossible to relay," she said.

I could relate. Spending time with horses always made me happier. Yet, it had been a long time since I'd done that. I frowned, suddenly *needing* to ride. It felt more important than anything else right now. I missed my horse!

Ok. So, I say "my" horse, even though the Knight horse is only nominally mine. He's Moon Dancer's stud colt who was sired by a demon horse—which makes him a "dark horse." You never really know what you're getting yourself in for with a dark horse. They can be incredibly talented—but also hugely unpredictable. Knight tended to disappear out from under me at the most inopportune times. Yet, this fact didn't stop me from loving him.

"Do you suppose Knight might come see us too, sometime?" I asked mournfully. "It's been ages since I've gone riding."

Moon raised her head as if she'd heard me. She nickered softly and Nan began to translate for her. But she didn't get far. There was a rushing sound as if a strong gust of wind had sprung up. Suddenly, Knight was standing next to his mother. His neck arched proudly and his nostrils fluttered with a long bluster. His black coat shone in the sun. He was *beautiful*.

I felt like jumping for joy. *'Where have you been all this time, big guy?'* I thought at him.

Knight shied violently at my thought-message. I don't think he was expecting me to be so enthusiastic about seeing him. He recovered quickly, though. His response was a mix of mental images and feelings—he'd been in training with Edona, the Celtic Goddess of horses. She'd made him work *hard,* and he'd learned plenty.

One thing about mental communication, it's efficient. Knight's relaying of his last few months away took only a few moments to complete. A picture really *is* worth a thousand words.

I was ready with my next question: "Want to go riding?"

Knight gave me a rough push with his nose: that was a definite yes.

Nan smiled. "We thought you'd never ask!"

Thirteen

I t was now late September; nearly two weeks had passed since that glorious afternoon of riding with Nan. Kellas and I were driving to Treman State Park for our daily workout. Trust me, I'd much rather have been heading to the stable. I had loved riding Knight since he'd returned. But now I had to train. Our lives depended on it.

"Archer has prelims this week, so he won't be joining us for a few days," Kellas announced. My heart sank at this news. I'd gotten pretty good at focusing my attention on the Swamp Monster during our runs, letting Kellas trail along like a fifth wheel. It made being around the Cait Sidhe a bit easier to bear. With no Archer, that technique was nonfunctional.

I looked out the window—and away from Kellas. It was late for a workout. The day had pretty much escaped us, what with one thing after another that needed doing. Plus, it was past the fall equinox. The days were now shorter than the nights. Dark came early. We'd come prepared with headlamps just in case we needed them, tucked away in the zipper compartment of our water packs. Still, I wasn't all that thrilled about running without Archer—or at night. I said as much...well, the part about not wanting to run in the dark, that is.

"You do realize we have a full moon tonight," Kellas said, without taking his eyes off the road.

I studiously ignored him.

He made a soft snorting sound through his nose. He knew I was upset.

As soon as we pulled into the Old Mill parking lot, I jumped out of the car and made a big show of warming up—doing high-knee lifts and jumping jacks (like somebody who was a real runner or something).

Kellas got out slowly and sent me a sardonic look that told me he knew what I was up to (ignoring him). Then, he started his own warmup routine. Only, he looked like a real runner who knew what the heck he was doing.

While Kellas had his back to me, I allowed my gaze to dwell on his body. Briefly. Very, *very* briefly. I wasn't about to be caught. That would never do! Also, looking at him made my throat hurt, like I'd swallowed too big a bite. I went back to warm-ups.

Gravel crunched, and I turned to see who was pulling in. A black, ugly-looking SUV had swung into a parking space at the far end of the lot. A large man emerged and began preparing for a run as well. Standing at the open back of his vehicle, he swapped out his shoes for sneakers and took off his sweat-pants, revealing shorts underneath. Then he pulled off his sweatshirt, leaving his chest totally bare. Tattoos covered nearly every square inch of skin, drawn taut over mountains of bulging muscles. *Huge* muscles. Like the ones body-builders have. I stood on one leg stretching my quads, and stared. I wasn't sure whether I found him attractive or utterly repulsive. His body was a caricature of a normal human's.

Muscle Man must have noticed me looking at him because he looked up and met my gaze. He smirked, like he knew how he affected people. Then he gave me that deliberate up-and-down look that makes you feel utterly naked.

I looked away immediately, my face flaming. No question in my mind. He was a nasty man. Completely repulsive.

"Let's go," said Kellas, heading for the trailhead.

Of course, he'd be completely oblivious to the whole silent exchange I'd had with Muscle Man! I quickly scuttled after Kellas, not wanting to get left behind with the human monstrosity—who, by the way, was still leering at me. Cringe!

The pace Kellas set was brisk, but I had no trouble keeping up. This section of trail was nearly flat. It wound its way past some gorgeous stonework and over a stone bridge. Even in the fading daylight, it was breathtaking. Still, it would be more enjoyable if Mr. Ick-Factor wasn't so close behind us.

When we got to the top of a long flight of stone stairs, Kellas slowed to check that I was still with him. I took the opportunity and ducked around him, flying down the steps faster than I'd ever done before.

Kellas quickly caught up. "Feeling speedy today?" he commented, right at my heels.

"Creepy dude...in the parking lot," I panted. "Just wanted...to put some... distance between us."

"Creepy dude, eh? Well, if that's what it takes for you to turn up the speed, I'm good with that!"

Darn him. He didn't sound winded at all! I nearly stumbled on a loose stone.

Kellas ignored this. "What made him seem so creepy?"

How do you describe that feeling—the one that comes from some guy stripping you naked with his eyes? I had no words to explain. I just shuddered and kept running. In fact, I may have even picked up the pace a click or two. *Down the stairs, down the stairs...*

Kellas grunted in surprise and matched my pace stride for stride. We ran past Lucifer Falls (high from recent rains) and down to where the path curved around a big bend, the shale cliffs towering overhead. I dropped to a walk, then stopped to catch my breath, hands braced on my thighs. I needed to get my heart rate down.

Kellas waited straddle-legged, hands on hips, his chest rising and falling quickly. Although not nearly as quickly as mine. *Uggh! For sure he was about to say something snarky.* He was facing back the way we'd come, a half-smile on his face.

Then it disappeared. Kellas went completely still, his posture rigid, every ounce of him on high alert. "That dude you were running away from. What did he look like?"

The guy had a full beard and dark hair all over his chest. The sides of his head were shaved, but a mohawk a couple inches long crested his skull. The overall effect? Scary. But since I was still trying to get my breathing back under control, I gave Kellas the short version. "Big...Muscly...Inked all over... his chest. Hairy."

"That him?"

Kellas's voice concerned me; it was unnaturally tense. I followed his line of sight and suddenly felt ill. Muscle Man was running down the steps we'd just descended. He was light on his feet—far too fast for a guy that size.

"Yes," I straightened up in alarm.

Kellas grabbed my upper arm and gave me a hard shove. "Move! Now!"

I didn't need to be urged. I took off like a deer in full flight, Kellas hard on my heels. Laughter echoed over the sound of the river and our pounding feet. Was Muscle Man mocking us? Hard to say. By then, my heart was beating so loudly in my ears it was a wonder I could hear anything over its thudding.

Kellas shoved me again, and this time I went sprawling to the rough ground. I skidded several feet on my hands and knees, scraping them badly. Worse yet, my face connected hard enough against the rocky trail that I saw stars. I was dimly aware that Kellas had collapsed beside me.

I scrambled to my feet almost immediately. Somehow my rattled brain registered that Kellas was still on the ground, hadn't even moved. I looked around wildly for the cause of his fall. The path was stony, but it was clear of debris. Kellas wouldn't have just tripped; he wasn't clumsy like me.

But then I saw it. An arrow stuck out of Kellas's back, the shaft still quivering from the force of impact. Blood squeezed out from around the shaft and spread across the back of his gray T-shirt. My heart was thudding even harder. But like before, another sound rose above its thundering. Laughter: cruel, mocking...drawing my attention to the stairs we'd just descended.

Muscle Man stood there, a longbow held low across his hips. "You may be fast, little girl, but no one can outrun an arrow," he jeered, walking unhurriedly down the remaining few steps. Dark energy was swirling around him as he approached, reaching out toward Kellas's fallen form. Its inky rivulets curled around the arrow and sank into the Cait Sidhe.

Kellas cried out and convulsed in agony.

I jumped between the shirtless giant and Kellas. "Stop right there! Don't come any closer!"

He stopped, a peculiar smile twisting his lips. "Do you know who I am?"

I glared at him while shaking like a leaf in my sneakers. "No! Should I?" My words gritted out past chattering teeth. I was like a rabbit facing down a wolf.

"I think you should. Everyone else does." His lips drew back from overly white teeth into a predatory grin. "Even girls who claim to be fearless." He gestured to the bold declaration printed on the front of my T-shirt.

I glanced down at the word. Yeah. FEARLESS. I sure didn't feel that way right now.

He carefully leaned the bow up against the shale cliff...intentionally leaving his hands free. Big meaty hands.

"I d-don't c-care who you are," I stammered. "You're evil!" I sooo hated sounding like a scared little kid.

The man responded with low laughter. "You're right there. But 'evil' is what I do best." That said, one of his enormous hands shot out. He grabbed me by the jaw and yanked me close, his breath hot against my cheek. "You're a tempting little tidbit, aren't you?" he growled into my ear. "I could teach you a thing or two..."

Utter revulsion animated my shaking limbs; Elias's careful instruction in self-defense kicked in. I broke free of the man's grasp, side-kicked him on the outside of his closest knee, and brought the side of one hand down in a chopping motion across the back of his neck. He stumbled and fell to his knees.

I'd stopped him from hurting me, but had brought him within reach of Kellas. With a snarl, the man reached out, yanked the arrow out of Kellas's back, and staggered to his feet—brandishing the bloody arrow at me. I danced back out of the way but he just sneered, gestured at Kellas, and pointed the arrow tip threateningly. "Shall I stab him again?"

Such a horrible grin. Too many white teeth.

"Might be fun," he added, his eyes narrowed, watching for my reaction.

It was anything *but* fun. His cruelty made my blood run cold.

Blood was pouring out of the arrow wound, a dark splotch rapidly widening on Kellas's back. My heart rate soared even higher: *How much longer before he bled out?*

The monster beckoned. "Come here, little tidbit. I saw how you were looking at me. You want some of this, don't you?" He flexed his muscles, then made a lewd, suggestive motion with his hips.

No, I most definitely did *not* want anything that pervert had to offer! The very idea made my supper rise high in my throat. I circled, trying to get closer to Kellas and farther away from this ogre.

But he circled too, lurching a little, favoring the knee I'd clobbered. Unfortunately, I hadn't completely disabled him. He lunged and caught me by my arm.

I screamed and bit him.

Cursing, he threw me backward like I weighed nothing—but not before I'd grabbed the arrow. The force of the monster's own throw ripped it clear of his grasp.

I landed hard against the cliff face, cracking the back of my head against the shale layers. I nearly passed out, but didn't let go of the arrow. Through blurred vision, I saw him pull himself upright—that horrible leer back on his face. He took a leisurely step toward me.

I don't know why I did it, but I snapped the arrow in half, right across my thigh. I was unprepared for what happened next.

The monster screamed, a deep, hideous scream of impotent fury. Ink poured from the broken halves of the arrow and drained from the tattoos on his body in dark sheets. His body flickered like a candle in a breeze, became translucent, then transparent, and then was completely gone, leaving only inky darkness swirling in eddies until that, too, faded and were was gone.

Shaking uncontrollably, I crawled over to Kellas and gathered him up in my arms. "Talk to me! Please don't be dead."

He didn't respond; his breath was coming in short, painful gasps. He wasn't dead...yet.

The gorge was so quiet and dark now, just the muttering of water running nearby in the creek, moonlight flickering on its surface. Nobody nearby who I could call on for help.

A huge raven swooped down from the cliff edge and settled nearby, ruffling his feathers.

The Morrigan? "Not Kellas! Please don't take him." I wrapped my arms tightly around Kellas, as though I could somehow defend him from Death herself.

A deep double bass sang in my head. *'Kindly stop insulting me. I am Huginn. But your Death Goddess is close.'* He pointed with his beak to another giant raven perched on a dead tree: the Morrigan. *'There is no time to waste. Call for help,'* he urged.

Emergencies require clear thinking—and I was struggling.

'Use your very fine brain!' the double bass voice grumbled. *'Who is good in a crisis? Who is always equipped with the tools of his trade?'* He sounded deeply annoyed. *'Must I do all your thinking for you? Think, child!'*

"Dad," I moaned. Oh gee, that was obvious! Careful not to let Kellas slide off my lap, I unzipped my water pack and drew out my cell phone. My hands were shaking so badly I nearly dropped the thing. Not that dropping it would have made any difference; the darn thing was deader than a doornail. Again. Story of my life. I appealed to the raven for help. "Would you please get Dad for me and tell him where we are? Tell him we need an ambulance."

'You would use me as a messenger boy?' Huginn ruffled his feathers, deeply annoyed. *'Waste your one favor from me on something like this?'*

I showed him the phone, its screen totally black. "My phone's dead." Cell phones hated me. I tended to fry their stupid little circuit brains in short order. No idea why. It couldn't be the moon magic. Nan had no such trouble. I probably should give up carrying them.

'Ha!' the deep voice grumbled. *'Fair point. I am gone on your errand, Raven Light Bringer.'* He spread his wings, lifted himself into the air, and was gone.

I wondered later why he'd been hanging around...

Fourteen

Then came the waiting—long, terrible minutes alone in the dark with my wounded friend, unable to do a thing other than hold him close. Kellas seemed to be breathing less frequently and in desperate gasps. I stroked his face, then patted it desperately. "Hang in there, Cat Man. Please don't die!" I stared at the full moon where it shone over the deep cleft of the gorge. *Gods, Dad, please hurry!*

Help finally arrived. Dad was there first, pelting down the stone stairs like he was in a race. His team was close behind, carrying a stretcher and huge bags of equipment.

Dad dropped to his knees next to me and Kellas. "What happened?"

"He's been shot. Arrow."

"We'll take it from here," he said, and I was kindly but firmly moved out of the way.

The next few minutes were a whirl of well-practiced activity, the paramedics working at top speed to save Kellas's life. They gave him a shot to relieve pain. An oxygen mask was settled over his mouth and nose to ease his labored breathing. A blood pressure cuff was wrapped around one of his arms. Working together, the paramedics lifted him onto the stretcher, then hooked the harnesses they wore to the corners. They lifted in unison—and we were off. Dad walked next to the stretcher, monitoring Kellas's vitals as the others navigated the stretcher up the stairs.

I was left to follow, unable to assist.

Back at the parking lot, the paramedics wasted no time loading Kellas's stretcher into the ambulance. Dad came over to where I stood watching helplessly. He handed me the car key he had grabbed out of Kellas's pack.

"Drive to the hospital," he instructed. "I'll tell Elias and your Nan to come get you there. Don't try to keep up with us. You aren't skilled enough yet."

Not skilled enough was an understatement. I had only recently obtained my learner's permit and had maybe five hours of practice driving under my belt. "I can't drive through Ithaca!" I protested. "The traffic!"

He nodded. "It's not so bad this time of night. You'll be fine." A shout from his crew had him moving away. "You've got this," he called as he hopped into the back of the ambulance. The last man closed the doors and climbed into the passenger seat up front. Flashing lights turned on and they pulled away. No sirens yet; they didn't have any traffic to warn.

Dad might have thought I'd be fine, but I sure didn't think so. I felt like I'd been gutted and hung up like a dead deer. I swallowed hard, then climbed into the Prius and talked myself through the start-up procedure. "Right foot on brake, push start button, turn on headlights, adjust mirrors..."

The car was incredibly easy to drive, but that didn't matter. I was badly shaken up. That sure didn't help. I backed up, then braked too hard. It made the car lurch, and I squeaked in panic. Driving the car at a snail's pace across the parking lot, I passed the evil man's SUV (unable to suppress a shudder at the memory of him), then down the winding back road to my least favorite highway: Route 13. I managed; I'll say that much. It wasn't pretty. So *not pretty* that a city cop pulled me over in the middle of town, his flashing lights nearly blinding me as they reflected off my rearview mirror. I pulled into a hotel parking lot and sat shivering uncontrollably as he pulled up behind me. He took a very long time getting out of his squad car. Letting me stew in my own juice, I suppose. I had enough sense left to pull the registration and insurance out of the glove box. Then dug my learner's permit out of my water bottle pack, which I'd dropped on the passenger seat earlier.

He strolled up to my window (already rolled down), leaned a hand on top of my car, and peered in. "License and registration," he said in a bored tone. I handed those over. "Wait here," he instructed and walked back to his car.

I sat there shivering. Considering the temperature outside was not that cold, I seemed to be having an awfully hard time staying warm. Could it be shock? It might easily be, considering everything that had happened. Wishing I had a blanket to wrap up in, I turned the heat up to 80.

The cop was back. "OK, young lady. I hope you have a truly fantastic reason for driving after 9 p.m. by yourself, with just a learner's permit."

I just nodded, struggling to keep my teeth from chattering. "Uh-huh. I mean, yes, I do, officer."

He waited, eyebrows raised skeptically, head cocked to one side. "And that would be?" he finally prompted when I stayed silent. "And why are you shivering? You've got the heat cranked up so high in there you could cook eggs. Are you on something? Crack maybe?"

"N-no, sir. It's just..." The shuddering was getting bad, not that I had any control over it. "My f-friend and I g-got attacked w-while we were out r-running, and he got really h-hurt, and the ambulance came and t-took him to the h-hospital. And he could b-be dying and I g-gotta get there, but I h-hardly know how to d-drive and I'm s-so scared..." I was rocking back and forth—in a full-blown panic attack.

"Easy, Miss...Callahan." He checked my learner's permit for my name. "Sounds like you've had a bad time of it this evening. Park your vehicle over there and get in my car. I'll take you up to the hospital."

It was my first ride in the back seat of a squad car, and nowhere I would choose to be ever again. I was locked in with bulletproof glass between me and the front seat; there were no handles on the inside of the doors. Up front was a laptop perched in the center console—and the dash was loaded with a great many lights, switches, and buttons. I wondered what they could all possibly be used for. It was fascinating...but it was also a very small, very secure *prison*.

The cop slid into the driver's seat and made a couple quick calls. The first was to the hotel explaining about my car. Then he called base to let them know what he was doing. The exchange was mostly in code, but I got the gist of it. "10-4, over and out." (Yeah, it's not just in the movies.) Then he turned on his roof lights and pulled smoothly into traffic, moving around other vehicles like an eel through a school of fish. It was an impressive demonstration of driving skills. He seemed incredibly relaxed; for him, it looked as easy as breathing.

"I'll n-never get this good," I said. Still stuttering! Argh! He glanced up at me via his rear-view mirror.

"Say again?" He reached over and flipped one of those switches I'd noted earlier.

I squirmed in my seat. "Your driving. I'll n-never get as good as you are, n-not in a million years."

That brought a big grin to his youthful face. "Sure you can. Join the department and we'll send you to school for it."

I shuddered and shook my head vehemently. "I'd be awful at what you have to do. N-no thanks."

"Never know until you try!"

I just shook my head again.

He chuckled, stepped on the gas—and the car bolted. The power under the hood was impressive.... No cap! The miles per gallon must be for crap, though.

We flew up the road to the hospital, ignoring all speed limits. He pulled up behind my dad's ambulance...still idling by the ER entrance...then came around to my door and handed me out like I was royalty.

One of Dad's crew came over immediately when he saw me getting out of the squad car. He and the young cop exchanged one of those curt nods guys make when they're being all professional and serious.

"I take it she had trouble downtown," the paramedic said.

"Not really, but she's obviously not a confident enough driver yet, so I pulled her over. Her car is parked at the Hampton Inn down on 13."

"Ah!" The explanation seemed to suit him. "Thank you, officer. I'll take over from here."

The cop gave me a parting grin. "Let me know if you change your mind about those driving lessons, Miss Callahan." He gave me a little salute and went back to his car.

The paramedic made a disparaging sound. "Watch out for boys like that one, Raven. They all think they're God's gift to women." He grasped my elbow and escorted me into the waiting room, guided me to a chair, and ordered me to wait there.

A lady in bright pink scrubs and a matching face mask came over almost immediately. She handed me a face mask, which I dutifully put on. She squatted down next to me. "A rough finish to your day, hmm?" she asked.

I nodded, then shuddered. Massive understatement!

"Your friend is in the ER undergoing tests. They suspect COVID. But it's been caught early. So, we can get him started on some drugs right away. That should help." She frowned when I started shaking my head when she said *COVID*.

"That's not what it is at all!" I protested. "He was shot with an arrow!"

She gave me a look that suggested I was not quite all there. "There's no wound, sweetie. Why would you say that?"

"But...." I trailed off, realizing that I was not going to get very far talking wildly about an attack by a mysterious man with a magical arrow that left no obvious wound—even after it had been violently ripped out of Kellas's back. Still, there had been all that blood.... Shouldn't that be there?

"You've had quite the awful shock, sweetie. Would you like a coffee, maybe? I'll bring you a blanket, too. And I'll check with Dr. Callahan for updates on your friend."

Huh? Dr. Callahan? Who was she talking about? "Coffee's fine, thanks," I mumbled.

She got to her feet and patted me on one knee. "I'll be right back."

It took a while, though. Things do, in a hospital as busy as this one. Nan and Elias arrived before Pink Lady came back. I was wrapped up tight in Nan's arms when the nurse came over. I let go of my grandmother and sat up by myself, scrubbing away the stupid tears I could no longer hold back.

Pink Lady handed me the promised blanket and set a paper cup of coffee on a nearby table. "Dr. Callahan has ordered tests, but it will take a little while to get results back. Meanwhile, your young man is being moved to intensive care; we're working to get him stabilized, but it's going to be touch and go for a while, I'm afraid. Do you have any questions for me?"

"When can I see him? Can I see him now?" I wrapped the blanket around me; it had been warmed up, which felt wonderful. "Please! It's important!"

Pink Lady smiled gently. "You'll be able to see your boyfriend as soon as we get him settled in. Only through the glass though. You won't be able to go into the room with him."

My boyfriend. She was doing some serious assuming, but I was too distraught to correct her. "But I have to..."

She held up a patient hand. "Soon," she said firmly. "While you wait, there's an excellent snack shop just down that hall." She pointed.

There was no bargaining with her. We dutifully visited the snack shop and armed ourselves with enormous apple Danishes and real coffee (not that gross stuff from the machine she'd brought). Then we went outside in the chilly night air, where we found enough privacy that I could whisper what had happened to Nan and Elias.

Nan looked like she had seen a ghost. "Dub," she breathed, after I had described Muscle Man.

Elias nodded in agreement. "God of Darkness. It must be. What you describe as ink is how he poisons people. It's not really ink, Raven, it's despair."

"Kellas is infected with *despair*?" I was horrified.

Elias nodded. "And you broke Dub's arrow. What made you think to do that?"

I glanced ruefully at the bruised line darkening across my thigh where I had broken the arrow. "I don't know why. I just did it. It was instinct or something. Like when I used the earworm against the troll earlier."

"Then he just disappeared." Elias scowled.

I nodded. "Poof."

Nan bit her lower lip, deep in thought. "Because of your quick actions, we might not have to deal with Dub for a while. It will take him some time to re-ink himself and make a new arrow. But if he's been here, chances are his brothers are as well."

I swallowed hard. "Are they all as creepy as he is? I mean, he acted like he meant to...you know..." I couldn't bring myself to say the word *rape*, but I was virtually certain that was what Dub had threatened. I couldn't shake off the way he'd called me a *tempting little tidbit*, like I was some kind of sweet treat he meant to eat alive. It made my skin crawl in horror.

Elias and Nan exchanged meaningful looks.

"Be honest," I warned.

Elias drew a deep breath in through his nose. "Yes," he said.

"But don't let that scare you," Nan added.

I started laughing, but there was no humor in it. "Too late for that!"

The automatic doors to the ER slid open and Dad came out. He jogged over to where we were standing and pulled me into a hug. My father didn't say anything. He didn't have to. Everything he was feeling was conveyed by the way he was holding me.

"How is Kellas doing?" Nan prompted finally.

Dad released me from his bear hug, ran a shaking hand through his hair, then ripped the medical mask off his face. He drew a deep, shuddering breath. "He's in critical condition. What the hell happened, Raven? We're testing him for COVID, but I'm sure it's not that."

I relayed my encounter with the terrifying man and how he'd shot Kellas with an arrow that was somehow not an arrow, and the ink that somehow wasn't ink that had entered Kellas's lungs.

He exchanged glances with Nan. "Dub?"

She nodded.

"This complicates things."

Ya think? I groaned. "Can you make him better?"

"Dub's arrow is not something we can treat with antibiotics, Raven. Not that I will be able to convince my colleagues of that. They will throw everything we have at him, hoping that something works."

"About that," I interjected. "Who's Dr. Callahan?"

He sent me a sheepish smile. "I am."

Knock me over with a feather. "Since when? All this time, I thought you were a paramedic!"

He made that wishy-washy head nod that said he was hedging. "I may be a bit overqualified for the position, but yes, I work part time as a paramedic. The rest of my team is overqualified too. They're all ex-Army Ranger medics."

Which explained the super-fit, buzz-cut, military bearing of his team-mates. Huh.

"The A-Team," Elias added. "It's even on their ambulance, see?" He pointed. Sure enough, "The A-Team" was painted in bold red letters on the side of Dad's ambulance.

"After that corny 1980s TV show," Dad added. "Kind of an inside joke."

I gave myself a hard shake. This was getting stranger by the minute. Did I even know the man I called my dad? "OK. Got it. Back to Kellas. What can we do?"

His shoulders lifted in a helpless shrug. "We wait and hope," he said.

To my way of thinking, that tactic seemed about as useful as offering thoughts and prayers after a mass shooting. "Surely there is something we can *do*," I insisted. "A healing potion, a counter-spell, a counter-curse, even?"

"If you can suggest something, Raven, I'm willing to try it. But this is ancient magic: hard to control and even harder to counteract." Then a thoughtful expression crossed his face. "Kellas may have recovered from an attack by Dub once before. Isn't that right, Mother?"

I was preoccupied with my own thoughts and didn't wait for Nan's answer. "It's despair, you say. His lungs are being destroyed by...despair?"

"Followed by the rest of him, by bits and pieces," Dad acknowledged, his expression grim.

So...we had to counter magically induced despair. But, *how*? "Is he awake? Can we talk to him?" I was answered with a grimace and a slow headshake. "Can we at least go see him?" Another minute headshake.

Ugh. If only I could have prevented this in the first place! At the time, all I could think to do was run away from what I thought was just a creepy dude. How was I to know he was the manifestation of human despair? Not exactly something you could fight, even with a sword of Fraegarthach's abilities. Not that I had given my magical sword a single thought at the time. But what if

I had tried? *I hadn't even tried.* Suddenly it was hard to breathe and my heart rate went ballistic. It must have cued the sword because I felt it hum in its hiding place against my back.

Nan noticed my panic. "We need to take Raven home. Now."

Dad nodded agreement. "And I need to get back to work." He laid a hand on my shoulder. "We're doing everything we can for Kellas. Try to get some rest, then come back tomorrow..." He glanced at his watch. "It's tomorrow already. Come daylight, then. Hopefully, we'll have better news by then."

I protested but wasn't given any say in the matter. Nan drove us back to her place and made sure I got ready for bed. She tucked me in with the admonishment not to show up downstairs until I had gotten at least five hours of sleep, then left, closing my bedroom door quietly behind her.

I lay on my back, staring up at the domed ceiling. Moonlight played across the arched beams and twinkled off the long mirror by my dresser. It was a mild enough night that I'd left the French doors open to the small deck outside my room, and I could hear wavelets lapping at the lake shore. Crickets sang. It was all very peaceful, everywhere but in my head. My thoughts churned madly about, seeking solutions for magical maladies—and endlessly blaming myself for Kellas being shot.

I must have finally slept at some point, because I woke up with sunshine pouring in through the eastern windows. I threw on fresh clothing and pelted down the circular staircase to the kitchen. It was empty, but someone had brewed coffee, and breakfast things had been set out. I took advantage of the bathroom being unoccupied, gobbled up a bowlful of cold cereal and milk, filled a travel mug with coffee (heavily doctored with cream and sugar), and went looking for Nan and Elias. I found them sitting on the back deck, looking out over the lake.

"Can we go?" I demanded without so much as a hello or good morning.

Elias leaned back in his rocking chair and sent me a dimpled grin. "Good morning to you too!" he teased.

Nan merely sighed, then struggled to her feet, turning stiffly to face me. She gestured in the general direction of the parked car. "By all means, let's go," she said.

A twinge of guilt assailed me as I watched my grandmother hobble across the deck. Morning stiffness afflicted many older people, I knew, and Nan became crippled by it each month. Yes, she magically rejuvenated as the moon waned, but.... I swallowed hard and followed her.

Elias caught up to Nan before she'd gotten ten feet. "I'll take her down; you rest."

I watched as Nan looked up at his face. His concern for her was writ large on his youthful features. Anyone seeing them for the first time would take them for mother and son, not long-time lovers. *Age was just numbers. Meaningless when love was involved.* I looked away as he bent down and gently kissed her, one large palm cupping her face. She nodded her assent to his plan and handed him her car key. He slid his hand down her arm in a final caress, then glanced my way and jerked his head toward the parked Prius.

I trotted after him, stopping just long enough to give Nan a careful hug; *careful*, so as not to hurt her aching joints. Then I piled into the car and we headed to the hospital.

～

I loathe hospitals, not that I've been in them much. I get how indispensable they are, and how they are there when you need them, but they are far from my favorite place on earth. I feel ill at ease in the sterility of it all, I guess. Not that you would want a hospital to be anything other than sterile. Don't get me wrong! But it's a long way from warm and inviting. Maybe that's it.

We made our way to the ICU, where we were told to take a seat in the waiting area. The place was quiet. There was just the hum of machinery, low voices, the occasional thump of a nearby elevator door, and squeaky shoes on polished hard floors as the medical staff went about their business. I sat opposite the nurse's station, thumbing through a year-old nature magazine and constantly glancing up at the young blond nurse who sat there scowling at his computer screen, occasionally typing vigorously on a keyboard. I glanced at the clock on the wall. We'd been waiting for 15 minutes! I hopped up and headed for the nurse. Before I got halfway, he was already holding up a pointer finger.

"One moment, almost there." He typed furiously for a minute more, then sat back with a sigh and gave me a tired smile. "Done. OK, let's see what I can do for you today. Name?"

I told him.

"Who are you here to see?"

I told him that, too.

The nurse's fingers rattled over the keyboard and stopped. He studied the screen. "Sorry. No visitors allowed," he announced. "The patient's condition is too...." He broke off and stared at the computer screen again. "*O que diabos é isto?*" His pale eyebrows lifted in surprise. "OK, scratch that. He's in negative pressure room 2." The nurse pointed to a glass-enclosed cubicle in the far corner. "You can look through the window, but you *cannot* go in with him. He's been heavily sedated and is on a ventilator to help him breathe." The nurse squinted at the screen, his eyes darting as he read the patient information. "Excuse me, miss, I'm on a second shift after being here since midnight and I'm a bit slow. Kellas..." he scowled and squinted at the screen "...odd...no last name. He is one of my new patients. I'm just getting up to speed on his condition. Hmm..." His brow furrowed. "Not COVID. They don't know exactly what's wrong, actually.... Which is why they must have made space for him in that room. Huh!"

I *knew* what was wrong. Not that I was going to tell him that. I'd probably get escorted to the mental ward if I did.

Elias joined me at the nurse's station. "We'll just go over and take a look," he said to the young man, and drew me over to the glassed-in room where Kellas lay. Not that we could see much of Kellas, however. He was a motionless lump under white blankets, tubes snaking from his body to various machines. It could have been anyone in that room.

Elias gave my shoulders a sympathetic squeeze. "They're doing everything they can for him."

Yeah. I got that. But what if it wasn't enough?

My face must have revealed what I was thinking because he added, "Remember, Kellas is not exactly human. He's tough. He can beat this."

Suddenly, I knew that to be a hopeful lie. I wiggled free. "No, he can't." I leaned my forehead up against the glass. "Nothing modern medicine has can counteract the misery Dub injected into him. He's dying, Elias. Dying of despair."

"You don't know that."

"Don't I?" Abruptly, I turned away from the window—and the miserable little cell where Kellas lay dying. Shoving my hands into my jeans pockets, I stormed out of the ICU, fighting the urge to scream.

Elias found me a while later, sitting on a bench near the entrance of the ER. He didn't approach, maybe because I had crossed my arms over my chest and was scowling at the ground in a *don't come close* kind of way. He just stood there watching me while I ignored him, until finally he sighed gustily. "Raven, come on. This isn't helpful. I'll take you home, OK?"

I got to my feet and stalked past him, knowing my behavior wasn't really fair to him, but I was angry. So very, *very* angry. We didn't talk the whole way home. I went straight to my room and shut the door the minute we got there. I buried my face in my pillow and screamed until my throat was raw and I could scream no longer. Then I curled up into a tight ball and let the tears come.

I visited Kellas every single day, sometimes twice a day. Day after day, it was always the same story. They'd tried something new and were hopeful it would help. Then it was always *sorry Raven, we really thought we had it this time.*

Kellas did not improve.

I got to know all the ICU nurses on the floor. They were all wonderful, caring people, and all were universally on the edge of burnout. The stress of treating deathly ill people all the time was taking its toll. The entire hospital was understaffed and its nurses overworked. I felt guilty that we were adding to their workload with what appeared to be a no-win case.

Kellas never knew I was there. My attempts to reach him telepathically did not work. I tried to play my lute to heal him, but the music wouldn't come. It wasn't because there was something wrong with my lute. The strings still sounded when I touched them; however, something was missing. It was as though—with Kellas so close to dying from dark magic—the music in *me* had died. I had no idea how to bring it back.

But I kept going. Just in case he woke up. Always hopeful this would be the time he did.

My family took turns driving me to the hospital, six miles one way. To save them from having to come get me, I offered to run back on the rail trail just downslope of the hospital. My suggestion was always met with a "no way you're going to risk that, kiddo." It seemed my family was even more rattled by Dub's attack than I was, and I was plenty rattled. So, I got taxied.

Even with his nutty schedule, Archer was my most reliable ride—and he stayed while I lingered by Kellas's cubicle. The Swamp Monster always had a massive textbook to read, and insisted he could do that anywhere.

Today was no different. He'd accompanied me to the ICU and curled up in a nearby chair with his textbook while I leaned my forehead against the glass surrounding the isolation cubicle and stared at Kellas's motionless form. I glanced over my shoulder. "Are you sure it's okay?" I was worried about Archer's grades suffering because he was taking so much time away from his studies.

He looked up from his book, a small smile on his face. "Stop your fussing, Raven. I'm happy to help. Besides," he added, "This way I get to spend time with my favorite girl."

I wasn't sure how to take that, so I nodded and attempted a smile.

"C'mon Raven. That was a compliment!" he teased.

I knew it was. If I'd learned nothing else about Archer, it was that he was choosey about whom he spent time with. "Thanks," I said, turning back to stare through the glass at the lump wrapped in white blankets. That was all I could see of Kellas.

A rustle of clothing next to me and an arm around my shoulders cued me that Archer had abandoned his studies. "Let's go, Raven. This staring through glass at our best friend is not helping you or him. C'mon. Let's go get a coffee or something, OK?"

I didn't resist, and he guided me from the ICU and outside, holding his car door open for me while I got in. He piled into the driver's seat and turned the Subaru's key. The car responded with a series of sputters and gasps. "C'mon sweetheart, you can do it!" he muttered and then breathed in relief as it roared to life, the entire body rattling ominously. "Each time I wonder if it will be the last," he explained.

Archer put the car in gear and drove out of the parking lot. "Now, what sounds good to you?"

Nothing did, to be honest, but he was trying so hard to cheer me up. "Ice cream?"

He burst out laughing. "At 10 o'clock in the morning? OK, if that's what helps, let's do ice cream. What's your favorite flavor? Oh, never mind. I know just the place."

A little while later, we were sitting outside the local ice cream shop on a beautiful (but chilly) sunny morning, digging into our ice creams. Mine was bittersweet, natch, because if that couldn't lift my mood, nothing could.

Archer was poking at his ice cream. He saw my look and managed a small grin. "I like it a little melty," he explained. Then he completely floored me with his next line. "What happened between you and Kellas?" he demanded. "And don't give me some stupid excuse. I have eyes. I can see."

I really hate crying, ya know? But his question, though obviously well-meant, brought me to tears. I ducked my head in a useless attempt to hide the wetness in my eyes.

"Ah, crap," I heard him say, and a moment later he'd laid a warm hand over one of my own. "It's OK if you don't want to tell me, Raven. But things have been sideways between you two for at least a month. I'd like to help if I could."

I sniffed and dug the heel of my free hand at one eye. "I'm not sure you can."

"Try me."

I poked at my ice cream for a bit before taking a deep breath and sighing it out. "OK, so here's the trouble: I'm too young."

Archer reared back in his seat with a look of disbelief on his face. "Come on! Really?"

I nodded. "And Kellas is too old."

Understanding flashed across his handsome face. "Oh. OK. I get it. What else did that dumb cat say to you that has you in such a tailspin?"

So, I told him. The whole sorry tale, even the bit about how Kellas had said I should go chasing after Archer instead.

Archer burst out laughing. "He's dumber than he looks, then!" he exclaimed.

I sat silently, wishing the ground would open under me and swallow me whole. My ice cream quietly melted in its paper cup.

Archer finally got himself back under control. "Look, Raven. Kellas probably thought he was being noble and selfless. That's a load of horse hockey. The cat is head over heels crazy about you; a blind man could see it. He's putting too much emphasis on age and not enough on chemistry. And it's not like he's ancient or anything. He doesn't age. He was never young, either. He's just... Kellas." He leaned back in his chair and fixed me with a level gaze. "And you! Well, you are probably the most mature, nearly 17-year-old I've ever met. So, OK, maybe you don't rush into an exclusive relationship anytime soon—you are a bit young for that, I agree—but that doesn't mean you can't be extra close to him." He laughed, a bit self-consciously. "And as for me, he's off there too. Raven, I'm Two-Spirit. Not the best choice for any young lady, even you. I'm floored he would have even suggested it. I thought he knew."

So...Archer was gay? I pondered that in silence.

Archer was frowning slightly. "You don't have a problem with that, do you?"

I shook my head vehemently. "Remember, I'm Hidatsa. Native. Half of me anyways. Two-Spirit people are gifts to our community. I just wish I'd realized that about you sooner."

He grinned, but it was a little lopsided. "Maybe Kellas is old-fashioned enough to think you could change my mind."

I made a face. "Might as well ask a tiger to change its stripes. This is who you are. And it's no skin off anyone's nose that you are what you are, either."

We got quiet then and applied ourselves to our ice creams. Thoughts raced through my head, like a cat chasing its tail.

Archer put down his spoon. "Out with it," he said gently. "Something in there is still bothering you."

I sighed, scooped up my last spoonful of bittersweet and stuffed it into my mouth. "It's like this," I said after swallowing. "You know all about the attack, right? I could have stopped Dub, and I didn't."

That brought on a puzzled frown. "How could you have done that?"

How to say this without sounding arrogant? "I have this sword…"

He made a disbelieving snort through his nose. "A sword, really? How could that have helped you? Against an arrow?"

"It's not your typical kind of sword, actually."

He just looked at me like there was a whole lot I hadn't told him. Well, true that!

I huffed in frustration. "It's Fraegarthach."

"Fraegarthach. Hmm. Naturally!" From the skeptical tilt of his eyebrows, it was obvious he didn't have a clue what I was talking about. "Continue, please."

Obviously, I wasn't convincing the Swamp Monster. "Things happen to me when I pull it out." Man, this was hard!

"Like what things?" And…now he had a wide grin on his face. Apparently, he found this very amusing!

I blushed. "I get big, like ten feet tall, and that sword, well…it's magical, and…well, I can fight magical creatures…and stuff." Way to sound like a nut-case, Raven!

That disappeared the grin. Archer took a quick look around, then stood up. "I think we need to continue this conversation in a less public place."

I could see his point. We dumped our trash in a nearby receptacle and got into his car—which started, thank the gods—and he pointed it back toward Nan's place.

"You are going to have to rewind here a bit. I'm not sure what you're talking about," he said.

So, I told him about when I'd become a Lunatic, when the trolls attacked, and then about Cerridwen and Tír na nÓg and the insane events that had happened while I was in the Celtic Other World.

Archer listened carefully to the whole crazy tale, never commenting, just nodding from time to time to let me know he was still listening. Finally, I ran out of words.

"So, you think you could have bested Dub with your sword, then?" he asked as he steered the car onto Route 89 North, past Cass Park.

"It makes sense, doesn't it?" I was fishing for confirmation of my worthlessness. It was my fault that Kellas lay in that horrible cubicle, unable to breathe on his own.

Archer was shaking his head. "No, I don't think so," he said. "I think you might have made yourself the target had you pulled Fraegarthach. He'd have known what it was and would have shot *you* instead. And, as much as I care for Kellas, losing you would have been far more serious. You are to take over for Amaris. No one else can do it."

If that was supposed to help me feel better, it didn't work. "No one can fill Nan's shoes. No one. Especially not me."

Archer grunted, frustrated. "And no one else has her power, either. Raven, can't you see? It's why they all make you work so hard. They know how important it is that you're ready to step up when the time comes. And it is coming. Soon. Even I can see that. And if an ordinary mortal can tell, you can bet the immortals do too. And some of them will try to stop you from taking over where Amaris leaves off."

I sat silently for a bit. "I don't think you are ordinary at all," I told him.

A huge smile pulled his lips back from lovely white teeth. "Why, thank you, kid!" We were quiet while he navigated the Subaru into Nan's drive and pulled up near the front door. "So, are we good then? You're no longer blaming yourself for Kellas?" he asked, sending me a sidelong look.

I drew a deep breath. "I guess."

His bronzed arm reached across me. He grasped my hand where it rested on the door handle. "Wrong answer. Try again," he said, his face mere inches from mine.

I squirmed in embarrassment. Maybe Archer had a point. "OK! You're right. It wasn't my fault."

"Better. Now it's back to nose-to-grindstone for both of us. Don't you waste another moment blaming yourself for what happened. Instead, put your brain to work finding a solution. Yes?" Then he placed a *friend kiss* on my cheek. "Believe in yourself, Raven. Because all of us do—Kellas most of all."

That might have been the end of my self-loathing, if only Erin hadn't been the first person I encountered when I entered the house.

The redhead was rinsing a mug at the kitchen sink and glanced around as I came in. "Back from your death watch?" she sneered, turning away to put the mug in the dishwasher. "I take it Kellas isn't dead yet?"

I honestly did not know how to answer that and silently headed for the stairs.

"Too good to talk to me now, princess?"

I halted, one hand on the railing, before turning slowly and glaring at her. "What do you want from me, Erin?"

She stalked toward me, her lovely face contorted in an ugly sneer. "What would I want from a loser like you? It should have been you in the hospital.

Not Kellas. He's worth a million of you." And then she used a word that I cannot in good conscience repeat. Basically, she called me a female dog.

"Don't say that," I warned, my voice shaking.

"I will if I want to." And just to show she meant it, Erin repeated the slur. "So, how long is it gonna take before you bump off the rest of us Cait Si? Seeing as how you've made such a great start already."

Ice formed in my veins. "I didn't…"

She drew closer, towering over me. "That's right, you didn't. You ran away and let Kellas take Dub's arrow. You didn't use any of your *moon magic*," she snarled, sketching air quotes for emphasis, "to do a thing to protect him. Did you? You're a coward and a fake. You should just go home to your mommy and let the rest of us deal with the mess you've made." Her face was now almost as red as her hair. "Things were great until you showed up and made it all about you, you little imposter!" She practically spat those last three words in my face. Hate was pouring off her like poison. She glared down at me from beautiful green eyes, her pupils the vertical slits like a cat's. "You make me sick," she said, shoving me hard.

I stumbled back against the post at the bottom of the stairs. Fraegarthach chimed softly in response—not that it registered over the roaring in my ears.

"Why are you still here, princess?" she hissed. Venomous. Hateful.

I turned tail and ran. Her bitter laughter followed me as I ran blindly across the lawn and into the woods beyond, headed I had no idea where. Away, that's all I knew.

～

I didn't stop my headlong rush until I crossed the road that ran along the upper side of our property. I slid into the same deep ditch Kellas and I had crossed when we'd returned from Tír na nÓg. Scrambled on all fours out on the far side, then up a steep rocky pitch, grabbing trees and hauling myself upward. By the time I reached the Black Diamond Trail, I was gasping for air. My heart pounded against my ribs like a trapped animal. Glanced quickly in both directions. Empty. No one out walking their dogs or getting in a morning run. I flopped down on a nearby bench, hung my head between my knees, braced my arms against my thighs, and let my hands dangle. Struggled to get my heart rate and breathing under control.

And, just when I thought things couldn't get any worse, they did.

I disappeared.

A few panicked moments later, I realized it had been two weeks since Kellas had fallen victim to Dub's arrow. I had entered dark phase. Invisible. Just pure energy.

Oh, crap.

Hiding in my room was not an option. No way I was going back to the house while Erin was there. However, it might be good to be near help if I needed it, and Dad was at the hospital today. Plus, I could go see Kellas again. Maybe even sneak into his room! I started off at a strong jog, thinking about how I sometimes bought Kellas flowers at the gift shop...not that I *could* buy flowers in this form....

And suddenly, that's where I was. In the hospital, by the gift shop. *How*, I had no idea, but I had done six miles in less than a second. This was seriously strange, but worth testing further. I focused on the cubicle where Kellas was fighting for his life, imagining myself inside, by his bed—and there I was. *Finally!*

I reached out and touched his shoulder.

He convulsed violently once, then again. Kellas tore the oxygen mask from his face and threw it halfway across the cubicle. He cried out in pain, thrashing wildly.

Alarms went off all around me. "Rapid response team to ICU NP 2, stat..."

I hardly heard them. Kellas's eyes had shot open and those baby blues looked straight at me, as if he could see me. The agony in them was more than I could bear. He made an unintelligible sound, then began convulsing again.

I was no longer alone in the cubicle. The rapid response team had arrived; there was nearly no room to maneuver. I brushed inadvertently against the blond nurse I'd met the first day. He jumped as if stung and swore mightily.

Dad...it had to be Dad...though it was a challenge to identify anyone in their full body protective suits...sent him a quelling look over his face mask. "Ian!"

"Sorry. Something zapped me," Ian apologized.

"Just focus," Dad ordered. And then they were fighting Kellas's convulsions, strapping him down, doing what they could to help him.

I started to leave. As I was slipping out, I heard Dad exclaim, "C'mon Kellas, you gotta fight this! You've done it before; you're the only one who knows how."

His words hit me like a runaway truck: *Kellas knew.*

And *that* is how *I* knew what I had to do. And there was no time to waste.

Sixteen

I had to find Kellas. An earlier version of Kellas, one who had fought Dub's poison—and *won*. Somewhere. Somehow. Some. Time. To do that, I had to harness my moon magic with the belief that *I could do exactly that.* Then hope Kellas could be convinced to tell *me* how. Knowing him, that might prove tricky.

I strode out of the ICU. "Where are you, Kellas?" I visualized his handsome face, smart-aleck grin and all. "Where?" Putting my head down, I broke into a run. I imagined the raised-eyebrow look he always gave me when I was being especially absurd. He'd be giving me that look now if he knew what I was planning. *Oh gods!* How badly I wanted to see that expression again. He'd always been there for me, fighting my demons, helping me, teasing me, pushing me to do better. I had to do this...for him. *I needed him!*

Desperation crashed over me like a tidal wave, and things went dark. I don't know what happened. But I was there, wherever and whenever *that* was, somewhere in the dark, in the middle of the woods.

Kellas jumped to his feet. He'd been slumped on a fallen log. "What the..." And the third word he said was *not* the sort I would repeat in polite company. One hand hovered over the dagger he always carried on his belt. He looked ready to use it.

"Kellas. It's me." I reached toward him.

He jumped back, ripping his dagger clear of its sheath. He crouched, ready to spring.

But I hardly noticed. I stared at my arm, transfixed. It was a silvery, glowing, ghostlike appendage. In fact, *all of me* resembled a light-up statue—surrounded by electric blue flames. Yikes! That's why I'd hurt Kellas in the ICU. That's what the nurse had felt.

"Who's *me*? And how do you know my name?"

I can be such an idiot! Of course, he had no idea who I was. Then I realized why he'd always called me by a name that wasn't mine. A name I had first resisted, and then grown fond of. "You call me Brannaugh," I said. "And never mind how I know you. I need your help."

His eyes narrowed. "Lady, I don't think I can be of any help to your kind."

My kind? What the devil did he think I was? But I had no time to play games. "I have a...friend...who's been poisoned by Dub's arrow. You are the only one who has ever survived it. Please, how did you manage that?"

He remained tense, but he rose out of his crouch and started to pace around me like a cat sizing up the competition. "That's really why you're here?" he growled.

"Yes, really." I don't have time for this! "He's dying, Kellas. I need to know how to save him." I kept turning so he wouldn't get behind me.

"This *friend*. I'm guessing he's a man since you keep calling him *he*." His voice was almost a purr now. "He's important to you?"

I nodded slowly.

A calculating look crossed his face. "How important?"

Oh, this could get complicated! "He means a lot to me."

A sneer lifted his upper lip, and his next words were so quiet I had to strain to hear them. "How much are you willing to give to save his life, *Brannaugh*?"

Was he taunting me? "You want *money*?" I exclaimed, horrified.

A quiet laugh greeted my distress. "Did I say money? Pah!" He spat to one side. "Money is meaningless. Are you willing to give *your life* for him?"

I stood motionless, staring blindly at the ground. Had someone sacrificed herself for him? Is that what it took?

"Brannaugh." He was suddenly beside me, his mouth close to my ear. "Answer me."

"Yes, I would. In a heartbeat!" I declared. Then warned as he reached for me: "You don't want to touch me!"

He did anyways. Because that is how he rolls.

My energy knocked him sprawling; the night air was crackling with electricity. He lay dazed on the ground, looking like a man who'd crossed two live wires. Stunned and disoriented, that is. It took him a while to get to his feet.

"What the hell was that?" Kellas demanded, once he could talk again.

"It's a bit like lightning," I said. "Pow." I tried not to grin, but failed utterly. "Not for a Cait Sidhe like you to play games with."

"Shhhh..." He managed not to swear. Instead, Kellas rubbed the back of his neck and put away his dagger. "Well, this is a useless weapon. Who are you anyway?"

"I told you. Call me Brannaugh. Now, would you please tell me your secret? Otherwise, Kellas will die..."

Ah, geez. Just like that, I blew it. I hadn't wanted him to know it was *his* life in danger.

But he wasn't going to pretend he hadn't heard me. "Kellas, is it?" he said quietly. "Would that be *me*? Because if that's the case, it's not a coincidence you're here. You're telling me that your *friend,* who you would willingly die for, is...*me*? And if you're willing to die for him...for me...that says a lot more about *you and me* than us merely being *friends,* lady."

"A future you." I pressed my lips together in a grimace, regretting my mistake. "You just haven't met me yet."

Kellas hitched up his pants (tan-colored, tied at the waist with a leather cord) and cautiously stepped closer. He gave me the side-eye. "It's a good thing you did, because you know what? I like my life and would rather keep on living it. And I'm rather intrigued that a creature like you thinks I'm worth dying for. Whatever the hell it is you are—besides being a fearless female who appears out of nowhere, glowing like the moon. So, I'll tell you, and you'd better listen well. I'm only going to say this once, *Brannaugh*." And he shrugged his shirt off over his head. Standing before me half-naked, his muscular torso was bare and white in the light thrown by my energy. White, except for the Druidic tattoos that snaked down from his shoulders along his collar bones in swirls and curls, and ended in two snarling cats facing off across his breastbone.

"You must pull the ink out of his...my...body, then put it into my skin. Like this." He pointed at his tattoos. "Use Druidic power symbols. They will neutralize the poison. You can't get rid of the poison, only neutralize it. Like I did." He frowned. "Can *you* do it? I'm assuming you have the training. After all, you have..." he gestured at me.

"An electrifying personality?" I supplied, unable to suppress a smirk.

He smiled ruefully, then sobered. "One more thing, Brannaugh. What you're going to do, it'll hurt. A lot. But you've got to do it anyways."

I stepped closer and saw how it took every bit of willpower for him not to flinch. I stared up into his eyes, locking their blueness into memory. "Thank you," I whispered. Then even more quietly I said: "Wait for me. *Please don't die*." That was for his future self, just in case he remembered. Then I was gone.

~

I appeared inside Kellas's cubicle, visible again—my almost 17-year-old glamour firmly in place. My father and Ian, the blond nurse, were there with

Kellas. Both men were startled: Ian stumbled and nearly fell, and Dad staggered. At least I hadn't materialized in toddler form.

"Raven!" Dad exclaimed. "How the hell did you get in here without us knowing?"

"It's complicated. No time." I leaned over Kellas's strapped-down body. "I know how to cure Kellas now. But it's gonna hurt him, he says. How are his pain meds? Can you give him more if necessary?"

The two men exchanged alarmed looks. "How did you find that out?" Dad asked.

"I time-traveled, found him, and asked." But asking was one thing. *Doing* was another. I broke out in a nervous sweat.

Ian was shaking his head like he thought this was impossible.

Dad looked even more alarmed than before. "And?"

"I have to pull the ink out of his lungs and put it into his skin. Like a tattoo. He says that neutralizes the poison." I could see he was unconvinced. It worried me.

Ian rolled his eyes. "Is she a medic?" he demanded. "What can she possibly do that we haven't already tried?"

Dad bit his lip, then stepped over to the glass walls and hit a button. Tiny internal blinds descended in all the windows, shielding us from the outside world. "*Feistigh,*" he muttered, and the door locked tight. "Ian," he said, catching the nurse by one shoulder. "You are not to say a word about this to anyone. Anything you see or hear today. Not. One. Word."

"Yeah, Ian," I said as I pulled Kellas's blanket down to the restraining strap. "If you do, you might end up a patient in the psych ward. We don't want that. The hospital is shorthanded enough as it is."

I drew a deep breath, steeling myself. My hands hovering over Kellas's chest, I could feel the bitterness of Dub's despair pushing against the power beaming out of my palms. I grasped the darkness to keep it from sinking back into Kellas, pinched the end of one thread as it tried to escape—then put the gentlest pressure on it, like a robin pulling a worm from the ground. I felt it fight me...then slip just the tiniest bit. I pulled it slowly, *slowly* out of him, then guided it along Kellas's skin with one finger, visualizing tiny needles injecting the ink.

Kellas groaned.

Dad stepped up to the tubes snaking out of Kellas's arm to a drip bag hanging nearby and pressed a button—injecting something. Then, he released the strap over the Cait Sidhe's chest and arms and pulled the blanket down to Kellas's waist, giving me more area to work on.

I was grateful for the hours I'd spent memorizing Druidic symbols and Celtic knots—patterns and designs that held sacred meaning. I inked protective shields on the skin over Kellas's deltoids and wreathed his arms in Celtic chains, power icons entwined. I inked a tree of life across one pectoral muscle, and adorned the other side of his chest with a dragon, just underneath the snarling cats. And in the center of his chest, right over his heart, I put a replica of my triskelion medallion, complete with the triple connected swirls and the three ravens, surrounded by a circular knot.

I was humming the entire time. Something about the music was helping the process. Odd, yeah...but it worked.

It took *hours.* Periodically, Kellas would groan and twitch, and Dad would increase his pain meds. Ian stood nearby, sometimes offering me water through a straw or wiping away sweat as it trickled down my face. He moved Kellas's arms so I could ring the Celtic chains front and back. It was exhausting work. I was tiring rapidly, and my hands were beginning to tremble slightly.

"Hang in there, Raven. Almost done," Dad whispered.

I wiped a drop of perspiration off the end of my nose. "You sure?"

"He's already breathing more easily," Dad assured me.

I risked a glance at Ian. "This has got to look truly weird."

"You don't say," Ian muttered from his position at my elbow. "*Eu vou ter pesodelos!*"

"You think *you're* gonna have nightmares!" I huffed a shaky laugh. "How do you think *I* feel?" I buckled down again. The strands of darkness had gotten wary and were becoming harder to grab. I needed to concentrate.

"Your daughter knows Portuguese?" Ian spluttered to my father. "Why didn't you tell me she knows Portuguese? *Ai que merda!*"

"Language," I warned him. He just laughed.

At last, I could not find any more inky darkness in Kellas's lungs. I scanned one last time, seeking any lingering bits, and found none. I straightened my aching back. "I think that's all of it."

"I think you're right," Dad agreed, checking his instruments. "But there's only one way to find out. We'll bring him out from under and see if he can breathe on his own."

I must have staggered then, because Ian immediately gripped me by both arms and guided me to a chair. "Sit. Stay," he ordered and turned back to help Dad.

Ian may have ordered me about like his pet dog, but I was well beyond caring. I slumped in the chair, leaned my head on the high back, and closed my eyes. I must have dozed off. The next thing I knew, Dad was shaking me gently.

"He's conscious and asking for you." I grunted in acknowledgment and fumbled to my feet with Dad's help.

It was only a step for me to reach Kellas's bedside. I leaned over him. My hair fell in a wave across his face and he sneezed. I shoved my hair behind my ears. "Hey, stranger."

"I...waited," he whispered. "I didn't...die."

I gulped hard and tried to swallow my sobs, but I couldn't stop a tear from spilling down my face.

He managed a faint smile and fumbled for my hand. "Hey."

"Hey," I echoed. Taking his hand in both of mine, I gingerly sat on the edge of his bed. His chest and arms were a raw, red mess. "Oh, geez, I am so sorry!"

He rewarded me with a crooked smile. "Needed doing." Then he grimaced as a fresh wave of pain washed over him. "How I hate...needles, though."

I sent him a wide, gritted-teeth look that expressed empathy. But bit back the multiple iterations of *I'm sorry* that threatened to spill out.

"Miss Callahan, we need to get Kellas cleaned up and moved to a different bed. This one is needed by a more seriously ill patient, and minutes count." It was Ian, still a bit in shock from the weird stuff he'd just experienced, but doing his best to be a complete professional.

Nodding, I got to my feet. "I'll see you once you're resettled." I basked in Kellas's answering smile, weak as it was.

Dad escorted me to the waiting room where we met up with Nan and Elias; he must have had a staff member call them.

Though Nan was white as a sheet, it was Elias's face that really caught my attention. "What happened to you?" I demanded. His face had been clawed from temple to jaw, and there was still fresh blood oozing from the scratches in places.

"Erin happened," was his brusque response. "How's Kellas doing?" He gestured at the bustling activity around the cubicle.

"I found out how to rid him of Dub's ink. That's what we've been doing for..." I peered at the clock. "It's 7:45? *P.M.?*" I glanced out the window. Dark out. Wow.

"Raven! Focus!" Nan spoke sharply. "You healed him? How?"

"Can we sit?" I begged. "I'm really tired."

Elias and Nan practically frog-marched me back to a chair, then settled on either side of me. They leaned in.

"From the beginning, and don't leave out any details," Nan instructed. She drew a symbol in the air. It shimmered a moment and then disappeared. "A silencing charm," she explained. "Now we can't be overheard. Talk."

I told them the whole thing, how I'd drawn out the poison and tortured Kellas by inking him with Celtic tattoos. "That's pretty much it," I finished up. "Dad thinks he'll be OK now. But he sure has an awful lot of tattoos."

Ian came over. "Your friend has been moved to a private room down the hall, if you'd like to go see him."

Nan and Elias rose to their feet immediately. I stayed put.

"Aren't you coming?" Nan asked, surprised.

"You go on, I'll be there in a minute," I told them.

When they came to find me a half hour later...I was sound asleep on a waiting room bench.

Seventeen

ellas checked himself out the next day, overriding the protests of hospital personnel. They finally relented when Dad assured them that Kellas would be looked after properly. Maybe they agreed more quickly because of the oddness surrounding his illness. Or maybe they just had more than enough to do, dealing with an influx of COVID patients. Archer picked Kellas up and drove him to our house. Nan set Kellas up in a spare bedroom and threatened him with mayhem if he did not remain in bed.

I gathered my schoolbooks and established my study area by a window in a corner of Kellas's room. Not that we talked much. He spent a great deal of time sleeping. Dad said it was necessary for his lungs to recover. Just removing the ink wasn't enough; his body had to heal from the damage caused by Dub's despair. We kept the bedroom extra warm because even having a sheet touch Kellas's wounds caused him discomfort. The new tattoos were an oozing, nasty mess—slow to heal, even though Kellas was on some strong antibiotics.

I played my lute to help him heal. I'd finally regained that skill. It made sense: magic requires believing in yourself and your abilities. I had lost faith in myself after Dub's attack. It had taken my desperate attempt (and deeply fortunate success) at time travel to get that back.

I admit to spending an inordinate amount of time admiring Kellas while he was sleeping. I didn't want him to know just how beautiful I thought he was. His beard had grown while he'd been in the hospital. He'd always been just a little scruffy before. The new beard looked nice, though. It softened the hard edges of his face. I wondered what it would be like to kiss a man with a beard.

He finally caught me watching him. One moment his eyes were closed and his breathing slow and even, and the next, his blue-eyed gaze was on me. There was a sneaky smile on his face. "Like what you see?" he asked. His voice was still gravelly and lower than usual, the result of his illness.

I must have turned six shades of red. "Yes, actually! I do good work."

That brought out a chuckle. "It wasn't the canvas you were admiring, then? Just your artwork? Are you sure?"

I bit my lower lip and pretended to be reading my chemistry book. "I'm studying."

"Yes, I know," he teased. "And it isn't chemistry, either." Then he gave me that one-eyebrow-raised look I'd so missed. "Or maybe it is, but it's not the sort you can find in that book you're pretending to read."

I snapped the book shut and set it aside. "OK, you win. I was watching you. Happy?"

A growling purr left his throat. "Ecstatic."

I rolled my eyes at him.

Kellas laughed. "Come here, Brannaugh." He patted the bed and I sat down next to him—carefully. He wrapped an arm around my waist and pulled me closer. "Look at me," he ordered.

I had been studiously avoiding doing just that. It took some willpower, but I finally met his eyes.

"First things first," he said softly. "Thank you for my life. I admit, when you showed up in 1756, I didn't think it was possible. But you did it."

That explained the rough homespun clothing he'd been wearing.

"Next, I know you ratted me out to Archer; he told me what a total idiot I am." He gave me a rueful smile. "Still, you can forget about going after the Swamp Monster. It looks like you've put your mark on me in permanent ink." He pointed to the center of his chest. "A particularly painful place to ink a tattoo. Or maybe you knew that? Maybe you wanted to make sure I wouldn't forget about you, huh?" I blushed and hung my head.

He jiggled me with his arm until I looked up again. "What?" I demanded.

"I won't lie to you, Brannaugh. I'm a male Cait Sidhe, with very active hormones. And I've catted around a fair piece—very nonexclusive, you might say." He fixed me with an intense gaze and lightly caressed my arm with his free hand...the one not already clamped possessively around my waist. "That night you found me? I'd had a fight with Erin. I was covered in scratches.... It's how she fights. She wanted me all to herself. No sharing. I wasn't having it."

I drew a shaky breath. "I can understand that. I wouldn't want to share you, either." *Oh gods, had I really just said that?*

He laughed, a soft huff. "I doubt you'd tear into me with your claws, though. But since that night when you came out of nowhere, shining like the moon...and told me you would willingly die for me...." Kellas gazed at me with the most serious expression I'd ever seen on him. "There hasn't been *anyone* else, Brannaugh. No one. I've waited all this time for you, just like you asked me to. It's been worth every lonely minute of it." He sighed, then chuckled. "Not that there weren't times I questioned my sanity. Especially when the First World War started, and the Morrigan herself offered to protect me from death if only I.... Well, you know."

I didn't know, but I was a decent guesser. He'd turned down the Morrigan's advances because of me? And was he blushing a little bit?

He hurried on. "But I knew I'd survive even that war because you'd showed up years earlier and told me I was still living in the future. Or more precisely, *dying*—from Dub's arrow, instead of a German bomb. I never actually knew *when* you had come from."

"But..." I hesitated. "When I first came to Nan's house, you were *mean* to me!"

He snorted. "When you showed up—my dream girl, who I'd been waiting something like 264 years for—you were a little kid! What a kick in the...umm, never mind."

Now, he was definitely blushing. It was kinda cute.

Kellas continued. "Any chance of telling you exactly how I felt was going to have to wait years more. Until you were mature enough to handle it. Cait Si are not usually patient creatures, Brannaugh. I'd already been waiting hundreds of years. So, yeah, I was a bit of a jerk about it."

"You can say that again."

Kellas's seductive growl sent heat rushing to my face. "I'd rather make it up to you."

"How?"

He reached up, caught me by both shoulders, pulled me close, and kissed me.

And, oh, baby, what a kiss. Never mind that it was also my *very first*. It about blew my mind....it.... Oh geez, forget it! I'll just say it was...magical. That's the only word close to describing how that cat could kiss.

He broke away sooner than I liked, but only to breathe a single word against my lips. "Peppermint."

"Lip balm," I whispered back.

He laughed softly. "I like it. Spicy. Like you," and he pressed his mouth against mine again.

I returned every touch of his lips with as much fervor as I could summon, which was *plenty*. I had wanted him to kiss me for months.... Months! OK, that's not 264 years. But for me, it sure felt like it. And now...I knew what it was like to kiss a guy with a beard.

It ended abruptly when he pushed me away with a shout of pain. "Ow! What did you do that for?"

I was clueless. "I was kissing you! What do you think I was doing?"

"Your butt zapped me!" He was shaking one hand.

"Serves you right for feeling my butt up!" I accused him. Although, in truth I hadn't noticed—I was all about that kiss.

"I got a little carried away," Kellas admitted sheepishly.

"Oh!" I exclaimed, realizing what had happened. "Fraegarthach."

"The Protector was protecting," he agreed. "Guess I know where that sword draws the line." A disgruntled frown darkened his face. Frustration. "I've waited so long for you, girl."

"I know." I reached down to touch the medallion I'd inked into his skin.

He flinched. "Careful," he cautioned. "Your *electrifying personality* could stop my heart."

"Trust me. I won't." I slowly drew my fingertip around the outside of the medallion, then delicately touched its center.

A tiny shiver crossed his skin. "Now who's being mean?" he muttered.

I drew back, then smiled. "Turnabout is fair play," I teased, then gathered my study materials, preparing to leave.

He lifted up on his elbows. "Where do you think you're going?"

I headed for the door. "Out. Because you need your rest. You won't get it while I'm here."

He chuckled. "Is that a threat or a promise?"

I stopped by the door but didn't turn to face him. "What do you think?"

"Brannaugh," he said, the warmth in his voice an unmistakable caress. "I will wait as long as it takes."

I turned, put my books down on the end of his bed and bent over him, my hair swishing down and tickling his face. "That, you incredibly annoying, self-absorbed, frustrating Cat Man, is probably the sweetest thing you've ever said to me!" I kissed him again. And...umm...probably a few more times after that. But who knows, because I kinda lost count. It's nobody's business but ours, anyways.

~

October grew colder and damper. Orianthi and I brought our evening practice sessions inside, setting up near the living room fireplace. We were often joined by Nan and Elias, and occasionally, by Erin. No one spoke of the fight we'd had. She always stayed as far away from me as possible. Archer dropped in when he could get away. Tonight, he was curled up near Kellas, who was bundled up in a blanket by the fire.

Kellas was recovering slowly. He was finally able to sit up for a few hours at a time. It was a bit unsettling to know he was there listening so intently while Orianthi and I practiced. I made a show of ignoring him, but it pleased me to know how much he liked my singing.

Orianthi and I were struggling to perfect the lyrics of our latest song. They just weren't coming together like we wanted. We were arguing (well, arguing in the sense of disagreeing) when Dad walked in. He had the weird-sprawling-energy man in tow. I could *feel* the guy before he came through the door. *Ugh*!

"Apologies for the interruption," Dad said. "This is Emmitt, and he has something to tell us."

Emmitt was as unprepossessing a character as I think I'd ever met. He was only about my height (when I'm my proper age) and dressed in clothes so old they had faded to a uniform gray color. They hung raggedly around his emaciated figure. And—not to be rude or anything—he stank. Body odor of the nastiest sort, and something else. Rubbish, perhaps? A sweetish, rotten stink. He might have been in his 40s, but was bent over like a much older man. Probably the result of his living conditions, which, if he were homeless, pretty much said it all. Hard to bathe when you don't have a house, hard to keep good posture when you're wandering about the street wondering when your next meal will be...or if you'll even get one. Did I mention his sprawling weird energy? It was just like that night months ago on the rail trail.

Emmitt's eyes darted about the room as if he were on high alert. First, his gaze fell on all three of the Cait Si in turn. "Kitties," he said softly. Next, he turned to Orianthi. "Trees...you're a forest fairy." Then he looked at me. He started to smile, then laughed. "Ho, ho! They don't know what you have! Ha ha! Song Bird can take them on. No more nasties eating us! No more ghosties making us cold and stealing our laughter. No more...." His voice faltered.

"No more what, Emmitt?" Dad prompted gently. "What have you seen?"

Emmitt started trembling. "No! Cannot say! Words make him worse. We must pretend he is not real, or he will become real."

"Pretending doesn't make something go away, Emmitt," Dad said. "Pretending won't help us stop him. Please tell us what you saw!"

Emmitt looked on the edge of tears, but he nodded shakily. I felt a rush of empathy for the poor guy and his predicament, not that I knew how to help. He struggled to get a grip on himself. "For you, Kind One, I will tell. But you must promise me he won't eat me! Promise!"

"We will do everything in our power, Emmitt. I promise you," Nan spoke softly.

He looked at her. She had her 40-something glamour on, but he must have seen right through it. "Ancient One speaks truth, but can she back up her promise with strength when it is needed?"

Nan looked devastated. "I do what I can, Emmitt."

"Amaris is as wise as the mountains," Archer broke in. "We do well to listen and heed our elders' council, as they have our best interests at heart."

Emmitt turned his sad gaze on the Cayuga. "Swamp Bear. I see your heart, and it is torn between two worlds."

"Who is this nutcase anyways?" Erin stood up, bristling violently. "He has no business being here."

Nan hushed her. "He has information we need, Erin. Please sit and let him speak." Erin closed her mouth and sat back down on the chair. But her arms were crossed tightly across her chest, her face a mask of suppressed annoyance.

Emmitt cringed at Erin's outburst, and he looked even sadder than he had before. "You're right, Pretty Kitty, I do not belong here. I do not belong anywhere." Tears trickled down his face. He glanced at my dad. "I'm sorry, Kind One, I must leave. I am not wanted; I cannot help you." He started shuffling toward the door.

Everyone started talking at once, which only sent Emmitt scurrying away faster. Any hope we might have of learning more was nearly gone. Under my hands, Fraegarthach vibrated powerfully, startling me. Its suggestion was unmistakable. I leaned over my lute and began to play.

It was a song Orianthi and I had just recently worked on, one about welcoming refugees. Orianthi recognized the opening notes and started singing as if we'd planned this. It had the effect of hushing everyone instantly, but I was still afraid it wouldn't stop Emmitt. He'd already left the living room. Dad had followed. Maybe he'd be able to convince the homeless man to return and tell us his news. All I could do was play and hope.

We finished the final chord. I stayed bent over the lute for a moment longer, feeling the vibrations slowly fade in its wooden heart. When I finally straightened up, Emmitt stood directly in front of me, less than an arm's length away. He was staring intently at me.

"Hello!" I squeaked. "A little social distance here, please?"

He nodded gravely and slowly backed away to exactly six feet. Emmitt was seriously literal for someone who could see what he saw and live how he lived.

"You called me, and I came back," he said quietly. "I will tell you what I saw. It was like a man but not a man...an ancient evil made of darkness and hate. It was calling the ghosts from their haunts and gathering ghouls from the depths of the earth. The Ancient One and the tree that guards peace are in danger. Because it sets people against one another, it does. Hate and misery make it stronger. It hates love because it has no heart to hold love in." His voice faltered. "It's a sad thing to have no heart, Song Bird."

I sat there frozen in fear by what he'd just told us. The fire at my back failed to warm me. Nan got up from her chair, came over, and touched Emmitt's elbow.

He flinched. "No touch! No touch!" he whimpered. "Touch is bad."

Nan apologized immediately. "If you would like to stay, I have a small apartment over our barn that you are welcome to use. Nothing fancy..."

He nodded, the hangdog look settling back over him like a well-worn jacket. "Just tonight, Ancient One. I want to get back to my things. Others will take them if I do not guard them well."

Dad offered to show Emmitt to the apartment, and the two of them left.

Erin rose to her feet with a grumpy huff. "A lot that helped us!" she declared. "An ancient evil? Ghosts and ghouls? Ancient evil wanting to kill you, Amaris? What *hasn't* wanted to kill you since Cerridwen 'blessed' you with her moon magic? Story of our lives, really."

I was sorely tempted to say something nasty to her. Seriously? Didn't she see how much it cost Emmitt to tell us...and how scared he was?

"Now, we have a better idea of what we are facing," Nan responded calmly. "This explains why your patrols have found nothing. Ghosts and ghouls are hard to track. And Emmitt's information," she emphasized, "informs us as to *when* we might be attacked."

"How so?" I asked, uncertain how she'd figured that out.

"This ancient evil is very likely Dother," Nan explained. "No heart? Sounds like him. Ghosts and ghouls operate after dark only. So, we can anticipate a nighttime attack. We have a second full moon this month, a blue moon, and it lands on Samhain, October 31st. That only happens every 19 to 20 years. Very rare." She started pacing back and forth, a frown furrowing her forehead. "It's also when the veil between worlds is thinnest, so spirits can cross over easily. A particularly dangerous time, in fact." She stopped pacing and looked earnestly at me. "I am grateful that with COVID, most Halloween gatherings are being suspended. Otherwise, there would be even more opportunity for widespread disaster."

October 31st was also my 17th birthday. I wondered if she'd forgotten that tiny detail. If Nan was right and we were attacked, I could kiss yet another birthday celebration goodbye. "What *do* we do?" I asked tremulously.

"We wait. Watch. And prepare as best we can," Nan said.

Our group broke up shortly thereafter. Archer hurried out, probably needing to study something or other. He was always taking extra classes. Or maybe he just needed to get away from the craziness that always seemed to surround us. Not that I could blame him for that! Erin left too (no great loss, that!). Then, Nan and Elias said their goodnights and disappeared into their bedroom suite. Dad headed for bed as well. He'd been on duty for close to 30 hours, what with the shortage of medical personnel. The COVID pandemic was burning many of them out and they were quitting left and right. Orianthi also disappeared somewhere.

I helped Kellas back to his bed. He was tired enough that he didn't argue with me about it. Then I went into Nan's office to call Mom. The time difference from east to west was enough that it was still fine to video call her and Iku, so I did.

"You all are expecting an attack on your birthday, again," Mom stated flatly. Her expression was a weird combination of frustration and worry mashed together. "I hope this doesn't become standard practice."

"Me too," I fervently agreed. "Iku, do you have any ideas how to help with, you know, the ghosts and such?" I felt borderline ridiculous talking about ghosts and ghouls like they were a real thing, and not just a fairy tale meant to scare kids into behaving.

She looked thoughtful. "You know, there is something that could do the trick. I will get to work gathering the materials and ship them out to you."

Mom looked completely flabbergasted. The sheer amount of what she preferred to call 'woo-woo' was shaking up her worldview big time.

"It's OK, Mom," I tried to assure her. "You'll get used to all this not-normal stuff—eventually." I thought about how I'd been overwhelmed at first by little things like flying horses, shape-shifting cats, and hellhounds with glowing red eyes. It was a darn good thing I hadn't immediately known the sheer extent of crazy that my moon magic would expose me to.

A new worry rose. Mom didn't have even an ounce of magic to help her deal with all of this. I suddenly felt terribly worried for her. I wanted to make sure she would be safe—and it must have shown on my face.

She scowled, sending me a far-too-familiar aggrieved look. "I just can't believe you would prefer to stay with your father! But I guess you're old enough now to make these decisions for yourself."

What that admission must have cost her! As difficult and ornery as she could be, I loved her. "It's just for now, Mom. I'll try to make it home this summer." She harrumphed, but didn't push things. We signed off shortly after that.

I climbed the stairs to my room, deep in thought. I found Orianthi sitting on my bed, tears streaming down her face. I ran to her and pulled her close in a hug. She clung to me like she'd never let go. I leaned my cheek against the top of her head. "Talk to me?" I asked softly.

She snuffled against my shirt. "Emmitt said they want to kill me and my tree. I don't want to die! I'm just getting started; there's so much I want to do!"

A fierce protectiveness toward Orianthi overwhelmed me. I would have fought a never-ending legion of ghosts barehanded to save her. "They won't even get close to you, little sister! I promise." Then something struck me. "And you can help too." I set her away far enough that I could look her straight in the eye. "I've done it before, in my dreams. We can stop the ghouls with our singing, you and me and Fraegarthach. We just need to figure out which songs will be the most effective. But not now. Now, we need to sleep."

She snuffled again and nodded, scrubbing her eyes to dry them. I handed her the box of tissues from next to my bed so she could blow her nose properly. "C'mon kid, you can sleep with me tonight. My turn to look out for you." I went over to my dresser and pulled out a T-shirt. "This one OK?"

It wasn't the first time she'd slept over, and she always wanted one of my T-shirts as PJs. "The horse one," she insisted. "The one that says, 'I ride like a girl.'"

I pretended to pout. "That's my favorite!"

She looked downcast. "OK. Whatever…"

I laughed at her. "Don't be silly. Of course, you can have that one!" I dug it out and handed it to her. "Last one into bed is a rotten egg!"

There was lots of dashing and giggling, pushing and shoving as we went through our bedtime ritual of teeth brushing and so on. But ultimately, I made sure to let her win. After all, she was my little sister.

Eighteen

The following day, Elias dropped me off at the hospital with a big box of gifts for the ICU staff that we'd pulled together. It was a lot of homemade stuff: several kinds of cookies and maple candies. Also, there were a couple gallons of apple cider that Elias had squeezed—the best I'd ever tasted. And organic apples and pears from Nan's trees. It made for a very full, heavy box. I was struggling to carry it as I made my way past Admissions and back toward the elevators.

A door marked "utilities" opened as I staggered by, and a very large man in olive-colored overalls stepped out, pulling a cap down low over his forehead. He stopped just short of running into me. "Oh, hello, young lady!" he exclaimed. "Wow, that box looks heavy. Want some help with that?"

His words were friendly, but something about the guy made me wary. I sent him...Fred, if his name tag was correct...a quick smile and shook my head. "Nope. I'm good, thanks," I told him, and hurried on. At first, I thought he was following me. I veered toward the elevators and heaved a sigh of relief when he continued down the corridor.

I was sooo glad when I reached the ICU and could finally set the box down on one of the waiting room chairs. Ian was on duty and immediately came over. "Hey there!" he said. "Long time no see. How's your boyfriend doing these days?"

I grinned at hearing Kellas referred to as my *boyfriend*. Especially because that was *finally* the case! "Better." I said, and gestured at the box. "We put some things together for you guys. There's a card in there too." I pulled it into view, then put it back. "It's not much, but we wanted to let you know how much we appreciate all you did for Kellas."

He scanned the contents of the box appreciatively. "Looks pretty yummy to me!"

Then the lights went out.

They didn't stay out for long. Emergency generators kicked in. Ian blew out a sigh of relief. "I hate it when the power...."

And the lights went out again. All the machines helping people stopped. A moment turned into two. The power did not come back on.

The ICU was instantly in turmoil. Medical personnel dashed about, doing what they could to help their patients. Some were screaming.

I grabbed Ian's arm just as he was taking off. "The generators! Where do I find them?"

He sent me a crazed look. "Out back. What are you thinking?"

"*Someone* disabled them."

Disbelief crossed his face, then anger. "Let's go," he declared and took off, running for the stairs.

I followed him. "Shouldn't you be with your patients?" I demanded as we galloped down a long set of concrete steps. Our footfalls echoed off the walls.

"They're dead if we don't get the power back on," he called over his shoulder. We reached a heavy door posted with '**Emergency Exit Only. Alarm Will Sound**.' Ian didn't hesitate; he shoved it open and we charged through. If there was an alarm, I didn't hear it. It probably needed electricity to function.

Two maintenance men cowered near the other side of the door. Neither one was the guy I'd seen earlier. "Don't go out there. There's a man with a gun," one of them warned. "I'll get security." He and his companion ducked through the door we'd just come through.

"Don't let that close!" Ian exclaimed, but it was too late. The door clicked shut after them. There was no handle on this side. We were caught outside the building. The hospital walls surrounded us on three sides. The fourth side was open to a sloping lawn facing a line of trees.

"Where are the generators?" I whispered as we stood there, not moving.

Ian held a finger to his lips, then gestured to the corner of the building. "Around there."

I started moving stealthily toward the corner.

Ian grabbed me by the arm. "Where are you going?" he demanded in a low voice.

"To stop that guy and get the generators back on. Where d'ya think I'd be going?" I retorted.

"He's got a gun!"

"And I've got a sword." I gritted my teeth, knowing there was no other way I could play this. At least Ian had seen my kind of crazy before. I reached over my shoulder and pulled Fraegarthach from its hiding place, transforming into my Celtic warrior avatar. Behind me, I heard Ian draw in a sharp breath.

"What the...." He paused, stunned. "Are you Wonder Woman's little sister or something?"

I wish! I hand-shushed him without looking back, then eased up to where I could look around the corner. There were the generators. And standing between us and them...was the man I'd seen in the hallway earlier. Fred. Or someone who was wearing Fred's clothes.

Ian hovered by my elbow. "That's not Fred," he whispered.

"My suspicions exactly."

"Where *is* Fred?"

"Dead, probably." I am nothing if not blunt.

A sibilant hiss passed through his teeth. "You're a cold one."

"Just being realistic." Should I tell Ian more? Or had he already been exposed to enough 'crazy' just seeing me assume my avatar form? I decided full disclosure was more useful. "That man over there? My guess is he's not."

"Not what?"

"A man," I answered and stepped around the corner.

Gods. Dub and his brother must have been identical twins. Same size, same body build. Same features that might once have been handsome but were now warped with cruelty. He turned toward me as I stepped out of hiding. "Ah! A hero come to save the day," he sneered. "What kind of idiot brings a sword to a gunfight, *hero*?" He patted the stock of the AK-47 cradled against his chest.

"Dian, I presume?" I managed to keep my voice even.

The god of violence gave me a mocking bow. "The same," he said. "Aren't you the clever one."

"Step away from those generators," I warned.

"No," he said, and smiled. "I like them off. More people dying, you see. I can hear them screaming. It's music to my ears." He bared a set of perfect white teeth.

"I will stop you."

"With a sword?" He threw his head back and roared with laughter. "You're slaying me with your jokes, *hero*."

My grip tightened on Fraegarthach, and I took a step toward him.

His expression changed to anger. "Very well then. Since you are so willing to throw your life away, I'll humor your death wish." He didn't even raise the gun to his shoulder, just squeezed off a burst of bullets in my direction, like it didn't even matter if he aimed or not.

Fraegarthach leapt into action, deflecting the bullets, sending them screaming in every direction, where they pockmarked the concrete walls surrounding us. One ricochet sliced Dian on the cheek, drawing blood (and a curse) as the god ducked.

Thank the gods there were no windows overlooking the generators.

Dian straightened; his eyes narrowed. "You are becoming more interesting, hero. Who are you, anyways?"

"That's on a need-to-know basis. *You* don't need to know."

"Maybe I do."

I shook my head. "No, you don't. Get away from those generators."

Dian bared those perfect white teeth again. "Make me." And this time, he took aim.

Fraegarthach sent every single bullet straight back at him. They riddled his torso, jerking him about, but he neither fell nor died. He also didn't take long to recover. Ripping back the front of the overalls he was wearing, he exposed the tactical armor underneath. "Ha, ha. Joke's on you." Then he dropped the gun...dropped it! And charged me.

Bracing myself, I leveled my sword's point. And just as he reached me, I let loose with a bolt of electricity strong enough to power the City of Los Angeles for a day.

Dian screamed high and shrill as the bolt passed through him. Then, he exploded into a cloud of darkness that blew outward in a filthy mess, before dissipating in the breeze. Gone, just like that, except for the lingering sweet smell of ozone.

I stood frozen, heart pounding in my ears.

"The generators!" Ian bolted past me to the closest one and quickly found the override switch. And threw it. The machine rumbled back to life. The power at the hospital came back on.

My hands shook almost uncontrollably as I fumbled to get Fraegarthach over my shoulder and back into its hiding place. I resumed my normal form, my glamour firmly in place.

Ian approached me cautiously. "You OK?" he asked.

I didn't have an easy answer to that, so I just shook my head. "We're going to have to come up with a plausible story."

He nodded slowly, agreeing with me.

"Short and simple," I said. "When we came out, the gunman ran away. The maintenance guys will have reported he had a gun, so we can't leave that detail out. You turned the generators back on. The end."

"And why would a gunman be so afraid of us that he would run away?"

I shrugged. "I don't know. Maybe they should ask him?"

"Play the dummy, then."

"Works for me." I said.

Ian slowly shook his head. "You are...not ordinary."

I sent him a crooked smile. "Nobody is."

Security officers arrived then, and they were not gentle. Both Ian and I were ordered to lie down on the ground, then roughly shoved there when we did not move fast enough to suit them. We were handcuffed, then dragged inside where we were put in separate rooms. Then we were interrogated by the state police for what seemed like hours. It wasn't until the maintenance workers confirmed that neither of us was the guy with the gun that the cuffs were removed.

We were hailed as "heroes." A search was mounted for the gunman, not that they ever found him *or* his gun. Somehow that had disappeared too. The assumption was he had taken it with him. I didn't disabuse them of that. Gods and magical weapons do not exist in the dimension where most humans live. That was movie stuff.

When I was finally released, Dad was waiting for me in the hall outside the room they'd held me in. He immediately escorted me upstairs. Ian must have been released before me, because he was already surrounded by reporters. He looked a bit shell-shocked by their clamoring attention. Dad stuck me in a corner by a potted palm and went over to rescue him. "You will excuse us, please." He gripped Ian's arm firmly above the elbow and drew him away. "My office. Now," he instructed us, and we gladly left the media behind.

Dad perched himself on the edge of his desk, facing the two of us. "Please tell me what really happened," he said.

Ian and I exchanged an uneasy glance. I shrugged and pointed at Ian. "You tell him. You're the one who got the power back on."

Ian laughed without humor. "I only flipped the switch. You got rid of the creep who had shut them down."

"'Got rid of,'" Dad repeated. "He didn't run away."

Ian shook his head. "She *exploded* him. Poof. Big black cloud."

"So, our police force is out there looking for nothing." Dad scowled.

"You want to tell them about Dian?" I asked. "We'd all end up in the mental ward."

Ian nodded in agreement.

"So it was Dian. *Wonderful.*" Dad said wearily, his tone indicating it was anything but wonderful. He rubbed one temple, like he had a headache coming on. "I understand why you told the story you did. But will it hold up?"

I shrugged. "Did we have a choice?"

Ian came to my defense. "Your daughter is awesome, Dr. Callahan. She pulled a sword out of nowhere and...."

Dad waved his enthusiasm down. "I had my suspicions about what she did. I just worry about the possible consequences *of one of my nursing staff knowing about it!*" His voice rose as he stressed that bit. Like it freaked him out. He glared at me but addressed Ian. "You know you can't tell anyone, right, Ian? Keep this to yourself."

"Yes, of course, sir." Ian managed a wry smile. "I'm a DC Comics and Marvel fan, guys. I know the rules. Secret identities need to stay secret, even Wonder Woman's little sister's alter ego."

"Especially her little sister's." Dad remained grim. "And stick to the story as you told it. No elaborating."

Ian sobered. "The dude ran away. I turned on the switch."

"And why were you accompanied by my daughter, hmm?"

Ian and I exchanged glances again. That was an angle that hadn't occurred to us.

"I...wanted to help?" I suggested. "I'd brought presents for the staff, and followed Ian when the power went off."

"I can see the headlines: '*Impetuous daughter of head surgeon helps save the day.*' Great." It sure didn't sound like Dad thought it was great.

"Head surgeon?" I repeated.

"There's a bit you don't know about me," he said.

I was starting to get angry. "Like with Mom? Things you didn't tell *her?*"

"Raven..." There was a warning note in Dad's voice.

"Whoa, you guys. Maybe don't fight in front of the staff?" Ian interjected. He stepped back, looking uneasily between Dad and me.

I glared at him. Dad just sighed. "He's right. This is neither the time nor the place." He looked at Ian and made a dismissive gesture with one hand. "I'll arrange for someone to cover your shifts for a couple of days, Ian. Go visit your folks in Ohio or something. Enjoy Halloween. Let this blow over."

Ian brightened. "That's great, Dr. C! It's been years since I spent Halloween with my family. Thanks."

Dad nodded and his mouth tightened in a forced smile. "You can go."

Ian wasted no time leaving, but he sent me an apologetic grimace before he left the room.

I watched him go, then turned back to face my father. Head surgeon?! You'd think he would have had the decency to tell me. I crossed my arms over my chest and fixed him with my best glare. "What choice did I have, Dad? People were dying."

He rubbed his face with both hands, then dropped them onto his lap. "I know, Raven. It just makes keeping things quiet much more difficult. We don't need widespread panic."

I huffed. "Oh, it's OK if it's just us weirdos who are panicking?"

"Basically."

I threw up my hands. "Great! Just great." I stalked past Dad's desk to his window and stared out over the expanse of still-green lawn that sloped down toward the lake.

There was a shuffling sound as he got to his feet. "Raven…" he started.

I rounded on my father, finally letting my temper get the best of me. "So, when were you going to tell me about this?" I indicated his office, but the gesture encompassed the entire hospital. "The ambulance, the head doctor stuff? How about telling me who you really are, *Doctor* Callahan? Because your daughter ought to know, before it wrecks another one of your relationships. Right?" Dad's expression turned bleak, and he shook his head in frustration.

Oh, too bad, so sad! I plunged ahead anyways. "How much did you keep from Mom? I saw how you locked the door that day; I've seen that spellwork before. When were you going to tell me you have magic? Who are *you?*"

"Keep your voice down, Raven!" Dad's voice was low, but carried an unmistakable warning. "I understand you're angry, but you mustn't undo all that your grandmother and I have done since we came over from Ireland."

"'*We* came,'" I repeated. "You came over with Nan? That's 400 hundred years ago, if I remember correctly. You're not 40-something, are you?"

Dad pressed his lips together and shook his head. "No."

I made a rude noise through my nose. "Would have been nice to know!"

"We were trying to protect you."

"By keeping important stuff from me? Gee, thanks." I studied him, scowling. "So...was your age the only thing you didn't tell Mom about? Does she know you can use magic? That you are a Lunatic also?"

He raked a shaking hand through his curls. "I'm not like your Nan or you. My magic is the learned kind only."

"You don't change with moon phases like we do?"

He shook his head.

So not fair! I flounced over to his desk and plopped down on its polished wood top. "But I daresay you did not spring fully formed from Nan's head, like Athena did from Zeus."

A rueful grin lifted the corner of his mouth. "I was a baby once, years ago. I just age more slowly."

Gods. "Poor Mom."

His eyebrows quirked up in agreement. "She didn't handle this as well as you are."

I laughed, but there wasn't any humor in it. I wasn't handling this well *at all*. Mom must have *really* gone ballistic.

"Understandable," he continued, "considering what happened to her as a very young child."

"What happened to her?" I demanded. "Or are you going to keep that a secret, too?"

"Maybe she should be the one…" he started, but I held a hand up, stopping him.

"No! No more secrets. What the heck happened to her?"

He stood gazing at me for a long moment, then shook his head and sighed. "As part of our federal government's 'Native assimilation campaign,' she was forcibly taken from the reservation, with other Native children, across the Canadian border to a so-called 're-education school.' The priests there physically and emotionally abused her and the other children." He grimaced, acknowledging the horrified look on my face.

A car alarm went off in the parking lot. An ambulance siren wailed in the distance. But I sat silent and still on the desk, attempting to make sense of this latest revelation.

Dad went over to the window and stood, staring out for a while before he began speaking again. "It was intentionally cruel cultural genocide. And it went on for over one hundred years. Your mother was caught up in the very end of it. Hers was the last school to be shut down." He turned back to face me. "Your mother was returned to Iku, irrevocably changed."

Oh. My. Gods. Secrets upon secrets. "I want to go home," I said in a low voice. I was beyond tired. Heartsick, I wanted to be done with all the crazies, the secrets, the lies.

Dad reached for me. "Raven, please try to understand."

"Argh!" I interrupted him with a strangled cry. I threw up my hands, then clasped them over my head before dropping them to my sides. "I *am* trying! I just don't get why you hid so much from me. Give me some time to think things through, OK? It's a lot to get used to."

He dropped his arm to his side. "Fair enough," he said quietly. "I'll call Elias. I believe he's waiting out in the car for you."

Nineteen

When I got home, I ditched my studies and went riding on Cayuga Lake. For me, riding is basically taking a break. And boy, did I need one! Ever ridden on the surface of a lake? When it's not frozen? It's quite the experience! As the offspring of a night mare and a demon horse, Knight was not bound by the usual rules; water supported him quite nicely when he wanted it to.

Cayuga Lake is long and narrow, formed when the glaciers receded after the last ice age. It's the longest of the all the Finger Lakes in Central New York, and only three and a half miles at its widest. It was deep too: 435 feet. What better place to run wild?

To keep our lake surface outings from confusing the locals (it *would* be odd to look out your window and see a horse and rider dashing by on your waterfront!), Nan had taught me how to modify my glamour so I would blend into the background. It wouldn't make me invisible, just less noticeable. I'd mastered that one right away. Go figure. Maybe my wallflower tendencies were finally coming in handy.

Despite Knight's dislike for practicing, we had done a bunch since he'd returned...despite his endless complaints. I told him it would help me become a better rider, and he (astonishingly) accepted that line of bull.

Knight coached me as we rode: my legs were too stiff, my hands should be softer, I needed to shift my weight off my right butt cheek because I was sitting unevenly.... He was terribly picky, and quick to let me know if I screwed up. Usually, this meant getting dumped into the lake—which, in late October, was darn cold. It was easy to get back on, though; he just sank into the water and swam back under me, once I apologized. The affection between us grew by leaps and bounds—although, the first time I threw my arms around his neck and kissed him on the cheek, he was very surprised.

Today, I was not in the mood for practicing. I needed speed; I needed distance. And the dark horse was more than willing to cooperate. I urged Knight into a flat-out gallop. We flew northward, rooster tail sprays of water kicking up from his flying hooves. We were faster than the motorboats, even seemingly faster than the jets in the sky above. Knight's muscles slid smoothly under my thighs. His neck stretched out, lungs pumping like bellows, long mane whipping me in the face as I leaned forward over his neck. Joy poured off him and soaked into me, easing the tightness around my heart—chasing away the pain. Horse magic. There's no substitute for it.

In record time, we reached where the lake was widest, then carved an arc that headed us south again. Knight dialed it back, dropping to a distance-covering, smooth canter that ate up the miles. I let him choose his path, his speed; I was just along for the ride. My hands lay relaxed on my thighs, my mind quiet. I wasn't thinking about murderous gods or family dynamics. Just me, my horse, and the lake. Exactly what I needed.

Coming up on the edge of Nan's property, Knight suddenly put on the brakes and dropped his head. I was totally unprepared and went flying over his front end. I splashed down into about ten feet of cold water and came up gasping and spitting. Knight whinnied mockingly, then sprang into the air and disappeared.

Blasted demon spawn of a horse! I swam to shore and clambered up over the pebbly beach, then headed for the house in an awkward jog, sopping wet and shivering like crazy. Dad and Nan were drinking coffee in the kitchen.

Dad took one look at me dripping all over, and winced. It wasn't the first time I'd come in like that. He wasn't keen on Knight's manner of teaching me, but wisely kept his worries to himself (except for the occasional comment about how riding in a wetsuit might be beneficial). "Hustle up and get dried off," he encouraged. "Then come back here. Nan and I have something to share."

That lit a fire under me; the Gods only knew what sorry news they were going to share. I headed for the bathroom. Showering and dressing in warm clothes in record time, I bounced back into the kitchen. Needing a bit of warming up from the inside too—and fortification—I helped myself to coffee.

This whole thing with the Old Gods felt like being under siege. It was unfair. We weren't challenging anyone's place in the world, just doing our own thing. But then, that's true of most conflicts. One side decides they want what someone else has, then start a fight to take it. (All good fun.... Not!) But what exactly did the Old Gods want from us?

Coffee in hand, I turned to face my family. "So, what's up?" I demanded.

Dad and Nan exchanged glances, which did nothing to reassure me. Dad spoke. "We've been discussing what you said about keeping things from you and decided the best course of action would be to fill you in."

OH. Wow! This was unexpected. Keeping my face carefully blank, I nodded. "OK?"

Dad made a wry face at my subdued reaction but continued—determined, if not enthusiastic. "So, you know your Nan's story. Mine starts later. I was... planned. A woman's body is not prepared to bring a baby to term when she spends part of her time as a young child every month."

I nodded again. "Yeah, I know enough biology to see that being an issue." My own periods had stopped. Not that I minded missing out on that bit of loveliness every month.

"But Cerridwen badly wanted a successor to her moon child, especially as your Nan was obviously starting to age. So, for months Cerridwen held the moon phase at its most ideal for conception and pregnancy." He took a swallow of his coffee and set the mug down. "Are you following me?"

I was, although the whole manipulativeness of the moon goddess's actions was seriously creepy. I glanced at my grandmother. "You were OK with this?"

"I was. I wanted a child." Nan smiled. "And I was in love. I was not forced." She leaned over, put an arm around my dad, and rested her head against his shoulder. "And because if it, we have Michael. And you."

"Who was he?" I demanded.

It wasn't terribly clear who I was referring to, but Nan understood. "Taliesin is your grandfather, Raven."

I had just taken a slurp of coffee and about choked on it. Setting the mug down on the counter, I gasped until my gag reflex was back under control. "Taliesin is my *grandfather*? Does *he* know this?" I wheezed.

Nan was beaming. "He does, and he's the reason you and your father have such a strong connection with music." Dad nodded in agreement.

My hand went to the necklace that lay underneath my sweater. "My medallion? Is that why he..."

Finished with her coffee, Nan set her mug down and pushed it away. "I would lay odds on it. His own grandchild. What a gift to him that you stumbled across his cabin and spent time with him!" She linked her fingers under her chin and leaned her elbows on the counter, her eyes crinkled in a smile. "He'd have wanted to give you every advantage in the fight ahead. No doubt he realized life would be a challenge for you."

I stood silent for a moment, mulling that over. Needing to know more, I asked, "What happened between you two? You're with Elias now."

Nan's face registered her sorrow. "Taliesin died, Raven. Despite his mother Cerridwen being a goddess—which made him a god also—he chose to live as a mortal after your father was born. We thought we would grow old together. As it turned out, that wasn't the case. Elias came much later, when your father was still a young child."

But my brain had skittered off on a tangent. "Taliesin died in AD 596," I mused.

Dad smirked. "She's trying to figure out how old I am."

"Can you blame me? You look 40. But..." I did some quick mental math. "You're probably about 1,400 years old. Geez! No wonder Mom freaked out!" And then, being the nosy nerd that I am, I had to know. "Were there...others?"

Dad shifted on his stool and suppressed a smile. "Others, as in...? What do you mean?" Obvious as heck he was hedging.

"You know. Before Mom." I huffed. "Other women." I did air quotes. "Lovers." I could hardly bring myself to say the word.

"Ye...s. There were." Now his grin turned awkward. "I am...fairly human in that regard."

Eek. Why had I even asked? And why wouldn't he? Even though I could hardly picture him as anything other than my dad, I could see how he would appeal to women. It wasn't just that he was good-looking in a ruggedly handsome way; he was kind and smart and accomplished, and.... Well. Let's just leave it at that.

I drew a deep breath and steeled myself for what I needed to ask next. "OK. Because Taliesin was a god when you were conceived, and Nan is mortal, but with magic, what does that make you, Dad?" I needed to get this sorted out while he was still willing to answer tough questions.

He shrugged. "It makes me a demigod. But with something extra because of your Nan's moon powers. Kinda hard to say just what."

"And that makes me what, exactly?"

"Technically, you're a demigoddess—but with something extra. You have moon magic. And, you wield Fraegarthach." Dad shifted uneasily and sent a sidelong glance at Nan. She patted him on the knee.

I realized I didn't have much time left to pry things out of him. "Moving right along...do you have other children?"

Dad ducked his head, and his shoulders shook. At first, I thought he was crying. But when he looked up, I saw Dad was laughing. "That's definitely 'moving right along,' fledgling."

Nan made a noise that sounded distinctly like a snort. "She is *your* daughter!"

Dad readily acknowledged Nan's comment. "The short answer is yes. You've had many brothers over the years." He blinked rapidly, like he was holding in strong emotion. "The longer answer is...they're all dead. They were all born mortal. I remember every single one of them and miss them all. But I could not mourn forever, Raven. I would have gone insane."

I remained silent for a moment, giving him a chance to regain control before I continued. "Did any of them have kids?"

That brought back the shadow of a smile and he winked at me. "Good question, fledgling! The answer is: only one."

"And?"

"And what?" Dad was being deliberately annoying. I could see it in the twinkle that lurked in his eyes as he got up from his stool. He came around the counter and set his mug in the sink next to me.

"OMG, Dad!" I exclaimed, throwing my hands up in the air. "Were there any *survivors* of that lineage? Might I have a living relative down the line somewhere? A great, great, ever-so-great grandson of yours, or something?"

Dad pulled me into his arms and hugged me. "That would be Archer," he said.

Eek. Double eek. Triple eek, even. I wiggled free of his hug. "Does Kellas know that little factoid?" Because if he had, and still sicced me on Archer as an alternative to him, well, that was just plain *awkward*. And what did that make us? Cousins? No. Maybe I was his aunt, just many generations removed. Oh, that was *very* awkward!

"Probably not." He waggled his eyebrows and chucked me under the chin. "As you know, we tend to keep secrets."

Oh, OK. Better. Phew! I gulped the rest of my coffee and turned to rinse my mug out at the sink. "So. I'm the only girl? Ever?" I turned in time to see a sad look cross Dad's face.

"Only you." Regret etched lines around his mouth.

Nan broke her silence. "We knew you were special right from the moment you were born."

"How? What clued you in?" I asked.

Dad's eyes got a faraway look in them. "I delivered you. Margaret wanted a home birth, so it was just me and your grandmothers there. You were small, maybe five pounds, and it was an easy delivery." He put an arm around my shoulders again, and I let him pull me close. "You entered the world with your whole body shining like the moon. And unlike most babies, you never cried. You just looked up at us with eyes that belonged to the oldest of souls."

"So, you at least suspected I would be like Nan." I paused, letting this sink in. And I knew what happened next. "You told Mom...and she started asking awkward questions. Didn't she?" I heard Nan groan.

Dad nodded. "She did. I wasn't prepared. I did...poorly." He sighed, then put me out at arm's length so he could look at me. "Raven, what happened between your mom and me...that was my fault. I tried to make it up to her, but as I told you earlier today, she had been badly betrayed as a young child by the people who were put in authority over her. Meg wasn't able to forgive me for what she perceived as just another betrayal of trust." He released me and ran his fingers through his hair. Upset.

"So, you divorced." I said that as gently as I could. Divorce is not an easy subject.

"Actually, no. We didn't." He crossed his arms over his chest and leaned back against the counter, staring blankly at the floor.

I sent him a startled look.

"She never filed the paperwork," Dad said. "We're still married; we've just lived apart since you were six." He shook his head and looked back at me. "I'd give anything to go back and fix things. But she isn't ready to forgive me. Not yet, anyways."

Right then, Dad's phone began to ring. At first, he ignored it. When it stopped and then started up again, however, he pulled it out of his pocket with an annoyed grunt. "Yes?" His expression went from annoyed to still in the space of a second. "I see. Anything else I should know?" He paused a moment, listening to the person on the other end. "OK. I'll be there in ten. Call up the rest of the team. Red alert." He punched the off button on his phone.

"What's wrong Michael?" Nan asked, quickly getting to her feet. She remained standing by the kitchen island, tense.

"Emergency, I gotta go." Dad strode across to the front door, grabbed his sheepskin coat off the peg and swung it over one shoulder, reached for the door and stopped. Turning around, he strode back to me and pulled me into a fierce hug. "We'll fill you in on anything else you want to know when I get back. Meanwhile, stay here. In the house. Don't go out." He headed for the door again.

I beat him to it and blocked his path. "Why? What's happened?" It was obvious he didn't want to say, but I wasn't having it. "Tell me!" I insisted. "Or I'll go find out on my own, I swear."

"Raven," Nan took a step toward us, "Let your father—"

Dad drew a deep breath, "OK, but you still have to promise to stay here." He scowled, angry. "Ian's been kidnapped. We're guessing it was people working for the Old Gods. It was caught on camera at the mini-mart where he was filling his car up with gas." He looked at Nan. "I think it's time for those emergency measures we discussed."

"Agreed," she responded.

Kellas joined us in the kitchen, his face furrowed in concern. "I couldn't help but overhear. How can I help?" He left it at that, but it was evident he wanted to be included.

Dad briefly dropped a hand on the Cait Sidhe's shoulder. "Keep Raven here, Kellas. I'm counting on you to keep her safe. If the Old Gods took Ian, they're most likely planning to use him as bait. They're after Raven, and we can't let that happen." He pulled me into another hard hug and kissed the top of my head. "Stay put. I mean it." And he was gone.

Yes, I immediately started after Dad. Yes, Kellas stopped me, blocking the door with his body. I tried to push him out of the way, but he just slung one arm around my middle and lifted me off my feet. And didn't let go. Kellas had gotten stronger, almost back to normal, and I was unable to break free.

"Let me go!" I snarled.

He shook his head. "No."

"Why not?"

"Two hundred sixty-four years of why not," he countered. "I lost you once. I'm not letting that happen again."

I couldn't find a way to argue with that.

Twenty

I let Kellas guide me into the living room to wait. Nan went out to Orianthi's tree and brought the dryad into the house, then left with Elias—without bothering to tell me where they were going. But not before she repeated Dad's warning about not going out.

Archer showed up an hour later with a large package for me that he'd picked up from the post office. It was from Iku. With nothing better to do, the four of us left behind crowded around the dining room table to open it. The box held small, tightly wrapped bundles of white sage. There were sweetgrass braids as well. Seeing these, Archer went to the kitchen and started rummaging through the drawers, looking for matches.

Iku had included detailed instructions on how to use the herbs most effectively: First, we were to smudge the whole house with the white sage, directing the smoke into all the corners and around the doors and windows. Then, we were to follow it up with a sweetgrass smudge, together with a prayer in Hidatsa, which she'd put on a digital voice recorder and included in the package.

I struggled to learn the unfamiliar words, but Orianthi picked them up quickly. It was a little annoying. Maybe my medallion wasn't doing its translating job as well here as it had in Tír na nÓg. But no matter. If the ghosts commanded by Dother tried to bother us, we now had ways to deal with them.

After we finished sorting out the contents of the package, there wasn't much to do except wait for news. I fretted, pacing back and forth in front of the living room windows, staring out into the growing darkness and fuming under my breath. Orianthi sat by the fireplace playing with a set of toy horses that Nan had fished out of a bin of my old toys. The dryad sang softly to them, putting them through their paces—occasionally remonstrating one of them for being naughty. Archer had his nose in a textbook—of course! Kellas lounged in one of the easy chairs and watched me pace.

"You're going to wear a path in the floorboards if you keep that up," he said after a while.

I rounded on him in irritation. "What would you have me do instead?"

Kellas sent me a lazy smile and lifted one quizzical eyebrow; my face flamed red. "You have to ask?" he drawled.

Archer didn't even look up from his book. "Little pitchers have big ears, Cat Man. Chill."

Orianthi just smiled to herself and continued to sing to her ponies.

I went back to pacing. "Where are they? What's happening? I hate this!"

The chair creaked under Kellas as he pushed himself up out of it. A moment later, he snaked an arm around my middle and pulled me up against his side. "You're driving the rest of us crazy, lady. Let's go somewhere else and let them have a few minutes of peace without you being a nervous wreck." Dragging me into the kitchen, he grabbed me by the waist and lifted me effortlessly onto one of the counter stools. "Stay put. I'll make us some dinner," he said, heading for the refrigerator and opening it. "What sounds good?"

"I'm not hungry."

He gave me a sideways look and closed the fridge door. "Of course you're hungry. You're always hungry. Now, what'll it be? Hamburgers? Spaghetti? Those are my specialties. My cooking skills have limits."

But I wasn't hungry, not even a little bit. Instead, there was a sick lump in my gut that sat there like congealed oatmeal. I just shook my head and looked down at my hands where I'd folded them together to stop them from trembling.

"Brannaugh." Kellas was by my side in a few swift strides. A moment later, he'd wrapped his arms around me and pulled me close. "It's going to be OK. The A-Team will find Ian and get him out of wherever it is they took him. That's what they do best."

Returning his embrace, I buried my face in his shirt front. I hoped he was right and that these weren't just empty words. "Where did Nan and Elias go off to?"

"I don't know."

I groaned. "I hate waiting. I'm no good at waiting."

Kellas made a soft sound that might have been a laugh. He tipped my face up, forcing me to look at him. "I stink at it too," he said, then added in a husky voice, "I'm going to wear the face off you, my cailin álainn."

Kellas leaned down and kissed me. I might not be all that experienced in this regard, but I think he's exceptionally good at kissing.... And then, of course, the phone rang. Worst possible timing!

He broke off our kiss with a muttered curse and grabbed the phone off its charging stand. "Kellas here." He stood listening intently, then wandered off to the far side of the kitchen before saying anything. "What do you need?" Another pause. "OK, can do." Yet another pause. "Yes, I understand. I'll try, but don't yell at me if she doesn't listen. See you soon." He hung up the landline.

I sent him a steady stare through narrowed eyes. "If that was Dad saying he needs your help and he expects me not to come, that man is sorely mistaken. You know that, don't you?"

A boyish grin greeted my declaration. "I know. Let's tell the others and go, shall we?" Kellas grabbed my hand and led me back into the living room.

Archer merely nodded when we told him we were leaving. "Orianthi and I can hold down the fort. Don't do anything stupid, Cat Man."

Kellas laughed. "Who, me?" He bumped fists with the Cayuga. We made our way out to a shed near the driveway, where I helped him gather the climbing gear Dad had requested. Heavy loops of thick rope, helmets, locking carabiners, and awkward-looking harnesses got piled into the back of the Prius. That was just the stuff I recognized. Dad had taken me to a local climbing wall a few times over the years, but I was far from an expert.

"What does Dad need this stuff for?" I asked as we pulled out of the driveway.

"He and the A-Team intend to do a bit of spelunking, from what I understand."

"Umm...what's that?" Spelunking? Not a term I recognized. I looked over at Kellas, waiting for a response, and saw he was tapping his index fingers on the steering wheel. Was he nervous?

He stopped and shifted in his seat. "The A-Team is going down into the salt mines under the lake. Michael got an anonymous tip about some curious stuff going on down there. One of his guys is a computer expert. They hacked into the mine's security cameras and saw Ian being dragged in."

"There's a *mine* under the lake?" I exclaimed, horrified. How could I be so completely unaware of this? You'd think I'd have known about a mine under Cayuga Lake.

Kellas nodded. "It's the deepest in the U.S. Goes down 2,300 feet below the lake in places. That's almost a half mile." He sent me a quick glance, like he wanted to see how I was handling that information, then shared more. "There's seven miles of tunnels down there, on four levels." The finger tapping resumed. "That's a lot of territory for the Old Gods to hide in. And the team can't go in by the front door. It's all heavily guarded. But they hope to find Ian down there someplace."

"Why would anyone put a mine under a lake? Wouldn't there be leaks?" I was having a hard time wrapping my head around everything he'd told me.

Kellas used the turn signal and passed a slow-moving truck. "Worse. How about a roof collapse?" He looked grim. "It's happened elsewhere. There are anomalies in the stone under the lake up by Frontenac Point, something like a fault line." A muscle tightened in his jaw as he clenched his teeth. "There are credible concerns that the roof could collapse. The mine would flood and the entire lake would be seriously damaged. It's why the company isn't allowed to mine in that area."

"But why would anyone think a mine under a lake was a good idea in the first place?" I demanded.

Kellas stopped for a red light. "Money. Lots of it. Rock salt is a valuable commodity. New York State uses it to salt the roads in winter." He sent me a quick look. "It's not all bad, Brannaugh. The mining company provides hundreds of high-paying jobs and does a lot of good things for the community besides."

I sank against my seatback, stunned. This was just a bit too much to absorb. "I never knew."

"It's a lot all at once, isn't it?" he agreed.

We'd reached Ithaca. I hadn't noticed how far we'd gone already. "Where are we going?" I asked, as we waited for the lights to change.

"Up toward Lansing. There's an airshaft there that's been under construction for the past year, and it's still not finished. We're hoping it isn't as heavily guarded as the rest."

Oh, this was just getting better and better. Not! The lights changed. I remained silent as we navigated Rt. 13 traffic. Exiting near the middle school, Kellas turned the Prius northward on 34B and stepped hard on the gas pedal.

Something Kellas had said was bothering me, though, but I couldn't put a finger on what exactly. I finally stopped trying and told myself it would come to me—if I didn't work at it so hard.

We didn't meet many cars coming the other way. But anytime we did, Kellas cussed under his breath. "I hate the low beams on this hunk of junk," he muttered.

I had to admit, they really didn't dispel the dark very well.

"A good thing I can see at night better than most," he added, sighing in relief as we passed an oncoming car. "Ah, there's the team!"

Our high beams had glanced off the figure of a man standing by the side of the road.

Kellas pulled up next to him and powered down the passenger window. The paramedic who'd marched me into the ER weeks ago leaned down and looked in on us. "What's she doing here?" he demanded. "Doc said not to bring the kid."

Kellas laughed without humor. "Doc was dreaming. She's as bullheaded as he is."

The paramedic snorted in derision. "Pull in here." He stepped back and indicated a grassy path that led into a field. Kellas guided the car after the paramedic, pulled up behind the ambulance, then killed the power and lights. Someone opened the hatchback and the gear we brought was dragged out and distributed.

I got out of the car and started toward the back...and ran immediately into Dad. He twirled me around, marched me back up front, did one of those *guide the perp's head under the roof of the car* moves, and shoved me down in the passenger seat.

"You're leaving." His tone left no room for negotiating.

"Dad! I can help!" I protested.

He snorted in disgust. "No, you can't. It's too dangerous, and I won't let you. This is a military-grade operation. You don't have the necessary training."

"And you *do*?" I yelled as he slammed the door in my face. Fortunately, the window was still open, or it would have mashed my nose. "Dad!"

He leaned down and looked me in the eye. "Yes, I do. And now that is something else you know about me."

We delayed our departure long enough to see Dad and his team of four rangers fade into the darkness. Kellas climbed in and started the car up, guided it carefully across the bumpy ground back onto the highway, and turned it south toward home again.

"We could only *pretend* to leave," I suggested.

Kellas only laughed. "Your dad wasn't born yesterday."

True, that. Darn it! "There's something seriously wrong about this whole thing.

Something stinks." I was muttering quietly enough that I didn't think he could hear me, but Cait Si have good ears.

"You can't blame Michael for wanting to protect his only daughter," he said.

"Oh, I can blame him all right. Just watch me! But there's something..." Then that *something* hit me like a ton of bricks. "That tip? It's bogus. They're walking into a trap." I grabbed Kellas's arm and the car wobbled dangerously. He cussed vehemently; I let go.

"Don't ever do that again!" he warned. "The road drops off a hundred feet here. This wimpy piece of junk would be a mass of crumpled metal if we went over in it."

"Sorry." I was, but it was a fleeting thing. "Kellas, we've got to go back and warn them!"

"No can do. Besides, I bet they already surmised that and are taking precautions. This ain't their first rodeo, Brannaugh."

I wondered if this cloak-and-dagger stuff had played a part in Mom's decision to kick my dad out. Maybe it hadn't been all because of me, after all. I could vividly imagine how Mom would react to such nonsense. I know I certainly didn't appreciate being actively excluded from the rescue party.

When we got back to Nan's house, I left Kellas and Archer discussing the situation in low tones in the kitchen. Orianthi had curled up on the couch in the living room and fallen asleep, cuddled under a warm red blanket. I brushed my teeth and headed upstairs to my bedroom like I meant to turn in. It was still early, only 8-ish, but I needed space to think. I stood by the French doors overlooking the lake and watched the full moon rise over the eastern horizon, large and luminous. The Samhain Blue Moon was upon us. I was officially 17. Great. Another crappy birthday.

A mist formed as the air cooled down over the slightly warmer water of the lake. I stood there admiring the scene as the spectral fog rolled upward, over the lawn, and toward our house. It was very pretty, the moonlight illuminating it with a lovely glow.

But when it was a mere 100 feet from our back deck, I saw human shapes lurking within the fog. "Ghosts!" I yelled, pelting downstairs. "Get those smudges lit! They're nearly here!"

I heard a scream coming from the living room. Orianthi! I darted in. Mist was seeping in around the French doors, getting larger and fuller by the moment, assuming human form. I grabbed Orianthi's arm and dragged her with me into the kitchen. Archer and Kellas were there, lighting bundles of sage as fast as they could. I grabbed one and handed it to Orianthi, then shoved her behind me and caught up two bundles, one in either hand. Archer and

Kellas joined me. The three of us stood back-to-back surrounding Orianthi, sage bundles outstretched as ghosts invaded our home.

Sage smoke may be cleansing, and the best way to chase off ghosts, but it's still smoke—not great stuff to breathe. We were all coughing in moments, our eyes stinging. It did stop the ghosts from getting closer. However, they hovered at the edges of the smoke screen, doing what ghosts do: moaning, shrieking, and being generally unpleasant. It didn't help that the smoke detectors started clamoring as well.

I had to shout to be heard over the din. "We gotta push the smoke toward them if this is gonna work!" I waved my hands. It wasn't very effective.

"I've no idea how we're going to do that!" Kellas wheezed.

"Blow it?" Archer suggested. He puffed a few times before breaking down in a coughing fit.

"I can do it," Orianthi volunteered from behind me. She poked her little face between me and Kellas. Then, very gently, blew a long breath outward. A breeze sprung up and teased the smoke in a swirling dance that played it outward, upward, and around. It drove the ghosts back, forcing them to retreat or be touched by the sacred smoke. They squealed and shrieked when it touched their misty bodies.

We chased them around the entire house. As we passed the electrical panel near the stairs, Kellas flipped off a breaker, silencing the incessant beep-beep-beep of the smoke detectors. The smoke drove the ghosts back out through the cracks and crevices they had come in through and prevented them from re-entering. However, over time, the smoke dissipated. We had to light more bundles; we were running out of sage. The ghosts remained outside, making awful faces at us through the windows.

"That's all of it," Archer rasped, shaking the last bits of smoke from the final bundle. "We're flat out. Now what?"

"Sweetgrass," Kellas stated, and pulled out the only two braids we had. He and Archer took those around, smudging everywhere we'd already been. Orianthi followed them, singing the Hidatsa prayer. Slowly, slowly, the smoke thinned out those same crevices the ghosts had entered through. As the smoke cleared, the ghosts started crowding nearer, nasty evil grins on their misty faces.

Nan arrived on the back deck riding Moon Dancer, crashing down in their midst like an avenging angel. "*Ag magadh atá tú, spiorad olc!* Away with you, evil spirits!" The ghosts scattered, wailing in despair as her curses hit them.

Bran, Nan's hellhound, was there, too, eyes blood-red, white streams of saliva dripping from his open jaws. He slashed and snapped at the misty monsters, tearing them apart until they were no more. Even the normal variety of mist fled.

As of one mind, we all ran out onto the deck. I was dimly aware that Archer had picked Orianthi up. She was clinging to his neck, terrified. Kellas crowded my elbow, protective.

"Raven!" Nan's voice held an edge of panic. "Call Knight. We're needed at the mine. Your father and the others, they're in trouble. There's no time to lose!"

"Knight! I need you!" I yelled, then grabbed my grandmother's stirrup. "What's happening, Nan? What can we do?"

"I'm making this up as I go," she snapped. "Archer, take Orianthi to your grandparents. She'll be safe there. Kellas, go with them."

"But who will guard my tree?" the dryad wailed. "They want to kill my tree!"

"I'll do it." Archer declared, his voice hard. He set Orianthi down. "It's our tree, too. Our contract. Our peace." He meant the Haudenosaunee. "Tell my clan, Kellas. Have them come prepared."

"There's bows and arrows in the shed, Swamp Monster," Kellas told him. "If you prefer guns, those are locked up in the safe. You know the combination." Then the Cait Sidhe grabbed Orianthi's hand and ran with her to the car.

Knight arrived with a snort and a rear, excitement flashing in his eyes like fire. Yeah. That's not an exaggeration. Fire it was. If there was any doubt about his demon parentage, that put any lingering questions I might have had to rest.

I grabbed a handful of mane and swung on bareback. No time for saddles or handy stuff like that. Good thing I'd been practicing!

"This way," Nan called as she launched Moon Dancer off the deck skyward, Bran in hot pursuit. Knight leapt after his dam, and we sped eastward across the lake like two swallows. We quickly arrived where the ambulance was still parked, quiet and dark. Nan dismounted gracefully; I just threw a leg over Knight's neck and slid to the ground.

"Now what?" I whispered, not knowing where Dad and his team had gone nor what Nan had planned once we found them.

"I told you. I'm making this up as I go." She led me across the road and down a long driveway toward a clump of dark buildings, Bran trotting along at our heels.

Everything was quiet, unnaturally so. "Shouldn't there be guards or something? The mining company wouldn't want just anyone to waltz on in, I should think." I was still whispering, but it seemed loud.

Nan put an arm out to stop me as we reached the corner of a building. "Make yourself less visible," she whispered. "There were guards. They've been taken. Now hush and follow me." She disappeared, as did Bran, blending in perfectly against the metal siding of the building. "Watch for motion," she cautioned. I saw a slight shimmer in the air as she raised an arm and pointed at a door that stood ajar a few feet away.

I followed the shimmer, but it was not easy. I had to concentrate like mad. I hoped I was as well disguised as she was.

There were red emergency lights spaced at large intervals inside the building. The lights cast strangely shaped shadows across the concrete floor. A low, continual hum came from an enormous metal fan that was blowing air down a large square hole. The fan must have been 12 feet in diameter.

"This is Air Shaft 4," Nan told me in an undertone. "It's incomplete. Once it's done, they'll remove the building and put up a huge metal tower to support the salt elevator they'll install. Meanwhile, there's a temporary lift. We can go most of the way down on that. But the last hundred feet or so, we'll have to belay ourselves." She drew in a deep breath. "They might hear the lift coming down and investigate, but it will appear empty. Hopefully, the assumption will be that the lift malfunctioned. Once we're on the ropes, we can disguise those and ourselves to escape notice."

I thought about the enormous area below. Seven miles of tunnels.... "Where are they?"

She drew a deep breath. "North. There's a place where no tunnels were supposed to have been dug, near an anomaly in the rock. It's on a level that isn't supposed to exist because it's too high up under the lake. The rock layer there is very thin."

Nan took my arm. "Come on." She stepped onto a flat platform that had only the scantest of safety rails around the edge. Bran and I followed. She pushed a button on a control panel and we started down. The lift made just the quietest whirring. The company's workers certainly kept the lift well-maintained. A good thing, since it went down something like a couple thousand feet.

The air the huge fan was forcing past us was frigid. Like standing in a gale-force wind on a winter day. I felt half frozen before we had even descended 50 feet. My thin jacket didn't protect me much from the cold.

No one stopped us because no one was watching. When we had gone as far as the lift could take us, we found the climbing gear Dad and his crew had left. The shaft became narrower here. I could stretch my arms out and almost touch the sides. We strapped ourselves in. Bran needed no such assistance; he just stepped off into thin air and disappeared down the shaft. I had a moment of vertigo when I stepped off into nothing at the top of my belay, but that went away quickly.

We didn't have far to go and were soon at the bottom. Here, the air was drier and smelled of salt, like the sea. It was much warmer, too. Topside, the air had cooled to below 40°F. After the cold outside and the arctic blast in the shaft, the mine itself promised to be downright balmy.

Nan had gone on ahead of me, not that I could see where she or Bran were. Besides being disguised, we were in deep darkness. There were very few lights in the shaft and even fewer down here. There was just the faintest sound, like rock being disturbed, that let me know where Nan was. I touched bottom shortly after her, unzipped my jacket, and gratefully shucked off the uncomfortable harness.

A small light bloomed: Nan had pulled up a moonbeam in the palm of her hand and sent it upward, hovering overhead some yards in front of us. "This way," I heard her whisper, and the light moved away—barely more than a will-o'-the-wisp. Nan remained invisible, as did I.

At first, her light did little to reveal the space we were making our way through. Although, I was aware of a vastness around us, like a huge cavern or a stone cathedral. Giant stone pillars supported the ceiling. The farther we went, the more the tunnel narrowed, with a low, rocky roof. Here, Nan's light reflected off ugly, hulking machinery—long, squat things with heavy, wide tires and enormous bucket loaders on the front. I wondered how they had gotten these monsters down here in the first place. But we were on a rescue mission. There was no head space for simple curiosity.

We stayed close to one of the walls. When I laid my hand on it to balance myself, it felt rough and left a gritty feeling on my skin. The ground under my feet was littered with rocks; not smooth. It made walking quietly very tricky.

Conveyor belts supported by thick metal cables attached to the rocky ceiling ran through the entire length of the tunnel. Power cables draped in thick loops; heavy duty mesh was secured to the wall where the rock was crumbling. Reflective, bowl-shaped silver disks were held in place above us by what looked like massive bolts drilled into the rock. We passed an old-fashioned telephone haphazardly stuck to the wall. Salt dust frosted every surface. The smell never lessened; I could taste it on my lips whenever I moistened them nervously.

Being underground was not my thing at all. And the fact that millions of tons of water lay above the rock over my head, just made me feel more claustrophobic. I could feel my heart beating faster thinking about that little detail. How the miners managed this day after day defied imagination. Either they were immune to the feeling, or they simply gave it no thought. It sure wasn't anything I would want to do...but maybe they didn't have other options. They had families to support. The job paid well, so they just stepped up to the challenge. I shuddered. Give me the sun and the sky any day over burrowing into the earth.

My attention came back to where I was. I saw Nan's light stop and grew dimmer. "We're close," she whispered. "I can hear them up ahead."

I fumbled around until I found Nan's arm, then muttered in her ear. "What's the plan?"

"Let's see what they're up to." She took my hand, and we eased forward to where we could look around the corner. Light was spilling from beyond yet another bend in the rock. Very slowly, placing our feet carefully to avoid disturbing loose rocks, we moved closer until we could see around the bend into a larger cavern, one that resembled the size of the first we had passed through.

However, this space resembled a throne room with carved arches. The stone walls were smooth and clean; torches burned brightly at regular intervals. On the far side of the room was a dais, complete with a stone throne. A large man reclined indolently upon it, his hands draped over the arms.

He must have been seven feet tall, if not taller—although, with him seated, that was only a guess. He had broad shoulders under a black T-shirt, his chest was deep and powerful. Tight jeans showed off muscular thighs. Heavy boots, well dusted with salt, covered his feet. He was beautiful in a magnetic, terrible way. Power rolled off him like thunder, catching my attention and holding it fast. I was mesmerized, like a mouse by a snake. Dother. It had to be. The resemblance to his brothers was obvious.

Nan pinched me hard enough to leave a bruise, but it broke the hold Dother had over me. I had no idea how she knew the god affected me that way, but I was grateful.

Dad was on his knees before the throne, his hands bound behind his back. His teammates and Ian were nearby, also trussed, laid out like mice in front of Old Brown, the owl in Beatrice Potter's *Squirrel Nutkin*. Like an offering. A sacrifice.

Lined up behind the throne were a dozen or so strong-looking men in hard hats and blue jeans: miners. They stood at ease, like in the military—their hands clasped behind their backs, legs straddled, gazes empty. There was something seriously awry with them, but I didn't know what.

Dub and Dian stood on either side of my father and his team; they had regained a semblance of physical form but remained mere shadows of their former selves. Somehow, though, I knew they were rebuilding their bodies. After all, they were gods. Unkillable. The thought made my blood run cold.

Dother spoke, his voice deep and powerful. "We meet again, son of the moon witch. How is your mother these days? She must be getting up there in years, no?"

Dad said nothing.

Unbothered by his silence, Dother only chuckled. "I expect she'll show up soon and I can see for myself. But, the more immediate issue is, what shall I do with you all, hmm? I can't have you littering up my mining operation." He gestured lazily at an odd-looking machine that squatted to one side. "My drill for placing explosives," he explained. "I didn't even have to bring one in. These kind folks use it in their own mining operations. Imagine that, will you? Blasting with anhydrous ammonia under a lake. Risky business, don't you agree?"

Dad did not respond, but Dother didn't seem to notice. The god was building enthusiasm for his own plans as he spoke. "I was told by one of these fine gentlemen," he gestured toward the miners "that they have been ordered not to drill in this area, that the rock above is unstable and could fracture, causing the lake to collapse into the mine, flooding it and destroying the lake itself. Now, doesn't that sound like fun?" He leaned back against his throne and smiled smugly. "I think so."

"Sounds like something you'd enjoy." Dad's voice was low, but I could hear the undercurrent of anger there.

Dother threw his head back and laughed. "Oh, yes. I shall so enjoy watching. Death! Destruction! Environmental catastrophe! And it can all be blamed on human greed, human frailty. Human stupidity." He leaned forward as he said this last bit, the smile gone, replaced with savagery. "Humans make my job so incredibly easy!"

A hand on my arm was pressing me back, pulling me away from the scene playing out before us. Nan drew me well back from the cavern before whispering in my ear. "You need to go sound the alarm. They need help here."

"Go where? Call who?" I demanded. "What can I tell them that won't make them dismiss me as a nutcase?"

"Call 911, then the Environmental Protection Agency's rapid response number. You can find it online. They take reports of threats very seriously," Nan assured me.

"My phone's dead."

Nan groaned. "Here's mine. Try not to fry it, too." She handed me her cell phone. "Now, go! There's no time to waste."

I nodded and went.

Twenty-One

I flitted back through the mine as silently as I could, making sure to note the things we had passed earlier: the old phone, the conveyors, the machinery. This helped guide me through the rabbit warren of tunnels, back to the bottom of Air Shaft 4. I used the belaying rope to climb up to the elevator, then sent it whirring up and out. Glad to be free of the claustrophobic confines of the mine, I made my way out of the steel building into the open, where I started seeking a decent cell signal. Fortunately, that wasn't a problem.

I dialed 911 and waited. Then, waited some more. Puzzled, I hung up and dialed the number again. Yes, it rang through, but then there was utter silence, like the line was dead or something. I tried a third time; same results. I gave up, looked up the number for the EPA and called them instead. Again, same results. What the heck? Then it occurred to me. Dother would have anticipated the possibility of someone calling for help. He'd have done something to mess up the signals, somehow.

I took off at a dead run, up the sloping driveway to where we had left the horses. I found them grazing in the meadow. "Knight, we need to go get help!" I gasped. He came over immediately, as did Moon Dancer. She pushed a picture of my Nan urgently into my consciousness, questioning. "She's in the mine." I gestured north. "That way. All the way to the end." Moon Dancer snorted and disappeared in a burst of moonbeams. I swung up on Knight's back. "Let's go..."

I'd hardly blurted that out when Knight launched himself aloft with the speed of a comet. It did not take us long to reach the city. Knight took us directly to the Ithaca Police Department. How he had known where we needed to go was something I'd have to figure out later.

Unfortunately, Knight nearly landed on an officer who was just exiting the building. The cop overreacted, of course. Nearly being landed on by a horse coming out of nowhere is enough to push a few swear-word buttons for the calmest of people. And this guy wasn't the calm sort to begin with. He cut loose with a whole sentence full of cuss words.

As the officer didn't seem to be ready to stop his irreverent soliloquy, I pitched my voice higher and talked right over him. "They're going to blow up the salt mine; we need help," I told him as I slid off Knight's back.

His response was to grab me by the upper arm and rush me into the police station. "I don't know where you get off riding a horse into my town, but it's against all regulations. Your parents are going to hear about this." His face was nearly purple with rage. (Just my luck to run into this guy first!)

I twisted out of his grip. Now it was my turn to be upset. "Did you not hear a word I just said?" I enunciated. "They are going. To blow up. The salt mine."

He scoffed and reached for me again. I fell back into a defensive posture, elbows tight to my side, fists up, legs bent. "Are you listening?" I was yelling now. "Am I going to have to thump you to get your attention? They are rigging the salt mine with explosives and they have *hostages*!"

Our spat had gained us plenty of attention. A number of uniformed police officers had hurried into the front room. The one who'd given me a ride to the hospital a few weeks ago was among them, thank goodness. "That's Doc Callahan's kid," he told the others. "What do you mean, there are people rigging the mine to blow?" he asked me. "Who are they?"

I eased out of my defensive crouch and sent the angry cop a last sideways glance to make sure he wasn't going to try to grab me again. "I think they're terrorists." It was unlikely anyone would believe a bunch of Old Gods were responsible for this! And besides, they fit the description. "They kidnapped one of Dad's nurses and Dad and his team went into the salt mine to rescue him. They got in through the unfinished air duct."

I strode over to the nice cop and grabbed one of his hands in both of mine, giving him the biggest pleading puppy-dog eyes I was capable of. "You've got to believe me!"

The young cop's forehead furrowed with a conflicted frown, like he was torn between skepticism and wanting to ride to my rescue.

I shook his arm, hard. "They found out explosives are being placed under the weak spot up by Frontenac Point. But they got captured. They're hostages, along with about a dozen mine workers. But the terrorists did something to them. It's like the miners have been hypnotized or something. They're...not themselves."

"This is what happens when amateurs try to handle situations like this," the angry cop grumbled.

My cop shook his head. "Callahan's team are all ex–special forces. They knew what they were doing." He turned back to me. "Sorry, kid, I never got your first name."

"I'm Raven. Can you get a hostage team down there? And a bomb squad? Right away?" My voice choked up. "It's my *dad!*"

He pulled his hand free and patted my shoulder awkwardly. "We'll call in the SWAT team and get them out. Don't you fret."

Things got busy then; there was a lot of shouting and running, guns, gear, and sirens. It was a lot more than I could process. My cop grilled me about the situation, a lot of who, what, where, when, why, and how questions—which

I did my best to answer. Then I was hustled into a corner out of the way, where I guessed they expected me to stay. Like that was gonna happen!

I slipped out during the melee and found Knight waiting in some deep shadows around the corner of the building. He'd gone unnoticed by the police. "Let's blow this popsicle stand," I muttered and wheeled him back north. I don't think anyone saw us leave.

Knight took me right inside the mine this time, floating us straight down the shaft like he himself was an elevator. It was a tight fit near the bottom where they hadn't finished widening it yet, but he managed. Knight made it quite clear that was as far as he would take me, though. He gave me giving his familiar "wiggle-woggle-itchy" shake the moment we touched down at the bottom. It was obvious I was to get the heck off. Then he faded into the shadows and snorted quietly. I understood his meaning: *I'll be here when you get back.*

I resumed my blend-into-the-background glamour as we approached the mine. Unfortunately, I hadn't yet learned Nan's clever spell for pulling up a moonbeam. As it turned out, it didn't matter. At some point, red emergency lights came on, dimly illuminating the tunnels with an otherworldly glow. They were placed far apart, so the spaces in between were still slow to navigate—but I knew where I was going. That helped.

A sound I could not place echoed down the corridor. It was a constant grating noise, like someone running a very large blender on high. I followed the sound. It was coming from where I knew the Old Gods were gathered— where Dad and everyone else was trapped. The sound stopped just as I reached the cavern.

I eased into the spot where I'd left Nan an hour earlier, hoping I would find her, but she wasn't there. I took a deep breath and looked around the corner into the brightly lit cavern.

The A-Team and Ian were no longer laid out like offerings in front of Dother's throne. A quick glance around found them in one of the alcoves, trapped behind a metal grate that covered the entire front of the alcove. At least they were no longer trussed up like dead meat. However, Dad was still on his knees before Dother, still bound. He was swaying just the tiniest bit, like he was stunned. There was a large miner on either side of him now; one held a long silver-colored rod that had two prongs jutting from one end.

"Let's do this again, my friend. And *try a little harder* this time, yes? Where is the moon witch?" Dother sounded bored, maybe even a little annoyed, but also eerily patient.

Dad straightened up as best he could. I could see the effort it was requiring of him. "She's not here. I don't know where she is. And even if I knew, I wouldn't tell you."

Dother grunted. "Hit him again, Dub."

One of the miners grinned in an all-too-familiar baring of teeth. If there had been any doubt in my mind that the man was possessed by one of the twins, that grin dispelled it. "Gladly," he said, and stabbed my father with the end of the silver rod. There was a horrible sizzling, crackling sound. My father jerked violently, collapsed to the floor, and lay spasming.

I clapped both hands over my mouth to keep from crying out. Ian threw himself at the iron grate that held him and the others captive. "Cut it out! You'll kill him if you keep it up!" Dad's teammates were all yelling threats mixed in with some truly foul language.

Dother laughed. "You humans are so amusing. What does it matter if I kill him, or any of you for that matter? You're all going to die anyways. Why not hurry things along a bit?" He pointed at the man not holding the cattle prod. "Pick him up, Dian."

The other miner bent and hauled Dad back to his knees but had to hold him there, because he was as limp as cooked spaghetti.

"Hit him again," Dother said, a murderous expression on his face. "Make sure he dies this time."

"No!" I was hardly aware of screaming this as I bolted to my feet, my right hand reaching back to pull Fraegarthach.

"Ah, there you are," a familiar voice said behind me. And something very hard and heavy collided with the back of my skull.

I regained consciousness painfully; someone was dragging me by my hair. It had grown back with unusual rapidity after the Lughnasadh incident, and after three short months it was nearly down to my shoulders. I was starting to understand Nan's comment about the advantages of short hair. This would be one of those.

I struggled, trying to free myself and get back on my feet. My captor kept kicking my feet out from under me. They dragged me over to Dother's throne, where I was dropped like a sack of potatoes next to my dad, who lay unmoving. My father's eyes were closed, his breathing rapid and shallow. I was unsure if he could hear me, but I jackknifed my torso closer anyways and put my mouth close to his ear. "Help is coming." It may have been the quietest of whispers, but it earned me a booted foot in the ribs, forcing the air from my lungs in a pained gasp.

"The moon brat!" the familiar voice crowed. "I knew she would be hanging around, the arrogant wee princess!"

I knew who it was now. She'd called me that not so long ago. Erin…a *traitor*?

"Get her on her feet," said Dother, a note of amusement in his voice. "I want to see the child who so thoroughly unmanned my baby brothers."

Dub's and Dian's possessed miners grabbed me by the arms and hauled me to my feet like I weighed nothing, then abruptly released me, cursing. I dimly wondered if they had been zapped by Fraegarthach, like Kellas once had. And whether these two were aware of how stupid they sounded when all they did is was swear. My vision was unfocused, and it made me even more nauseous than I already was. Blows to the head are unadvisable. I'd had far too many knocks to the bean lately as it was. It made me very weak, weaving slightly as I tried to look at Dother.

Dother was not alone on his throne. Erin had draped herself, catlike, across his lap. Aware I was watching, she nuzzled him under his chin, then planted a very messy, open-mouthed kiss square on his mouth.

He tumbled her impatiently off his lap. "Not now, kitten. I'm busy."

Erin gathered herself up with as much dignity as she could, then laid a possessive hand on the back of his throne. She glared at me like it was my fault he'd tossed her off his lap.

Dother leaned forward. "How very unremarkable looking you are," he mused. "One wonders how such a small and insignificant creature has put so many stumbling blocks in my path."

Small and insignificant. Wow. Nice guy! "You'd be surprised," I said, startling myself nearly as much as it did him.

He recovered quickly. "Really?" he chuckled. "Aren't you the spunky one." He rose with the liquid grace of a tiger and descended from the dais. "Put him with the others," he instructed, shoving Dad with a booted toe.

His brothers obeyed without hesitation, hauling Dad to his feet and dragging him to the prison alcove. They threatened Ian and the A-Team away with the cattle prod while they opened the cell door far enough to shove Dad through. He collapsed as they released him and would have fallen to the floor had Ian not caught him. The grate was closed and locked again.

Dother paced around me, peering closely at me with calculating eyes, like he was memorizing everything visible about me. "You really are a tiny thing."

"David and Goliath," I retorted, but it was straining every nerve in my body not to let him see how terrified I was. I desperately hoped that the SWAT team would arrive soon. From a distance, Dother exuded unmistakable power; up close, he felt like imminent death. Tremors started rippling throughout my body despite my best efforts to hold still. No doubt the Morrigan was lurking nearby, death being her thing.

"What shall I do with you, hmm?" He stopped in front of me, a thoughtful expression on his face. One arm was crossed over his middle, the other elbow braced on it, his chin resting on one fist. "Shall I give you to Dub, as compensation for you depriving him of his favorite arrow? He seems to find you oddly attractive—I never have understood his taste in women!" He dropped his arms to his sides and resumed pacing around me. "Or maybe I will give you to Dian, to repay him for that lightning bolt you exploded him with? They'll both fully regain their bodies in time; I daresay they will want to make you pay for the inconvenience you put them through." Then he gave me a smile that shot pure terror through me. "Or! Shall I keep you for myself?" That smile said clearly what being *kept for himself* would entail. I shuddered at the thought. "You might prove amusing, at least for a little while," he added softly.

At the edge of my vision, I could see Erin's face darken in rage. Not one to share, Kellas had said. Not that I had any desire to compete with her for Dother's attentions, whatever dark and awful things he might have in mind.

"Or!" He turned and stepped back up to his throne, seating himself with effortless grace. "I could use you as a bargaining chip, ransom you in exchange for the moon witch. She's the one that matters." He made a dismissive gesture with one hand. "You are, as Dub puts it, only a *tasty tidbit*. Your brand-new magic will increase my own by only a fraction. Hers, however, will make me unbeatable. I could rule the world."

He scowled then and turned toward the miners, who were standing idly by the drilling machine, their eyes vacant. "Don't you have a job to do? Get the blasting caps and explosives loaded into the holes and wire up the detonating cord. Must I do all your thinking for you?" They jumped into action, hurrying to follow his instructions. He turned back to me. "I was only joking, small one. Of course I must do all their thinking for them. I've deprived them of conscious thought. Nice little robots, all of them."

He considered me through narrowed eyes for a beat. "Now, where were we?" He tapped a forefinger against his lips. "Oh yes, that's what I shall do with you." He beckoned to the two miners his brothers had taken over. "Dub, Dian, string her up. Over there, where the prisoners have a clear view of the show. Humans have such lovely emotions. I will enjoy feeling them wash over me. And yours, little one," he said with a nasty smile on his lips, "will be even more enjoyable. Erin, dearest, bring me my tool kit."

I hadn't drawn Fraegarthach while I had the opportunity. I wanted to, truly. But my body would not obey my mind. I felt frozen—could not move so much as a pinkie. It was probably because of the effect Dother had on me. Like earlier, when Nan had pinched me to break his hold over me. At any rate, I didn't...couldn't...resist as the twins took me by my arms and dragged me to the alcove Dother had indicated. This time, it didn't bother them to touch me, like I no longer could zap them with my sword's power. Fear had somehow deprived me of that ability.

They tied my wrists to two ropes hanging from the upper arch of the alcove opening so that I was suspended with my arms uplifted in a Y, my feet barely touching the ground. That would have been awful enough, except then Dub leaned in close to my ear and whispered some very explicit and horrible things he had planned for me should I be given to him. Then he deliberately ran his open hand over my breasts. The shock unfroze me, and I smashed the side of my head into his face with all the force I could muster. He yelled in pain and staggered back, both hands going to where blood was spurting liberally from his nose. Dian roared with laughter. Dub swore, wrapped his bloody hands around my throat and squeezed.

I must have blacked out momentarily, because when I came to, the miner Dub had been occupying lay in a broken heap to one side. Dub himself was back to being barely more than a glaring black ghost hovering nearby.

"You will not harm this child!" Dother roared at him, the force of his words shredding Dub's misty body even further. "That," he declared, turning his back on his brother, and fixing his quelling gaze on me, "is *my* job." He held out a hand to Erin, who was hovering nearby, a black box open in her hands. "The dull one, kitten. I don't wish her to bleed to death. At least not yet."

She extended a long, wickedly curved blade to him. Something that looked like rust was smeared liberally along the edge.

"I've changed my mind." Dother had cocked his head to one side, studying me with the calculating expression back on his face. It made me feel like my blood had turned to ice. "I shall require a larger area on which to work my magic. A razor, please."

Her lips drawing back in a furious snarl, Erin replaced the first blade and handed him something that looked like a scalpel. He examined it carefully, then nodded. "This will do. Now, I recommend not wiggling, little girl; you would not want me to slip with this!" He reached up and slowly cut the sleeve of my jacket away from my right arm, then across the front of it and through the zipper. He repeated the process with the other sleeve, and my jacket fell to the floor. "Now this bit of attire," he whispered, taking hold of my T-shirt. There was more threat in those seemingly harmless words than any of the explicit nastiness Dub had spewed in my ear earlier.

I was shuddering violently despite trying to hold myself very, very still. His eyes met mine, and he smiled. It wasn't a nice smile. "I am beginning to see what Dub found so alluring about you," he said, his words almost a caress.

"Your emotions are so very...fresh. Shall we see what you have hiding behind this?"

"You're d-disgusting." I managed between teeth clenched against the chattering.

He just laughed softly. "I am only getting started, darling." He delicately sliced down one sleeve and across the front of my T-shirt.

"Animal!" someone yelled from the prisoner alcove. I had no idea who.

Dother never stopped grinning. "Yes, I am," he agreed in the mildest tones, then he grabbed the collar of my T-shirt and violently ripped it completely off. His gaze lingered over my nearly naked upper body. Sighed. "What a disappointment!" He slipped a forefinger under my running bra strap and tugged on it. "This does nothing to enhance your charms, my dear. You really ought to find someone to fit you properly. I would suggest something lacy and barely there." His touch was icy-cold, leaving the patch of skin where he'd touched me feeling like it had been frostbitten.

"It does the job it's meant for," I forced between my teeth. What was keeping the SWAT team? I didn't think I could manage to stay brave in the face of Dother's emotional torture much longer.

He huffed a small laugh. "Shall we rid you of these ugly jeans as well?"

Something like a growl emerged from Erin's mouth.

I shook my head vehemently. I'd worn the scantest of my panties this morning. It was bad enough I was strung up in front of an audience in only my running bra. No way did I want everyone to see what I had on under my jeans.

He laughed again. "Oh, very well, I'll grant you that at least. I'm not a complete monster, after all."

Oh, wasn't he!

"But what's this?" His attention was suddenly caught by the leather thong around my neck, the one that held my medallion. It had slipped behind my bra, mostly hidden. He reached for it. I reared back, not wanting those icy fingers to touch me *or* my medallion.

Fortunately for me, his attention got distracted. He strode away to the far side of the cavern where the miners had stopped loading the explosives. He picked two of the men up like they weighed nothing at all, despite the lighter one being a minimum of 220 pounds (best guess). Then he smashed their heads together and tossed them, insensible, against the far sides of the cavern. "Get to work, you worthless bits of rotting meat!"

'Brannaugh, listen up,' Kellas's achingly familiar voice spoke into my brain. *'Amaris is waiting above the lake with reinforcements. Hang in there. When I cut you down, take Rhiannon's ring off your pinkie and throw it up against the ceiling, while calling out the following as loudly as you can:*

"Hail Rhiannon, hear my cry,

Open up the earth to sky,

Send your moonbeams shining down,

So they reach me, underground."

'He's coming back. Be strong, sweetheart,' he encouraged.

Hope surged through me. Kellas was here, and he'd called me *sweetheart.* I felt a large furry body press up against the back of my legs, proving he was *very* nearby. All cats are invisible—when they want to be. I sure hoped he was.

The miners were now working feverishly, and Dother was striding back my way, his mood turning dark and dangerous. "Give me that," he snarled at Erin, snatching the curved knife from the box she was holding open for him and glaring at me from eyes that had gone red as fire. "We're running out of time here, so I'm going to make an example out of you, little girl. When that moon witch finally shows up, she will see just what I think of her and her nasty offspring."

Then he cut me in an ugly curving line from my hairline down across one eyebrow, barely missing my eye, but cutting deep over my cheekbone down to my jaw.

The pain was unimaginable. I must have screamed, although horror and shock temporarily lifted me out of my body and made everything surreal. Erin was cackling maniacally, taking pleasure in my agony. The men imprisoned in the alcove were shouting and cursing.... And then Kellas cut me loose with a single slash of his dagger. I collapsed to my knees, sobbing. "The ring, Brannaugh!" he yelled, before lunging at Dother, his dagger foremost.

Half-blinded by the blood pouring down my face, I pulled off the slender silver band Rhiannon had given me just three months before when I'd saved her from marrying a zombie and threw it with all my remaining strength at the ceiling.

"Hail Rhiannon, hear my cry!" I screamed the words Kellas had told me and watched as the tiny silver band tumbled over and up, hit the ceiling of the cavern...and stuck...growing sideways into an immense circle. It pushed back the rock, expanded rapidly upward, and thrust itself through the layers of rock salt and stone until it reached the bottom layers of the lake. Even then it didn't stop, but rushed upward through the water, shoving that back like it was nothing, creating a silver shaft that exploded out of the lake's surface before it stopped growing—allowing the glorious light of the Blue Moon to shine straight down into the cavern below.

For the briefest of moments, everything was a frozen tableau. Everyone in the cavern stared in a mixture of awe and horror as the ring bored upward through rock and water. However, the instant that moonlight shone where no moon had ever shed its light before, everything descended into chaos.

Nan came down the shaft, riding Moon Dancer. She was armed with a spear that sparked with an energy like that of Fraegarthach's. Two brilliant beings made of light energy rode silver horses on either side of Nan. They were so bright; it was impossible to tell for sure what they were. If I had to guess, I'd have said they were the moon goddesses Rhiannon and Cerridwen.

Dother tossed Kellas aside as if he were no more trouble than an annoying fly and met their attack with a shout of triumph. He morphed into an even larger giant than before, but his lower body was no longer that of a man. Instead, it was the scaled body of a dragon; heavy leather wings sprouting from his back. In his hands was a black trident that hummed with an unnamable power.

Suddenly, Elias appeared, running over to where the others were imprisoned in the alcove. Dian threw himself after Elias, roaring in anger. Dub, no slouch, found himself another miner to inhabit and went after Kellas. The Cait

Si had barely enough time to transform into their avatars before the twins were upon them. Elias was the largest lion I'd ever seen. And Kellas...well.... Kellas did justice to panthers everywhere.

Then there was Erin. Screaming in fury, she threw herself on me, knocking me to the ground and wrapping her hands around my neck. "Die, you little...." And here she repeated the female dog expletive. But what else could I expect from her? She's a sweet one. Not that it mattered now; I was fighting for my life. I broke her grip by shoving my forearms between hers and clawing at her eyes. Street-fighter tactics. But as they say, all's fair in love and war. And this was definitely war. We tumbled over and over, each trying to gain the upper position. Neither of us succeeded in holding it. I finally managed to smash her head against the floor. Her grip lessened enough that I was able to break free and scramble to my feet.

Not that I was rid of her, however. Snarling, she transformed into her tiger self, tail lashing in fury. And not your ordinary everyday tiger, either. No. Erin's Cait Sidhe avatar form was a saber-tooth. She was bigger and meaner. And wow, those canine teeth were impressive. Hers were a foot long, like curved blades with serrations on both edges.

There was no time to stare. She lunged at me, one huge paw reaching out and swiping me across the ribs as I drew Fraegarthach. Her claws raked deep, knocking me back and spinning me around as I morphed into my avatar warrior form. I rolled over and over on the floor, and only got to my feet an instant before she was on me again. Those terrible teeth were way too close for comfort. Unable to use my sword as a sword, I smashed the hand guard against the side of her head and leapt back as she dropped to her belly, dazed.

That's when I should have finished her, but we locked gazes. This was Erin, Nan's erstwhile friend. How could I kill her? I hesitated.

Big mistake.

She had no such qualms and immediately sprang at me, those terrible canine teeth wide open and aiming for my throat. I did the only thing I could; I cut them out of her mouth with a focused swing of Fraegarthach's blade.

I didn't know teeth like that could be so incredibly fragile. They broke off as easily as breaking icicles from the eaves of a roof. I watched in horror as Erin collapsed to the floor, reverting to her human form. Her hands were clamped over her mouth, where blood gushed liberally, spilling through her fingers. She was sobbing, curled up defensively like a hurt child.

A terrible cry yanked my attention to where Nan was battling Dother. She was bleeding heavily. They were still locked in a fierce battle, neither gaining the upper hand as they parried and thrust with their weapons, sparks flying everywhere like those of an arc welder. Sometime during their battle, the stone throne had been smashed to bits. The drilling machine Dother had forced the miners to use to place explosives was damaged, its segmented cranelike arm twisted and bent to uselessness. The miners had regained enough self-awareness to move away from the fray, albeit far too slowly, like sleepwalkers. The ones who remained unhurt were helping those who were incapacitated.

Kellas and Elias still battled the remaining two possessed miners. They were hampered by their desire not to hurt the men but still wanted to stop Dub and Dian from joining forces with their brother. They'd pushed the twins back toward the entrance of the cavern, distancing themselves from the battle behind.

My father and the others remained locked in the alcove. I needed to get them out. Now. Sheathing Fraegarthach in one smooth motion, I ran over and grabbed the bars.

Before I could say a word, one of Dad's men was pointing to a spot just outside of their cage. "The key! There! Covered in dirt. Find it!"

I dropped to my knees and felt around frantically. Nothing...

"More that way!" I looked up to see them all pointing a few feet away from where I was running my hands through the powdered dirt. I moved and continued to search. My fingers touched a hard, slender object. The key.

I lifted it, tossed it to them.... And there was a shout of warning.

It came too late. Erin fell on me, knocking me to the floor, one of her saber teeth gripped in one hand, raised high. There was a crazed look in her green eyes; the entire lower half of her face was covered with gore. With a wordless cry, she stabbed the tooth down. I twisted away as best I could and her blow, aimed at my jugular, buried the tooth between my neck and shoulder. Screaming in frustration, she yanked the tooth out and drew her arm back, intending to stab me again.

After that, things got a bit messed up in my head. Someone was screaming (likely me), and suddenly there were men everywhere. One person smashed Erin off me. Someone else pressed a hand against the wound in my shoulder, trying to slow the gush of blood pouring out. Then everyone was yelling in alarm. I was unceremoniously scooped off the floor, and we were running, running.... Behind us, a terrible rumbling sound swelled and grew while salt dust and stone grit blasted against us in a gust of super-heated air—pushing everyone from the cavern at a stumbling run.

As suddenly as it had started, the rumbling stopped. The air stilled, leaving dust swirling around us. Somebody coughed. Someone else swore under his breath. Dad appeared, leaning over me, horror stamped on his face like a mask. "We've got to get her to the hospital. Now!"

Then there was the sound of many running feet and rough shouts. "Everyone, face down. On the ground. Hands behind your heads!" More shouting. Confusion. I floated in and out of consciousness, so I didn't know exactly what was going on, other than the cavalry had arrived (in the form of the Ithaca Police Department SWAT team). They immediately assumed *we* were the bad guys.

They must have figured things out quickly, though. It didn't seem like all that long before I felt men gather around me, sliding their hands under my body from multiple directions. They lifted me on the count of three, then laid me back down on a blanket. I felt someone press fabric over my shoulder wound, then carefully wind something around my chest and shoulder to hold the makeshift bandage in place. It hurt terribly, and I groaned. "Hang in there, kid," I heard someone say (maybe one of Dad's paramedics?). Then they were lifting me, jostling me despite their best efforts to be gentle. I may have passed out. Mostly, I was in and out, like a bad dream.

More voices...

"My god, what happened to her face?"

"Shut up, fool. What if she can hear you?"

"What the hell happened here?"

"She was attacked by a giant cat."

"Did they actually collapse the mine?"

"No, the anhydrous never went off."

"But how do you explain all that rock?"

"Who were they, anyways? Iranians? Russians?"

I was dimly aware of the whirring sound the lift made as it brought me and the others up and out of the mine, the freezing cold in the air shaft, then of being carried out into the night, and the light of the full moon shining down on us. I was lifted into the back of my father's ambulance and settled onto the stretcher there. Then held down and strapped in place while I fought against the restraints, crying out in fear—until there was a prick on my arm and I tumbled down, down into darkness.

~

There were moments when I regained consciousness, although I was never truly awake. I heard voices, mostly, like ghosts who made their way on tiptoe through my mind.

Once I heard Dad talking with someone else: a man. He had an English accent.

"Can you repair her face so she won't scar?"

"Geez, Michael, there's dirt and crap ground into the cut so deep, there's no way to get it all out. She'll have that scar like a dark mark, forever."

"But you're the best there is. Surely you can…"

"Bloody hell, Michael, I'm a cosmetic surgeon, not a ruddy miracle worker. I know she's your kid and all, but…" Then, nothing.

Another time. Familiar voices: Archer and Kellas.

"If she dies, I'll never forgive myself."

"She'll make it, bro. She's a fighter. You've got to have faith."

"What if she doesn't?"

"Now you're being stupid, Cat Man."

I wanted to open my eyes, to speak, tell them I was alive, that I heard them, but it was as though my eyelids were stuck shut, and my lips could not move to form the words. I passed out again.

My dreams, at least I hoped they were dreams, were dark and ugly. In one of them, Erin visited me. She had new canine teeth, as long and silver and sharp as those of a vampire. The tips of the upper ones rested on the outside of her lower lip.

"Well, well, moon brat. Looks like you'll bear Dother's mark on your face for the rest of your short, miserable life." She laughed. It was an ugly sound. "Not that you will be sporting it for long."

I didn't reply. It's never a good idea to respond to bullying.

"Don't you want to *know* why? Oh, never mind, I'm going to tell you whether you like it or not. Remember Dub? Surely you remember Dub. I stole some of his poison and put it on that tooth of mine you so cruelly cut out of me. That's what's killing you, sweetheart: despair. He's incredibly angry with me for doing it." She chuckled, like it amused her to have Dub upset with her. "He still pines after you, strange creature that he is. He had such plans for you, his 'juicy little tidbit.'" She threw her head back and laughed. She sounded insane, truly insane. "You deserve to die. Filthy moon brat, thinking you could steal my man away from me!" Then she plunged her ice-cold hand straight into my chest, wrapped her claws around my heart and squeezed.

Alarms were blaring. *"Code Blue…"* There was the sound of rushing feet. People worked feverishly over me. *"Clear!"* A powerful electric shock convulsed my body and dropped me like a stone into insensibility.…

Later. Who knew how much later:

"Margaret!" A startled voice came from nearby, as well as the sound of a chair scraping across the floor, and eager footsteps. "You…came."

"Of course I came, Michael! Raven is terribly injured, possibly dying. Your mother *is* dead. I had to come. You must have known I would."

The sound of movement, and a soft exclamation of surprise from my mother.

"Michael…" then the sound of a breath being drawn in deep. "Oh my god, Michael."

My father was crying. The sound was muffled, like he'd buried his face against my mother. "I'm so sorry," he said, over and over.

Mom's voice was shaky as well. "Please stop, Michael, or you'll make me cry too…"

I drifted back down into dreamland.

Then the oddest one:

Kellas, talking in a low whisper: "She's not recovering, Michael. We've got to assume there's more going on than meets the eye."

"We've no proof she has been infected with Dub's poison. Just because the Morrigan insists she has, that's not enough." Dad was speaking in the same undertone as Kellas. "It's too risky. She's barely hanging in there as it is."

"I know what to do. I've done it. To myself, even! I've got to try."

"What if it kills her?"

"If we don't, she's dead anyway."

My father cut loose with perhaps the most imaginative string of cuss words I'd ever heard from anyone, let alone him. Then he groaned. "You win. If you find what you think you're looking for, where will you ink her? What design will you use?"

I felt Kellas's cool fingertips on the inside of my right arm. "Here. With my icon."

My Dad's breath left him in a long shuddering gasp. "Are you sure? Absolutely, positively sure you want to do that? I know what that means, Kellas."

"I've never been more sure of anything in my life, sir."

Another long breath in and out. "Very well, then. *Do it*. I'll make sure she doesn't feel anything."

A moment later, I was tumbling down, down into the dark and utter silence, again.

~

When I next awoke, I could open my eyes. Well, one of them, anyway. My left eye had a heavy bandage over it. Blinking from the light, I struggled to focus on where I was. The rustle of a page being turned drew my attention, and I slowly turned my head toward the sound.

"Ah, there you are. Finally awake."

It was the Morrigan, your friendly neighborhood death goddess, sitting normal as you please on a chair next to my hospital bed. "I was beginning to wonder if you were going to sleep the whole of November away," she said, setting aside the magazine she'd been perusing. "I really do wonder at the material humans deem worthy of their attention," she continued in a conversational tone. "Entire magazines dedicated to probing the private lives of Hollywood personalities. Honestly, I would think people would have better ways to spend their time and money."

I grunted, trying to reactivate my vocal cords. "*People* magazine?" I croaked.

She smiled and nodded. "You got it on the first guess."

I managed a half smile.... That cut on my face really interfered with smiling. I could feel the stitches pulling unpleasantly. "Some people really enjoy it, but it's not my kind of reading."

"Fortunately," she retorted.

"Where is everyone?"

"Sleeping. Or they ought to be. It's one o'clock in the morning. But enough chitchat. Now that you're out of the proverbial woods, there are things we must get worked out. First off: You can forget about that useless sister of mine. Cerridwen was unable to save her moon daughter, your Nan, and in a fit of pique, declared that she has washed her hands of you entirely."

"What?" I tried to sit up, felt my stab wound protest mightily, and fell back with a gasp.

"She blames you, of course. Completely unable to accept any responsibility for how things turned out for herself. Must always find a scapegoat. This time, that's you. If you weren't so completely under 24/7 guard here, my guess is that she'd already have tried to kill you."

"So, what else is new," I groaned.

The Morrigan snorted in agreement. "Two. I have retrieved my spear."

"Spear?" OK, color me confused.

"The one I loaned your Nan, the one she fought Dother with, and won. Unfortunately, she buried it under a million tons of rock along with herself and Dother, and it required a good bit of cleverness on my part to extract it. Fortunately, I am very clever indeed."

And a bit egotistic, too, I thought, but felt breathless. Nan had died. Down there in the mine. Buried under tons of rock. She'd sacrificed herself for the rest of us. I closed my eyes and felt the tears leak out, sliding down the side of my face and soaking into my pillow.

"She was valiant beyond all reason," the Morrigan said softly. "She's gone from this dimension, killed by the magma she called up out of the depths of the earth to fill the cavern that Dother had forced the miners to carve out. But she's not gone entirely. Trust me on that."

I tried to believe her and gave a slight nod, but the tears continued to flow anyway.

The death goddess drew a deep breath and continued with her list. "Three. I hereby claim you for myself. Cerridwen is unworthy of you. You are now *my* warrior champion and will remain so until you die, whenever that may be. Hopefully not too soon, because champions are hard to come by. Still, you seem to have a death wish, throwing yourself into one impossible situation after another. So, who knows? I shall have to educate you in that regard. Some fights are not meant to be engaged in. I shall see to it you do not enter any battle that you cannot win decisively."

That stopped the tears. I reopened my good eye and looked at her, incredulous. "You would do that? For me?"

She looked affronted. "And why wouldn't I? I knew from the moment I saw you that you were worthy of my patronage. Why else would I have

directed you to the all-knowing Taliesin? And that brings me to number four."
She shifted from her chair onto the side of my bed and stretched out her right
hand, laying it as gentle as a feather upon the bandage that ran across the left
side of my face. "This will hurt; there's no way to make it so won't, but I will
not have my champion scarred. It's not a good look. Makes you seem vulnerable. Now, take deep breaths. Try not to scream; we don't want the hospital
staff to intervene..."

It's hard to describe what happened next. At first, it felt like warmth, like
the sun on your face on a summer day. And then there was a ripping, a tearing,
a gushing of blood as the partly healed cut was torn open and laid wide, and
then something like millions of tiny pins being torn from my flesh...

I fainted.

When I came to, the Morrigan was gone. My face felt like it was on fire,
but the worst of the pain was gone. I put a hand up to the bandage and it came
away sticky. I looked. Blood. It made me nearly pass out again, but I fumbled
for the nurse call button and pressed it before letting my head drop back on
the pillow, weak as a new kitten.

Ian came bursting through the door. "You're awake!" he exclaimed trium-
phantly. Then he saw my bandage. "*Mãe de Deus, o que te aconteceu? Ay que
merda!*" which basically translates to 'Mother of God, what happened to you?
Crap!' Along with a long string of Portuguese that I shall not translate for you,
because it was liberally sprinkled with a great deal of *very* colorful language.
When he finally switched back to English, it was to tell me he would be back
in a jiff and that I was not to go wandering off. As if I could!

He was back in short order, and he wasn't alone. Dad came charging in
also, and about collapsed in relief when he saw me awake. He sat down in the
chair recently vacated by the Morrigan, picked up my right hand, and cradled
it gently in both of his.

"That's a mess, fledgling. What did you do to yourself?"

"I didn't. This is the Morrigan's work," I said.

"That's the Celtic Death goddess, isn't it? Well, she sure made a mess of you!" Ian was very gently picking at the edge of the tape that secured the bandage to my face. I winced as he lifted the tape free, pulling tiny facial hairs along with it. Ian apologized. "No help for it, sorry. I'd rip it off in one swift yank, but I doubt you'd like that either. Hang in there. We're making progress." He hissed in sympathy as he eased the tape off, then lifted the blood-soaked bandage away.

He and Dad stared wordlessly.

"Well?" I demanded. "How does it look? Like I've been filleted? Because that's what it felt like."

"No fledgling, it looks like you've been magically repaired," Dad said. "It's raw-looking and quite red, but the dirt is gone. It looks like it won't leave a scar at all."

I smiled, and this time there was no tugging of stitches nor any discomfort. I raised a hand to touch my face, but Ian blocked me. "Best not to touch. I'll get you a mirror if you like."

Dad nodded at that, and Ian left the room. We looked at each other until I could bear the pain in my father's eyes no longer. I looked away.

"We nearly lost you," Dad said finally. "It was touch and go for weeks. If it hadn't been for Kellas…. But that's history. You're on the mend now. The others will want to know. I need to go call them."

"Nan died." I hadn't meant for it to come out quite that bluntly, but I couldn't take the words back now.

Dad grimaced, then nodded. "She did. But she took Dother down with her. She wouldn't have done it if there had been another way."

"She sacrificed herself, didn't she?"

He nodded. "Sometimes, that's what it takes. Particularly when facing an immortal enemy like Dother."

"Will he come back?"

"Hopefully not for a very long time. But we have no way of knowing."

Ian arrived with the promised mirror, and I inspected my scar while he busied himself cleaning up the mess of nasty bandages. The left side of my face was indeed red and raw-looking, and there was the thinnest of red lines where Dother had cut me. But all in all, it didn't look like I would be called 'scar face' anytime soon. However, I looked wan and sickly. What's worse, I appeared to be about three years old. Oh, go stone the crows and spare me the details! "How long have I been in the hospital?" I asked.

"Weeks," Dad said. "It's November 17th."

"New moon?"

"Two days ago."

"It's why I'm here instead of one of the other nurses," Ian said. "Doc Callahan let me in on your secret, so I wouldn't flip out when you disappeared. We're trying to limit the number of us body-typical folks who know about your lunar tendencies. Your grandmother, Iku, is it? Is taking the other shift."

So...Iku was here as well as Mom. "Good to know," I muttered. I concentrated as best I could, attempting to assume my proper age, but beyond some rainbow flickers, I failed miserably. "I hate looking like a little kid."

"Save your strength. You'll get there." Dad rose, smoothed my hair back, and kissed my forehead. "What's this?" He pushed a lock of my hair to one side. "Well, look at that! You're going white, kiddo."

I brought the mirror up so fast I almost hit him with it. "What?!"

He gave a small lock of hair a gentle tug. "Here. See? It's growing in white."

Sure enough, my hair had turned white at the apex of the slash where Dother's knife had cut me. Something to remember him by, no doubt. The creep.

"You can always dye it," Ian suggested.

Maybe. Or maybe I wouldn't. Sometimes it helps to have reminders of one's own foolhardiness. And, who knew, it might look cool once it grew out far enough.

But I was tiring fast and it must have showed on my face because Dad took away the mirror, tucked me in, and warned me to rest. He'd be back later with the others.

Try as I might, I could not keep my eyes open any longer. I slept.

K ellas was there when I woke next. Maybe it was because he'd delib- erately eased himself down to sit on the bed next to me, or maybe it was because he'd lifted my right hand onto his lap, where he held it pressed against his belly. Maybe it was the pressure of his unwavering gaze... but I was aware of him even before I opened my eyes.

"Good morning, sleepyhead," he said.

I grunted something unintelligible and attempted to sit up. That was a mistake, because even though the Morrigan had fixed my face, that stab wound was altogether another matter. I gasped and fell back, mortified at my weakness.

Kellas gripped my hand harder. "Easy, tiger. You're not quite all there yet."

I groaned. "Please, anything but 'tiger.' Call me an idiot, call me stupid, but for gosh sakes, never call me 'tiger' again."

"I could never call you any of those things," he assured me. "But I promise not to call you 'tiger.' You're right, that one holds some nasty memories, no? How about I call you...let me think. I'll call you my beautiful bird: my cailin álainn. How does that suit you?"

I must have blushed bright red, because he chortled in glee.

"Beautiful it is, Brannaugh. My fearless girl." His voice deepened with strong feeling. "Don't you ever, *ever* scare me like this again, do you hear? I could not bear it."

"But it's OK if you scare the crap out of me, is it? Who was it I had to drag from death's door last month? I seem to remember it was *you.*"

"Well, you certainly got even with me," he scoffed. "But, as you're fond of saying, turnabout is fair play." His thumb flicked over the inside of my right arm, and I felt a slight sting.

I pulled away from him and looked at my arm. A small black cat sprawled as if asleep just above my wrist. "What's this?" I looked up at him, eyes wide. "You tattooed me?"

"It was that or watch you die," he said very softly. "The Morrigan warned me. There was some of Dub's ink on that saber tooth Erin stabbed you with. Or maybe some on her claws when she swiped you. But you were infected, as I was."

"But you didn't ask my permission!"

"You were comatose! How could I? I did ask your dad, though."

"Ugh! This is the 21st century, Kellas! You don't ask a girl's *dad*, you ask *her*!" I inspected the tiny cat on my arm, rubbing a fingertip across it. The cat stirred and stretched. He sat up and looked right at me with the smuggest, most familiar smirk in the world. Then purred. "Kellas! You marked me...with yourself?" My gaze flew to his face, now very close to my own.

"What else could I possibly have marked you with?" he asked...then kissed me. And just because I know you're thinking how weird and icky it is for a grown man to be kissing a little kid, let me assure you that any time Kellas is near, I am instantly my right age if not always in my right mind, because just being near that dude is enough to make me crazy.

I wrapped both arms around his neck and kissed him back. Somehow, with my Cait Sidhe bodyguard close, I felt much less vulnerable. Like maybe I could relax a little. Dother's attack had shaken me to the core.

We did not get to indulge in much kissing, however, because the door of my hospital room opened. Mom raised her voice in alarm. "Who is this person mauling my daughter? Michael! Get him off Raven at once."

Kellas broke away from possibly the most wonderful kiss I'd ever had in my life, and I glared at my mother. "Don't you ever knock?"

"I'm your mother! I shouldn't have to knock."

"I'm 17, Mom, and this is Kellas. Who, by the way, is my boyfriend. Kellas, this is my mom. There! You've been introduced. And you *might* want to get into the practice of knocking, Mom! Just in case you walk in on something you really don't want to."

Dad was grinning ear to ear as he hooked an arm around Mom's neck and pulled her close. "C'mon, Meg, it's just kissing. Let them have their fun."

She scoffed. "That young man was practically devouring our daughter's face!"

"I seem to remember that you rather enjoyed that sort of kissing," he retorted, and proceeded to demonstrate. She resisted initially, then relented and returned his kiss, with what looked to me to be a fair amount of enthusiasm.

Kellas and I exchanged astonished looks. Then he sent me a devilish grin. "Let's give them a little privacy, shall we?" He leaned in with a kiss that completely took my mind off my parents.

However, Mom is not all that inclined to public displays of affection, so she broke away from her kiss far too soon for my liking. But here she was, and ignoring her was not something I could do.

The initial awkwardness of the situation settled down, and she went straight to fussing over me. Kellas gave up his place on the bed and went to stand next to Dad. After I finally reassured her that I wasn't about to kick the bucket anytime soon, that my face felt fine, that the cuts on my ribs only stung a little, and that the stab wound was, in fact, getting better, thank you, she sat back and fixed me with an accusatory stare. "I thought having a girl was supposed to get me out of worrying about her getting into horrible fights. What in the world am I going to do with you?"

I made an 'I dunno!' face and shrugged my good shoulder. "Maybe accept it?" I suggested. "It's not like I can change what I am. If it makes you feel any better, I don't go looking for trouble."

"Oh, don't you?" Kellas drawled.

Mom twisted so she could look between the two of us. "Meaning she does?"

"Not intentionally, maybe, but she sure doesn't back down."

"Raven!" The 'mom voice.' Every kid knows the tone, I'm sure.

I glared at Kellas. Some help he was! I heard Dad chuckle too, so he got a glare as well. "When someone tries to hurt me, I hit back. OK? You want me to be some immortal's punching bag? Not how I play ball, Mom. And neither do you, may I point out! It's just that our techniques are a little different."

"Mine gets me paid. Yours gets you hurt."

"Oh, because you've *never* come home from a day at court going after some rich, entitled rapist, and spent the night crying, have you?" I snapped. Because that was the kind of lawyer my mother was. A prosecutor, a very talented one, and her specialty was going after powerful men who felt themselves to be above the law, especially when it came to women. Not a surprise, knowing what I knew now about her history.

"That's different." She was on the defensive now.

"Because it shouldn't bother me that my mom is crying? When is a wound to the spirit any less awful than a wound to the body? You, of all people, know better than that."

It shocked her; I could see that. She sent a look at Dad that said clear as anything she needed his support. And bless him, he was right there for her.

"That'll be enough, fledgling." He stepped forward and laid an arm around Mom's shoulders. Was she leaning on him just the tiniest bit? "This has been hard on all of us. We need time to process it and come to grips with this new reality. Meanwhile, please don't fight. It just takes too much energy away from healing."

"Can I come home?" I blurted out, because suddenly, that's where I wanted to be more than anything.

"Where's home, Raven?" Mom asked, her eyes getting moist.

"With you, Mom. *And* with Dad. With my friends. Can't I have all of that? All the time? Please?" Oh, how badly I wanted that to be how it was. "Dad loves you, Mom. He never stopped loving you. Please, please forgive him! Let's be family again. Here. In one place, together."

"But..." she hesitated. "My work!"

"You can do your work anywhere, Mom! You can fly out to Bismarck when you need to, or wherever it is you go when you're gone. Please." I pointed at my father, who was standing very still, a stunned look on his face. "Look at him; you can see I'm not lying about this. What about that kiss he gave you just now? Kisses like that don't lie. Please, Mom."

Mom looked at Dad, back at me, and then at Dad again.

"I wish you would, Meg," he whispered.

She got up off the bed then and stood there indecisively for a few painful moments. Then: "We can try. I can't promise either of you that it will work out, but we can sure try."

Dad wrapped both arms around my mother and pulled her close. "I can live with that," he said.

~

I did get to go home, but my family put me in the room Kellas had occupied until recently. I simply wasn't strong enough to climb the stairs to my loft. Iku set herself up as my nurse, sternly limiting how much time anyone got to spend with me, insisting I rest. She also pushed me to get out of bed and walk around a bit as I got stronger.

Archer and Orianthi visited often—Archer with boxes of chocolates that seemed to disappear faster than I remember eating them (because I very likely had help), and Orianthi with bunches of wildflowers that bloomed riotously out of season. Hey, she's a dryad. Dryads have that skill set.

With a fair bit of trepidation, I asked about her tree.

"Oh, my tree's fine," Orianthi said breezily. "We killed off a bunch of ghouls and sent the rest packing."

Ghouls. We. "I seem to be out of the loop here. What happened?"

Archer was grinning from ear to ear. "As Orianthi feared, our tree was attacked. A bunch of disgusting creatures walked on up out of the lake and came at us. It was a bit like shooting balloons, though. Hit them anywhere with an arrow and they exploded. Orianthi showed up...because she's about as good as you at staying away from danger...and hurled insults, acorns, and little green apples at them. It confused them. They're not terribly smart, apparently. Then, once the moon got high overhead, they melted away."

I wondered if that was when Nan had finally overwhelmed Dother. That made sense, at least.

"They made trouble in town, too." Orianthi added. "The papers put it down to Halloween mischief, but it was clearly the ghoulish variety. I mean, who goes around smashing kids' jack-o'-lanterns and stealing their candy? That's just plain mean."

I agreed with the "mean" assessment, although people could be plenty ghoulish when they decided to be.

Ian came too, his visits often overlapping with Archer's. It didn't take long for me to realize this wasn't entirely coincidental. They'd first met while Kellas had been hospitalized, and the attraction between them was certainly there.

Dad was around all the time. He'd been ordered to take a leave of absence to recover following Nan's death and my injuries, not to mention the torture he'd endured. It meant he and Mom had lots of time to get reacquainted... and just how reacquainted that was I discovered one evening while on one of my prescribed perambulations of the house. I came across the two of them in the living room, kissing. Passionately kissing, I might add. As I watched, Dad slid a hand up under the back of my mother's sweater *(onto her bare skin!)* and pulled her even closer. Geez, people! Get a room already!

I muffled a squeak as Kellas appeared out of nowhere next to me and walked me backward all the way to my temporary bedroom. "Let's not interrupt the lovebirds, shall we?" he whispered, shutting the door behind us. "They have a bit of...hmm...catching up to do."

"Yowza." I breathed. It gave me even more hope that in time they could reconcile their differences, but gads, the fireworks...!

"Impressive, yes?" He put both hands on my waist and pulled me up against him, not that I resisted. "Maybe with a bit of practice, you can get good at kissing too. What do you think? Shall we try?"

Stupid question! I stood on tiptoe, buried both hands in that messy black mane of his, and showed him I didn't mind practicing at all.

At some point, he broke away and pushed me out to arm's length. I think we were both rather breathless, and there was a seriously dazed look on his face. "Have pity on me, Brannaugh. Any more of that and I won't be able to hold myself back any longer."

I made a grumbling noise deep in my throat and unsuccessfully tried to push closer.

He made a small sound: part scoff, part laugh. "Nope. I made a vow. We need to do normal dating things first. I want to take you ice skating, go out for dinner and a movie. Maybe even take in a Cornell hockey game? They've been playing well lately. What do you think? A girl like you deserves fun stuff like that."

Oh, wow! Actual dating...that would be a novel experience! I bounced up on my toes and gave him a quick peck on the lips. "I'd love to."

"Then that's what we'll do." His eyes crinkled in a lovely smile. "Now you need to go rest up, and I need to go take a cold shower. A very, *very* cold shower!" Then he pressed a final kiss upon my forehead and quickly left.

Dang...

~

We saw my mother and Iku off at the airport at 'oh-dark-thirty' the next morning...a pilot joke about how ungodly early eastern flights tended to leave. It was to make connections in a timely fashion, or so I was led to believe. As this was on a private aircraft owned by Nan's businessman friend, I grouchily wondered if it was some sadistic desire on the part of the Embraer Phenom's pilot to deprive ordinary earthbound types of their beauty sleep. We went to the private section of the field where the plane was waiting, air stairs down, lights bright in the windows. A gangly teenager romped down the stairs and met us as we walked across the tarmac. She offered to take Iku's suitcase. "Nothing potentially hazardous, liquid, fragile, or otherwise a really bad idea to bring on board a fabulous aircraft such as ours?" she demanded, in a way-too-wide-awake and energetic tone.

I send her a wry look. "Caffeinated much?"

She tossed her long, curly mane and laughed heartily. "Only matcha for me! Coffee is for the uninitiated."

Oi. Serves me right to ask.

Iku chuckled. "Just clothing, dear. Thank you," she added as the girl lifted the suitcase effortlessly and galloped giraffe-like up the air stairs into the jet.

Iku's skills as a nurse and shaman were sorely needed. She'd been gone from Fort Berthold for far too long. Now that her house was habitable, (having undergone a year of repairs due to the troll attack on my 16th birthday) she could finally return. Mom had to go take care of some things, but would be back soon. She was going to arrange with her law partners to stay in New York; they'd been discussing opening a branch office there. She would close her house for the time being, then sell it later—should everything work out.

Mom and Iku finished saying their goodbyes and had boarded the aircraft, when a dark form materialized out of nowhere. It bolted up the air stairs just as the tall girl was about to retract them. She stuck her head out the cabin door. "Is your dog supposed to come with us?" she asked, surprised.

Dad waved a hand, indicating his OK. "Bran goes where he wants to." Then he said to me: "He'll protect Meg, just like he did your Nan."

The girl waved back and resumed closing the cabin door. Shortly thereafter, the engines started up and the slim jet trundled toward the runway.

Things quieted after that. Dad was busy moving out of his small cabin and into Nan's house, clearing out her belongings and putting his own in their place. He could only do a bit at a time before being overwhelmed with grief. It had to be done, and he did it, but it all came at an emotional cost. Nan's place was his now. The current plan was to get Dad's cabin ready for Mom to use, just until she and Dad were sure they were truly ready to be married again. Even if they chose not to be together, at least she wouldn't live so far away anymore. That was worth a lot to me.

Items of Nan's that Dad thought I might use (ceremonial artifacts, candles, moon charts), he gave to me. I did my best to find a home for them up in my loft. The house helped me find space for it all. Any time I brought another armload of her things upstairs, I'd find that new cubbies and storage bins had appeared in just the right sizes. Labels appeared on the outside of the bins each time I laid an item inside. One knifelike item was labeled, *boline*. When I looked that up online, I found it was used for cutting herbs, cords, and candles.

The last thing Dad handed me was a massive book with tooled leather bindings; it appeared to be extremely old. The title was stamped in old script with gold leaf, in a language I'd never seen before. It would take some doing to discover just what it was. Inside was the same. This was an assignment that would take time for me to complete. I hoped my medallion would be able to help, especially since there was an exact copy of it in the center of the cover. Coincidental? I'd find out eventually, I guess.

Mom returned just before Thanksgiving, and we prepared a bonfire, a big one this time, to honor my grandmother. We didn't have a body to bury. She was already under tons of rock beneath the lake. But we did our best to observe the rituals she would have performed. We shared honey and bread, drank a toast to her with her favorite wine, and tossed rowan branches onto the fire. Dad and Kellas told stories about her that had Mom and me at turns horrified and impressed. I'd barely known my Nan, and it made me so very, very sad.

I dreamed of her that night. I watched as she walked hand in hand with Elias (so *that* was where he'd disappeared to! I'd been wondering). They strolled along a narrow path that meandered over green hills and rock walls, past silver streams, and along the top of craggy cliffs. It looked suspiciously like I remembered Tír na nÓg, which made sense. That was the afterlife she'd grown up believing in. Nan looked to be 25 or so, and her step was sure and strong. She looked up at Elias often, laughing, obviously happy. He gazed at her like he would never let her go. At first, I thought she didn't know I was there, but then she looked straight at me, winked, and blew me a kiss.

I awoke in my own bed, my face wet with tears. I knew in my heart she was where she wanted to be. She was no longer in pain; she was happy. No matter how badly it hurt to have Nan gone, I wouldn't begrudge her that. I'd do my utmost to live up to her legacy, to continue the work she'd started over a millennium before, to show the world that her faith in me was not misplaced. I would be a champion for what was right, and do whatever it took to keep the bad guys at bay. After all, I am a Lunatic. That's what we Lunatics do.

Epilogue

Brett Goodwin was glad his shift was over. He'd been repairing a section of conveyor belt that had given way under constant use. The others on his shift had left a little while before him. Brett had been struggling with getting the newly installed mesh connectors to slide together properly, like the annoying teeth of a stuck zipper. When the metal rod he'd been working through the mesh connectors finally reached the far end, he grunted in relief and secured the rod so it wouldn't pull out. Now he could get out of this godforsaken hole in the ground and see the sky again. Brett gathered his tools and headed for the exit.

He wasn't a miner at heart. Brett had taken the job just a month ago because his little farm wasn't paying the bills as well as he and his girlfriend, Clarisse, needed it to. Actually, no...make that fiancée, now. His sister had come to dinner last week, and in the presence of her and Clarisse's two kids, Brett had asked Clarisse to marry him. She'd said yes.

The new job came with much needed benefits, like medical insurance. Until recently, it hadn't been necessary; now, with little Evan's leukemia diagnosis, it was critical. They had already racked up tens of thousands of dollars in medical debt. And the donations coming in from the GoFundMe campaign his sister had started up barely scratched the surface. Brett tried not to think about the looming debt as he left.

His way out led past the rockfall. The incident earlier that year that had caused it had shut down the mine for two weeks; some maniacs had broken into the mine and tried to blow a hole in the bottom of the lake. They'd kidnapped a bunch of the miners that had been on duty and forced them to do the drilling and explosives work. Fortunately, the plot had failed and the resulting rockfall had secured the area, saving the lake—and the region's tourist economy. It was an odd sort of rockfall, though. Instead of being a jumble of boulders, like one would expect, this was solid rock. No gaps. *Strange.*

The miners victimized by the nutcases hadn't been so lucky. They had all quit. A few were so badly traumatized that they were now on permanent disability. One had even committed suicide shortly after the incident. None of them would talk about what had happened. Brett couldn't imagine what they must have been through. While these circumstances had created the job opening he'd so badly needed, Brett wasn't happy about the other men's misfortune.

He gave an empathetic nod of his head and kept walking. Brett had been so lost in thought, it wasn't until he was halfway past the rockfall that he heard it: *'Treasure.'*

Brett hesitated; not sure he'd actually heard what he thought he'd heard. Before he could walk on, the voice came again.

'Treasure!' Almost like it was coming from inside his head instead of through his ears. *'You'll never lack for money again.'*

Brett stuck a pinkie in one ear and wiggled it. He knew the echoes down here could deceive you easily enough, bouncing from the walls of the mine in uneven ways, making voices sound in places distant from the actual speakers. But this was a first.

Treasure, though. Enough money to pay for all 3-year-old Evan's doctor bills, even buy Evan's older sister that pony she'd been begging for forever. Make it so his girlfriend...fiancée...never had to clean another house in that enclave of super-rich folks in the Heights. Brett had no use for people who had to call on others to do their dirty work. Clarisse had chided him about his attitude. It was a great-paying job, she'd told him; it contributed to their income. She was her own boss and could set her own hours, so she could be there for the children. Plus, the people she worked for were always pleased with her work. While this was her decision to make, Brett wasn't thrilled about it.

Now, he was hearing a voice that couldn't possibly be there, one that just happened to promise him exactly what he needed to solve this financial nightmare.

"Who are you?" Brett whispered. He must be nuts, talking to a disembodied voice in his head. Wasn't that the first sign of insanity?

'A victim of circumstance, like you.'

"This is crazy." Why was he even listening to this? No, he'd been underground for too long. It was messing with his head. Time to get topside. He hurried on; his family was waiting for him.

~

Brett avoided the rockfall area for nearly a week. But he had to return when the conveyor belt broke again. This time it took longer to fix than it should have, and his coworkers all left before he'd finished. It didn't help that his hands were trembling. He couldn't get his mind off the latest set of medical bills that had arrived yesterday—*co-pays*, they were called.

They were astronomically high. A debt collector had called earlier that week and frightened Clarisse so badly she'd still been crying when he'd arrived home at midnight, after his shift ended. He'd tried to reassure her that they'd get through it. He even took out a million-dollar term life insurance policy with some money from his paycheck—not that they could really afford it. But

Brett didn't want her left hanging if something happened to him. She'd been horrified at what he'd done, but not because he'd spent money that way. It upset her that he would even consider the possibility of dying; he was only 32.

He was lucky to have found a woman like her, Brett thought as he finished the repair. He was walking out past the rock fall when he heard the voice again. *'Treasure.'*

This time, he stopped. "What do you mean, *treasure?*" he demanded. "What treasure?"

'It's here, free for the taking. No one will be the wiser. Just dig for it. I'll show you where.'

"Yeah, right. Find some other sucker, fool!" He stalked out. But try as he might, Brett could not stop thinking about what the voice had said. What if there were some truth to it? What harm could there be in investigating further?

Even so, it was several days before he went near the rockfall again. This time, he didn't wait for the voice, just talked into the empty air. "If I dig, what will I find?"

"Enough to solve all your problems," the voice assured him. *"You'll never have to worry about money again."*

What the heck, I'll give it a shot at least, see if there was anything to it, Brett thought. He worked after-hours, while no one was near. He took the rock he'd removed and scattered it so it didn't attract attention. He told Clarisse he'd taken on another shift so she wouldn't worry about his absences. Brett hoped she wouldn't notice that his paycheck hadn't gotten any bigger. Hoped no one would remark on the hole he was making, one that grew steadily deeper with every hour he spent on it. Since third shift had been eliminated, there was no one to hear him working. No one ever noticed his excavation work during the other two shifts, either, which, frankly, was more than a little odd. But he chose to ignore the uneasy feeling it gave him.

It took the better part of a month, but just before Christmas, he finally broke through into a hollow spot. Just the tiniest breakthrough, maybe three inches in diameter, but there was an opening. Brett made the hole larger until he could reach in and feel around. Something seized his hand, something colder than anything he had ever felt in his entire life, something that flooded into his body, took control over it, and shoved his consciousness into a tiny corner of his brain.

"I'm back!" It was Brett's voice that was raised in triumph, but it wasn't Brett saying it. It was the something that had enslaved him and made him a prisoner in his own body. Not-Brett threw down the drill and pickax he'd been using and strode out of the mine, never to return.

He stopped at a 24-hour mini-mart on the way and bought a lottery ticket. Not-Brett neatly wrote "Property of Clarisse Whittaker, in the event of my untimely death" on it, then signed it. He wrapped it carefully in the plastic baggie Brett's sandwich had been packed in and shoved it deep into his jeans pocket. Driving north to a small park that Brett and his family liked to hike in, Not-Brett walked back in to a spot overlooking the lake. He clutched at his chest as his heart squeezed hard, then even harder.... The thing that had briefly possessed his body vanished.

Brett never felt the ground when he fell.

～

A white and tan rabbit hopped along, nibbling the tips of frozen grasses where they poked through a thin layer of snow and ice near where Brett's body had fallen a month earlier. The rabbit was painfully thin; a domestic bunny, apparently abandoned. Someone had probably lost interest in it and set it loose in the wild, assuming it could take care of itself. Some people's hardheartedness was difficult to understand. Why would they not have just taken it to the local animal shelter?

Brett watched it with the passive disinterest of one who knew that life was fleeting and death merely another form of misery to be subjected to. He existed as a ghost; there, but not there. Unseen, unheard, his body still lay unfound, despite the search parties that had combed the area. Clarisse had called in a missing person report when he'd not shown up at home. How could they have missed his body, laying in plain sight of the trail?! But none of this terrible mess made sense anyways. Brett had watched as the search crew found his abandoned F-150, then as they'd bumbled around, completely bypassing where he lay—barely covered with leaves and snow.

Time passed. No one found him. Once he'd even had to scare off a hungry coyote that had snuck close enough to chew on one of his legs. But the crows would not come near; crows sensed abnormal and stayed far away.

One day in January, Brett heard young voices approaching—a family from the sound of it, a couple of kids and their father. He almost moved away, unable to bear the happiness in their voices or his own heartbreaking loss. But something stopped him. That rabbit hadn't taken off at the sound of the voices, instead it merely sat up tall, its ears flicking back and forth, showing interest, not fear. Could he draw the family off the trail to where his body lay, using the rabbit as a decoy? A moment later, he took over the rabbit's body, pushing its consciousness aside as ruthlessly as that disembodied voice had shoved aside his own. It was not easy to do; the rabbit fought him with every ounce of its being. This made him wonder: Had he fought his own possession as valiantly? But now, a young girl appeared on the trail, skipping and kicking the snow up in powdery clouds. She spied the rabbit a half-second before her little brother did.

"A bunny!" she screamed, her voice shrill with delight. "Daddy! It's a bunny!" She took off like a rocket straight at him, her little brother a half step behind. "Bunny! Wait!"

Brett took off, running down the trail closer to the small hollow where his body was hidden. He hesitated long enough for the kids to almost catch up, then led them straight to where he lay. The father cautioned them not to scream, that they'd frighten the poor rabbit even more. Not that they listened. They were too excited.

When Brett got to his body he paused, waited for the kids to reach him, then forced the rabbit to hesitate long enough for the girl to scoop him up in her arms. Then he abandoned it and fell back, overwhelmed by the massive effort it had taken to possess the rabbit, even briefly.

The girl turned. "See Daddy? I caught it!"

She was leaving! How could she not have seen his body? She was practically standing on him! Her little brother was also too intent on the rabbit to notice the dead body within inches of his bright red boots. "I saw it too!" he whined. "It's mine too!"

Their father had a long-suffering look on his face as he made his way downslope to where his kids were arguing. But as he reached them, he stopped abruptly, sniffed and made a face. "Something's dead near here," he commented, looking around. He saw Brett's body, and a look of shock crossed his face. He hustled his kids back up to the trail. "You two stay put. I'll be right back." He came back down to where Brett's body lay, and using a stick, cautiously pushed leaves and snow aside to reveal a portion of the red-and-black-checked wool jacket Brett had been wearing when he'd died. The father made a choked sound and flung an arm up over the lower part of his face, then made his way unsteadily back up to the trail where his children continued to fight over the rabbit laying peacefully in the girl's arms. A tame bunny for sure, accustomed to small children and their loud voices. Brett heard him reassuring the kids they could keep the rabbit, but that they had to get back to where he could get cell service. He needed to report something he'd seen. He ushered his kids and their new pet back up the trail the way they'd come.

Brett had been found. Finally. Maybe now he could rest.

But, no. He'd watched the whole sorry episode of his body being brought up out of the woods, and taken to the morgue, where he was unceremoniously stripped, toe-tagged, and shoved into a refrigerated locker. Brett watched while the police went through his pockets and found his wallet and ID, truck keys, and the coins in his left front pocket. They also found the lottery ticket with the note that it belonged to Clarisse Whittaker. Then watched in despair as Clarisse and his sister came to identify his body, then left together, sobbing. Observed the mortician cut him open and determine the cause of death, a massive heart attack. (Good, now maybe the insurance company would pay what they owed poor Clarisse.) He stood by helplessly as his friends and family gathered at the funeral home (closed casket, thank God; the time spent rotting away in the woods had not been kind). Brett was grateful that his neighbor, a kindly older gentleman well versed in financial management, had helped Clarisse deal with the uproar over the lottery ticket; it had won them a cool $3.5 million. The neighbor had showed her how to invest it such in a way that she'd never have to worry about money again. Treasure, yes; the voice hadn't precisely lied. But it had failed to mention the cost exacted from human misery that such riches required.

Brett watched as his fiancée grew round with child, then as his sister held her hand while Clarisse delivered his baby in the spring. He hadn't even known she was pregnant. He listened as she named the baby boy Brett Junior, then watched helplessly as she kissed the baby's woolly little head and cried.

Afterwards, Brett left to wander the streets of the small city, restless, angry, and grieving. He took to making small, spiteful acts of meanness against the living: tipping over cups of coffee left sitting too close to the edge of a table; tripping an unwary pedestrian and then scattering the papers she dropped; dumping rainwater off a street vendor's pop-up tent onto a customer who'd just gotten his meal. All of these efforts weakened him a bit, but somehow soothed his frustration at being dead, if only for a short time. Nights found him at the homeless encampment behind the local Walmart, where teasing the dregs of humanity (as he thought of them, lazy, useless beggars!) was his only means to distract himself. He snapped tent poles, tossed possessions all over, and pulled knit beanies down over people's eyes. Stupid kid stuff, really. It was about all he could do anymore. Until the day, (or night, rather) that one of them saw him.

Yes, someone *saw him.* And then spoke to him. "What did we ever do to you to deserve your nasty behavior?" the man demanded. He was shorter than average, lean to the point of emaciation, the result of addiction and poor eating habits. He'd pulled his blanket close around himself to keep Brett from plucking it away.

That hauled Brett up short. *'You can see me? Hear me?'*

That brought a scoff. "Unfortunately."

He hunkered down near the man, a little distance away. The guy stank like garbage. *'How?'*

Bleary gray eyes peered at him from under three layered beanies. It was a chilly spring night, but honestly, three?

"Just lucky, I guess." The homeless man's tone indicated he felt it was anything but lucky.

"Wow." Brett was impressed.

"It's why I'm here, actually. Seeing you misty types makes people think I'm insane." The man shook his head in frustration. "They keep locking me up and filling me full of nasty antipsychotics. It's no wonder I turned to street meds! It's better if I'm higher than a kite—at least then I can tell myself it's all just imaginary." He grimaced and pulled his blanket tighter. "But today people were stingy with their donations, and I can't get my dealer to give me an advance. So here I am, lucid. And seeing you. Unfortunately."

Brett weighed the man's words. Donations. What the homeless called the charity they received when they begged on the street corners. There were quite a few of these people, all with cardboard signs reading 'Need money for food. Any amount helps. God Bless.' Always the 'God Bless' line. Always. It didn't make sense. *'Businesses are begging for workers, and paying good wages. Why don't you people just get a job?'* Brett demanded.

"Because we can't keep one," the homeless man said, "even if they hired us. Which they won't." He scowled. "Would you?"

Brett had to admit he wouldn't, not even for a summer vegetable-picking job. Besides being unkempt, the addicted were completely unreliable. But finally, here was someone to talk. Like it or not, Brett was terribly lonely. So, he took to hanging around the man, whose name he eventually found out was Emmitt.

Emmitt had been an academic, researching paranormal phenomena until jeered out of research by colleagues who felt his theories were too far-fetched, too fueled by psychedelics to count as true research. He'd lost hope then, and life had spiraled out of control until he lost everything and ended up on the street.

Brett started to draw parallels between his life and Emmitt's, and over time came to feel far kindlier toward the guy. He started nudging the homeless man toward the food kitchen for meals and toward the homeless shelter at night.

Brett bullied him into taking baths and washing his clothes. Pushing him to buy fresh clothing at Sally's Army down on Rt 13. Brett also found ways to get the man's drug supplier in trouble with the law, so Emmitt spent longer and longer without a fix. While doing so, he discovered the doctor and paramedic that Emmitt called "Kind One," who checked in on him regularly.

Dr. Callahan saw the changes Brett was causing in Emmitt, not that he knew the ghost was behind the changes. The good doctor did what he could to see that the homeless man got the support he needed to keep getting better.

Brett appreciated that. Here was someone whose education and social status didn't make him set himself above others. He treated all with kindness and respect.

It wasn't until Emmitt told him that Dr. Callahan was basically immortal that Brett began to wonder if perhaps his ghostly existence might be fixed. Immortal, eh? Maybe the doctor could help Brett move on from ghost-hood. Maybe even be able to deal with that creep Brett had been fooled into busting out. Because only something immortal could have done what that thing had: survive encased in rock and then taken Brett's body over—like he was nothing more than a rental car. Which the creep then trashed.

Brett needed Emmitt to relay his message. He waited for the right opportunity, and when it presented itself, pushed Emmitt to tell the doctor his story.

The doctor didn't act like Emmitt was just spewing insane nonsense; he did quite the opposite, in fact. When the homeless man got to the part about the voice in the rocks, the doctor had gone pale, found a place to sit down, then questioned Emmitt closely about the circumstances. When Emmitt had turned to Brett to find out the answer to some of the doctor's questions, he'd picked up on the fact that Brett was 'there.' If not quite 'all there.' Then the kind doctor talked directly to Brett. It felt validating. Like he was still worth listening to.

"I read your story in the papers," the doctor said. "Utterly heartbreaking. I am so very sorry. For what it's worth, you should not be so hard on yourself for what you did. Few have ever been able to resist Dother for long."

Dother. He had a name for the beast now. Brett wished he'd never taken that job. At least he'd owned up to the damage his actions had caused. Having someone else know what he'd done eased some of the pain, like confession at church, perhaps. He wasn't Catholic, but he could see some value in that practice.

As summer got underway, Brett took to wandering back up to his old place to check in on Clarisse and her kids. He watched Brett Jr. sleep in his cradle, rejoiced that Evan seemed to be going into remission, and was pleased with Jodie's happiness over her spoiled-rotten little pony. He was even grateful when his best friend, Roger, started showing up regularly, helping Clarisse with the little fix-its every old place needs on an ongoing basis. Although he couldn't watch when it progressed to something more than that. Love was for the living, not for him. Not anymore. He had no intention of getting in the way of her happiness. But it was hard on him, nonetheless.

And then, just as Clarisse's life was getting back on track, Roger suffered a terrible tractor accident and was airlifted to Syracuse Hospital. Brett went there to be with her. He stayed with Clarisse as she mourned yet another loss, because none of the doctors thought his friend would live. He watched as Roger's spirit finally lifted from his body. His friend was startled when he could see Brett.

'What the heck are you doing here?' Roger demanded. *'You died way back in December.'*

'I'm here for Clarisse,' Brett answered.

'Oh. I see.' But no. Of course, he didn't see. Not really.

'Are you leaving?' Brett asked.

'Nothing left for me here, I reckon. My body's busted up bad. I never wanted to live as an invalid. Didn't you hear the doctors? If I live, I'll never walk again.'

There were worse things than that, Brett thought, but he didn't say so.

'Well, there's my ride,' Roger said. *'Aren't you coming?'*

Brett pointed at the body on the bed. *'Would you mind?'* he asked.

His friend looked at him like he was insane. Well, maybe he was, just a little bit.

'Feel free,' he said, then rocketed up through the ceiling like a comet with no substance.

Brett slipped into his friend's body and felt the agony that radiated from his broken pelvis and crushed legs. He practically cried with joy at being alive. Badly broken, yes. But alive. He fought off the urge to fall asleep again and was awake when Clarisse came in for her daily visit. He rejoiced in her surprise and happiness at finding him awake and alive. He promised to do everything in his power to get well for her, to be there for her and the kids. "Whatever it takes," he told her.

"Even if you can never walk again, Roger?" she asked.

"I don't need legs to love you, girl," Brett answered.

And yes, she cried, but if the kiss she gave him then was any indication, she was fully on board with that.

"So good of you to join me, Raven Light Bringer," a man's voice spoke out of the total darkness that surrounded me. "I had hoped you would."

"Where am I?" I had dimension-hopped some place while dreaming, an occupational hazard of mine. Where that was, however, I had no idea.

"You are here, in my *demesne*. Where eventually, I hope you will stay." His voice was smooth and sweet, like liquid caramel.

I had no intention of remaining here if I could help it! This pitch darkness was nothing I cared to linger in. To illuminate where I was, I called up a small light in my hand, (after the craziness of the salt mine, I'd worked on that spell until I could cast it). It hardly made a dent in the pitch black; mostly it put a spotlight on me.

"Lovely as ever," the voice sighed.

His voice was vaguely familiar, although I couldn't place it at the moment. "Who are you?" I wished I could see who was speaking!

"Don't tell me you've forgotten already!" his deep voice mocked. "Not after I left such a lasting impression on you and your beloved."

Then I remembered, and it chilled me to the core. "Dub." The god of darkness...one of the three Old Gods who had tried their best to kill me on Samhain, my 17th birthday.

"That's me," he said.

I reached over my shoulder and put my hand on Fraegarthach's hilt. "Show yourself, you coward!"

A quiet laugh. "A bit difficult to do now. Thanks to you, I lack a physical presence."

"That's your own fault." I released my grasp on Fraegarthach. He couldn't hurt me in his current condition. At least I didn't think he could.

That elicited a deep sigh from him. "I see that now. I would like to make amends, if possible."

Amends? Wait. What? This was the god who'd come close to killing Kellas, who'd assisted Dother in his torture. Who'd threatened me with...nastiness. "Are you *kidding* me?"

A deep chuckle: warm, even pleasant. "I could not be more sincere."

This was just nuts. "I don't believe you."

"Oh, for crying out loud!" He sounded annoyed at my attitude. "I can understand your reticence, Light Bringer, but I assure you of the purity of my intentions. As proof, I will tell you what my brother intends for you and yours."

"Which one?"

"Dother, of course."

I scoffed. "He's encased in stone and unlikely to be planning much of anything right now."

"Unfortunately for all of us, my elder brother has been freed and has joined forces with the red-haired feline. Together, they plot...mischief."

My heart sank into my toes. Dother had escaped? So soon? "Why should I believe a word you say? And why is your brother being freed unfortunate for *you*?" I said that last bit aggressively. He and his brothers were why my grandmother was dead! *Unfortunate? For him? Really?*

That made him growl. "I swear to you; I speak the truth! They have already taken your Cait Sidhe beloved. Sadly, they will use him to revenge themselves." He sighed, and strangely, it did sound like actual regret. "He will suffer the tortures of the damned. You would do well to steal him back as soon as possible."

I was silent, mulling over what he'd said. "Why are you telling me this? What's in it for you?"

A soft chuckle. "We got off on the wrong foot, you and I. The moment I saw you, I felt you were the only one for me. Hence, I attempted to kill off the Cait Sidhe, and then failed when I underestimated your fierceness in protecting him."

"You were.... Are! Disgusting. The things you said and did...." I shuddered, remembering.

His voice became caramel again. "There was a time when domination was how a man courted a woman. What we wanted, we took."

I made a retching sound. "That's just vile."

"Hmm." He sounded...amused. "There are still many who would disagree with you."

I sure hoped not! Unfortunately, he was probably right.

He continued. "In time, I hope you will form a far better impression of me than you currently hold. I will show you that I can be your ally, your port in the storm, your rock. Eventually, I hope that you will come to love me even more than your Cait Sidhe, that you will leave him and become my Queen, shining your light in my dark *demesne* for all of time."

Not gonna happen, I thought, and woke myself up.

With much gratitude

For all my readers. You deserve a huge thank you. Without you, these books would just be a whole lot of whistling in the wind.

For my alpha readers/grand-girls McKenzie, Aislynn and Evelynn. You listened to the story well before it all pulled together and emphatically let me know when my descriptions had gotten "too mushy!" between Raven and Kellas. But you never once flinched when the going got tough for our heroine and her Cait Sidhe bodyguard. I could not ask for better feedback from the very age group this book is written for.

For my beta readers Stasia, Sandy, Pam and Charlie. Your input made this story much better in so many ways. Thank you from the bottom of my heart. Also, many thanks to my good friend Cat, who checked the Portuguese dialog for me. Brazilian and Portuguese versions of their shared language are very different!

For my copyeditor, Brendan. I'll get you liking fantasy yet!

For my extra-super-special, "let's get this right, Ann!" editor, Nichole. I feel very lucky to have found you. Note: If there is a mistake on *this* page, it's not her fault, because I didn't bug her to check it for me. She's worked hard enough on this project already.

For my cover artist, Cristiana Leone, who brought a pivotal scene from the book to life. It's hard to express just how exciting that is!

And, as always, for my husband/hiking partner Charlie, my anam cara, who by turns keeps me grounded, then drives me crazy with his teasing. Kinda like how Kellas is with Raven. *Dang!*

About the Author

A.M. Leonard has lived her whole life in Upstate New York…and anywhere else a good book can transport her. The daughter of two veterinarians, she grew up semi-feral on a rural farm, which gave her a lifelong love of animals and nature. When not creating a fantasy world where the good guys always win (eventually), her favorite things involve caring for plants and animals, wandering in the peace and quiet of forests and wide-open spaces, making music, and spending time with family and friends. Urban environments, noisy crowds, and heavy traffic are "not her favorites." Although she's extra fond of her dog, cat and horses, she is beginning to think pet rabbits are very cool, too. She and her husband live on a small farm surrounded by several thousand acres of state-owned forest.

Also by A.M. Leonard

The Lunatics Series

Hunter's Moon

9 798990 754423